RUNNING FROM ASPERITY

by

Melissa Kirk

GRACE WARRIOR TRILOGY

1

Charlene Publishing

RUNNING FROM ASPERITY

Copyright © 2018 by Melissa Kirk.

Cover Design by Jay's Photography & Design.
Cover Model - Mekisha D. McClure.

From the desk of Charlene Publishing.

Also available as e-book and audio

Printed in the United States of America.

Library of Congress Cataloging-in-Publication Data

ISBN-13: 978-0-9969231-6-3

First Edition

My mother, Jessie Marie, is the strongest woman I know.
I love you.

GLOSSARY
Shospokee words with pronunciations

*Amigota (Ah-mee-**go**-tah)* – Love

*Duwaniitehai (Doo-wah-nee-**tay**-hay)* – Pray

*Gehetmo (Ga-**het**-moh)* – War

*Koiyah (**Koi**-yah)* – Mother

*Kuha-cho (Koo-**ah'**-choh)* – Wolf, Wise One, voice of Almighty

Na (Nah) – Now

*Nahuto (Nah-**hoo**-toh)* – Son

*Nama heganda et'noo (**Nah**-mah hee-**guhn**-dah **et'**-noo)* –Save yourself

*Pai'tiompu (Pey'-tee-**uhm**-poo)* – Daughter

*Tüdampa (Too-**dohm**-pah)* – Coyote, Trickster, voice of Evil

*Wadonii (Wah-**dohn**-nee)* – Warrior who discerns

Tribal Chant – *Gehetmo* Dance:

*Wa hee na hai ho (Wah **hee** nah hey **hoh**)*
*Wa hee na hai ho (Wah **hee** nah hey **hoh**)*
*Wa hee na hai ho (Wah **hee** nah hey **hoh**)*
*Na ho! (Nah **hoh**)*

Translation – War Dance

Warrior kneel now, then rise,
Warrior kneel now, then rise,
Warrior kneel now, then rise,
Now, rise!

ASPERITY

When troubles come from every direction, pushing souls to their breaking point.

PROLOGUE

Whatever route it took, meant disaster.

The shift of the earth had caused the Mississippi River to run backward, creating a dam that rose high enough to block the late afternoon sun. It suspended, teasing, while it sought its new course. When it arced over the demolished School of Law, Linda scrambled to wrap her legs around the twisted sidewalk railing and brace.

The torrent tore her away, slamming her into the building, before changing its momentum and scooping her toward the river bank. Steel structure beams shot by like missiles catapulting out of the water.

Her lungs burned, begging for oxygen. She flailed in vain to find something to grab onto as an underwater whirlpool pulled her headfirst to its fury. Her body spun around the deep center until it was mercifully rejected from the swirl and thrust into still water.

Golden powder like Pixie dust drifted down, creating a shimmering curtain behind which a school of bluegill fish swam back toward home. Trapped sounds pressed against her ears, playing a composition of slow, deep pitches.

Help me!

Her petite mother appeared. The Shospokee Indian's prayer shawl swayed from side to side as she swam to a circle of light and squatted next to Linda, who as a child, sat.

The Child-Linda cried, "*Koiyah!* I can't do it."

"My *pai'tiompu*," her mother said. "What makes you worry?"

"It is not pretty." She held up the small dream catcher. Sinew strands crossed the round willow frame in an erratic pattern. A broken white feather tied to a string dangled below.

"I see beauty."

Linda tossed it to the ground and crossed her arms. "I have failed."

Her mother reached to comb the tangled black hair with her fingers and gently pulled it behind the small shoulders. "My Linda, you were put on this earth for me to love. For you to love me. The Creator of *Amigota* sees beyond what is not learned. The Spirit of *Amigota* looks to what can be achieved. You have yet to learn this truth about love. I see beauty in your work because I choose to see through the eyes of the Spirit. I see no failure."

Linda rose to her knees. "*Koiyah.*"

"What do you want, my daughter?"

"*Duwaniitehai.*"

Her mother smiled. "I will always pray for you." She spread her prayer shawl over them and twirled.

The swirl pulled away and morphed into a coyote. The ravenous animal stalked through the water, beams from his green eyes illuminating each piece of waste as he prowled for the choicest prey. Linda squinted in the blinding glare that stopped on her, aware that the predator just found his feast.

His head became that of a monster as he swam closer, and she stuck out her arms to protest his advance. He stopped and bared his teeth, the exposed pink tongue curled up in anticipation.

"Pray for me *Koiyah – Duwaniitehai!*"

10

Powerless, she watched her arms' betrayal as they surrendered to separate and float shoulder-high. Elbows bent, the slender hands rose only to jerk back down and repeat the movement. A stream of bubbles escaped from her nose and ascended. Her gaze couldn't follow.

"*Duwanii – te – hai.*"

Melissa Kirk

CHAPTER ONE

Ozark Ridge, Arkansas

Wednesday

Linda never questioned the road taken or regretted what she left behind. Every race was a win and today felt like a trophy day. Each run offered a new path. Take the low road to the left or bear up the hill to the right. Stay on concrete or sprint across the grass. Maneuver through chunky gravel or stretch your stride on a lonely road.

Today's 5K route was simple, its only incline near the Ozark Ridge First Methodist Church. A flat road led the runners the rest of the way through neighborhoods around the town courthouse. Streets blocked to traffic gave the runners plenty of room.

Long legs finally limber, she took a deep breath and pushed toward the last turn. A local group dressed in matching shirts with "Arkansas Kick It for Kids" printed on the back ran past her, but she didn't care. She was ahead of last year's time.

Passing the three-quarter mark, she shook her head at the volunteer's offer of water. The woman pointed across the street. At the far end of the city's park, a large herd of deer ran past the

13

swing sets where children watched, clapping and laughing. Moving in unison toward the fence, they cleared the hurdle one at a time, crossed the Trust National Bank parking lot, and disappeared behind the building. One toddler started after them, but an older child with the same bright orange hair scooped him up and sat him on the swing.

The July sun bounced off the windshields of participants' dust-covered pickups and worn-out minivans parked in the empty field where Bernie's Groceries once stood. A slick red Porsche broke through the glare and edged toward her. Its stern black grill crept closer, and she slowed, causing the runner behind her to do a quick side step.

"I'm sorry, Andy."

"No problem." He sprinted toward the finish poles.

Fighting the catch in her stomach, she maneuvered through the passing cluster of runners to the driver's window.

"Hi. You got off early for a Wednesday." She started to lean in to kiss Lostyn but decided he wouldn't appreciate the sweat.

Lostyn looked down the road. "There aren't many here."

"Most runners have already made it in, and the walkers are about half way."

He smoothed his mustache. "I'll be ready for dinner when I get home."

"I'll be right there as soon as I cross the finish line. It'll take me just a minute to complete dinner." She glanced down. "And shower, of course. Hey, there's chicken in the crockpot."

His nose twitched, so she added, "It's a new recipe with lemon and basil. You'll like it."

He rolled his neck. Thick jugular veins popped from beneath his chin, descending to disappear under the starched, white collar.

Aware her new runtime was shot, she pulled her ponytail a little too tight. "So, tell me. Did you sign the Vegas group?

"The meeting isn't until next week. Did you forget again?"

"I'm sorry. You're right, of course."

Frantic hands caught her attention, and she waved back at the race coordinator. "Looks like Renee needs me."

"I'm going home and counting on you to be close behind." He drove off, the car's narrowed tail lights glaring back in disappointment.

Renee motioned to a small group gathered on the sidewalk. Linda sprinted to the men squatted next to a little girl lying down with her knees pulled to her chest.

"What's wrong?" The child's pink tulle skirt was torn. "Let me see, Princess." When she gently pried the small bloody hands away from a gashed knee, the child cried out.

"I'm sorry. Did you fall while running?" The little girl nodded and tried to reach for her knee again, but Linda intercepted the trembling hands and held them together in hers. "I'm a nurse, and I'll help you. What's your name?"

"Amy."

Renee reached the group and tossed a roll of paper towels toward her before sliding down the nearest tree trunk, gasping for breath.

Linda hopped up, but the frazzled woman flung up a hand in dismissal, so she turned her attention back to the child.

"Okay. Let's get you fixed up, Princess Amy."

One of the men gave her a bottle of water to clean off the dirt. "It'll be okay. Look. It's almost stopped bleeding."

Amy opened one eye to inspect and sniffled. "It still hurts."

"I know it does, sweetie. Who came with you today?"

Amy's lower lip protruded.

Linda covered the wound with another paper towel. Renee should have been better prepared with a first-aid team on standby... and *No unaccompanied children allowed* posted!

She sighed. Lostyn was waiting for dinner. Renee was wheezing. Amy was alone. And she hadn't crossed the finish line.

~

Thursday

Linda waited at the red light, drumming her fingers on the steering wheel. The newly manicured nails sparkled with tiny dots, reflecting off the Indian eagle-shaped crystal hanging from the rear-view mirror. Its ruby gemstones were a lighter hue of her nail polish.

Her phone rang. "Hi, Mom." She cut into the outer lane, ignoring a blaring horn.

"What was that?"

"It's nothing. What are you up to?"

"The Nevada sun hid behind clouds today, so I went to the reservation to visit Mr. Shamo. He only sells his fruit there while he grieves for his wife." Her mother sighed. "It was as I thought. The gloom of the day weighed heavy on him. Pain still pierces his heart. I fear our friend will never heal."

"I'm sure he appreciated the visit."

"He knows Wadonii well. The good price he gave me on blueberries today will yield him fresh cobbler tomorrow." Her mother chuckled. "I will not disappoint. And I will freeze what is left so we can make pies when you visit. I tried calling yesterday. You are busy on Wednesday nights, I think."

She hesitated. "I the missed call. Blueberry pie sounds yummy, Mom, but I'm in traffic right now. Let me give you a call later, okay?" Breaking through the congestion, she sped up. The gray Impala with tinted windshields following her fell victim to the snarl-up. *Too bad.*

"Okay. Be safe. Watch for –"

Her phone went dead. "Great."

The car in the next lane swerved, causing her to slam on the brakes. Bags of groceries overturned into the back floorboard. "Oh well, great!"

The lane switcher weaved through traffic, causing the cars ahead to screech to a halt and block both lanes. Linda released her grip on the steering wheel, inhaling slowing to the count of four and exhaling to the same.

Her mouth suddenly watered at the thought of the blueberry pies. It seemed like forever since she'd been to her childhood home. She pictured the kitchen, with flaky-crust-covered pies in the oven, and freshly washed fruit spread across the counter-top. Nothing ever wasted, some fruit would be frozen and some dried.

Stems, roots, or seeds would lie on a clean cloth, waiting to be examined for their integrity. The little wooden stool would still be by the sink. Mom stood on it as a child, as had Linda and her son. Swiping away a rogue tear, she turned her focus back to the next several hours. Failure wasn't an option.

Turning onto Wantland Road, she hit the brakes again to avoid a coyote standing in the middle of the street. *Huh.* She'd never seen one in the neighborhood before. The animal held its ground, forcing her to steer to one side to reach the drive and pull into the garage.

The coyote appeared in the car's rear-view mirror. Standing at the garage door, the animal's tail raised high and rapidly flicked side to side. A chill crept up her back. She reached to push the garage door remote clipped to the sun visor and screamed.

In the side mirror, beastly eyes flashed at her. Yellow flecks of light danced in the narrowed spheres that slanted downward over a wrinkled muzzle.

The image vanished as quickly as it appeared. Linda swung around. The coyote stood on the drive, its flicking tail disappearing behind the lowering door. She shook the vision away in disgust. *It's a stupid coyote.*

She jumped out and grabbed the bags on the backseat, leaving the spilled goods that cluttered the floorboard.

The clock on the stove read 4:20. The crock-less meal would take forty minutes. Dinner couldn't be late, again. While peeling potatoes, she blocked from mind the coyote along with the gray Impala, now parked in its usual spot down the street. Instead, she watched a ruby-throated hummingbird guard the feeder outside the window. When a smaller hummingbird flew close, he

17

drove it away.

"Bully." She scraped the peelings into the trash and added the potatoes to the boiling water.

After a quick survey of the house to be sure everything was in order, she changed into a yellow-over-white double tee-top that lay nicely over her jeans. Lostyn would approve. He'd bought that particular top, commenting that the color complemented her skin. After reapplying foundation to cover the reddish-blue mark under her left ear, she ran a brush through the jet-black hair, grimacing while working it into a chignon. At least, it wouldn't be such an easy mark.

Back in the living room, she turned the television channel to the news and muted the sound. Folding the morning's paper in half, she set it on the end table by Lostyn's chair and flipped the lamp on low before returning to the kitchen window to wait.

The hummingbird was gone. So was the coyote – *Tüdampa*, as her mother called the canid. *"Tüdampa is the trickster. He will play games with your soul,"* the native Shospokee always warned. *"Spirits do not concern themselves with boundaries between worlds. They are here. You must protect your soul."*

She smoothed her hair. *Tüdampa* hadn't messed with her soul but certainly had tried to trick her mind.

In the neighbor's yard, Brianna practiced cartwheels. The young neighbor's blond head bobbed in count – one, two, and three – and over, landing on unsteady feet. The girl rubbed her thighs and ran back to the starting point. Repositioning herself, she took great care to point her toes forward. When she raised her hands and looked up, she saw her audience and waved shyly. Linda gave a big nod and then moved out of Brianna's view.

From the new vantage point, the neighbor across the street checked his mail. Lostyn always checked theirs. The young man bent so the little black and tan Yorkshire terrier could jump into his arms. He cocked the dog under his arm and went through the door his wife held open.

The couple was Nathan and Chandra Deal. Corky was the

dog. They weren't home most weekends, but during the week, Nathan always came home, checked the mail, grabbed the dog, and walked through the door held open by his wife. Linda never inquired further. No one needed to know more than that about their neighbor.

When the familiar red sports car turned onto the street, the Impala pulled away. She shut off the oven and pulled the pork tenderloin out as the timer counted down its last few seconds. While Lostyn gathered the mail and checked the flower beds as always for any stray weeds his wife might have missed, Linda positioned herself at the end of the counter, pointed her toes forward, and wiped her hands on her thighs.

~

Lostyn was on the phone when he walked in.

"Your mother," he mouthed. "You're right, Wadonii. A trip would do us both good." Noticing Linda's top, he winked. "I want you to know, I'm looking at the most gorgeous woman. Reminds me of her mother."

He listened for a minute before finishing the conversation. "I'll check my schedule, but I'm sure we have a free weekend coming up. I'll have Linda call you. Tell John Hugh hello for me."

Plugging his phone into the charging station, he crossed the room in three broad steps. He cupped his hand around her neck and pulled her close. "You do remind me of your mother – mysterious. She does it well, though. Years on the reservation, I guess."

Sunlight from the kitchen window highlighted the yellow hue on his amber eyes. "Wadonii said you sounded distracted when the two of you talked earlier." He cocked his head. "Problems today?"

"Of course not. It's been a good day."

Linda didn't blink as his gaze traveled down her neckline. He smoothed his mustache and leaned in, scratching her cheek with his shadow beard. The woody scent of his aftershave had faded, replaced with a light layer of salty perspiration and a hint of the aged, grassy smelling Cuban cigar he apparently chewed on during the drive home. Kissing her neck, he relaxed his fingers one by one, pausing before releasing his thumb. Orange flames danced in his eyes when they met hers again.

"You are gorgeous to look at, my love. Don't ever change."

She chewed her lip while he walked into the living room and turned a 360, stopping to read the newspaper headline.

"Small-town politics," he smirked. "People in this town are clueless." He disappeared into the bedroom.

She tossed the salad. Lostyn didn't like Ozark Ridge. He grew up in the town of 20,000, but even before they married, his dreams were bigger than what the entire population of Arkansas could fulfill. The manufacturing plant that he had worked for shut down twenty years ago. It shocked him, but he quickly landed a position with Hendrix Towers in Memphis.

The fact they hadn't moved to the big city sometimes made her wonder how serious her husband's plans were to leave small-town life, but his busy days and lengthy commute often interfered with any long-term planning. The town suited her, small enough to greet familiar faces, but large enough she didn't have to worry about anyone nosing into their private life.

He returned, wearing khaki shorts and a white T-shirt, his muscular arms pulling the short sleeves tight.

"It's pork tenderloin tonight. I know it's your absolute favorite and —" She pulled a peach cobbler out of the oven. "*Voila!* I know it's not as good as Mom's homemade, but with a scoop of French vanilla ice cream? Yummy."

"Keep it warm while we talk."

"Oh." She glanced around. Everything seemed to be in its place. "Okay." Shoving the meal back into the oven, she turned on the warmer and joined him in the living room. "Is anything wrong?"

He sat in his chair and turned off the TV. "Does having a

conversation with me bother you?"

"Well, no. I mean, of course not." She smoothed her top and sat on the edge of the sofa across from him. "What's on your mind, dear?"

"Terrance and Bradley have several decisions to make before the end of the quarter. They will be here Saturday to play golf. The fact they accepted my invitation shows how valuable my input is to them. They finally realize they would be idiots not to include me in the decision-making process."

He stood and paced. "After dinner, I'll go over my notes for tomorrow morning's meeting. The numbers are excellent, thanks to me. Hmm. I'll be sure to initial all five of the Resources Department's line items so they know I checked the figures. Yes, that's perfect." He tapped his forehead. "Always thinking. That's what keeps me ahead of the game. That's why I never fail to make a good impression on them."

"I'll have the house in perfect order, and I'll pull out my recipe book after we eat to work up an excellent menu. Whatever you —"

"You know how important first impressions are, don't you?"

She nodded.

"They won't like the drive, but they'll be happy about the golf course. Our club is small but adequate." His lips pursed. "Actually, the course is in great shape. More important, potential backers will be there, lined up to tee off."

He shook his head. "Few of them have much more than fat payments and slim wallets to fund their lifestyle. Not a problem, though. All I have to do is get a group of them to agree to tap into their savings. Then the bosses will milk them for plenty more — watched it a dozen times. I have to hand it to the old codgers — they are smooth. I'll exchange introductions, lay out a plan for big profits, and gather signatures when they bite. Add just one big player to the mix, and I can call it a lucrative day."

He propped an arm on the fireplace mantel. "Success

equals power, Linda, and attaining it is just days away. Saturday is the final test. I've considered all angles and have the edge. Tunica, Mississippi's casinos are still new players, but I have plenty of ideas to grow that gaming town all the way to Memphis."

"Isn't that a good thirty miles?"

"Do you doubt me?" He huffed. "The Vegas group will too. But, for a change, they will learn a lesson from *my* playbook. When we're done at the club, I'll bring the men home through the Willows Subdivision. That way, they'll see nice homes that aren't the caliber of ours, making this neighborhood look even better." He walked the circumference of the room. "I think a new entry table will help. Take care of it. And change that old picture for something updated."

In the portrait, her father sat, placing him eye level with a petite wife whose long black hair fell behind her shoulders. The woman's smile revealed how proud she was of the homemade dream-catcher she held up. The strands meticulously intertwined across the willow hoop, creating a spider web design meant to protect its owner from harm.

Lostyn crossed the room and stood between her and the safety net.

She swallowed. "Do you have something in mind?"

"I'll trust you to make that decision. Spare no expense."

"I'll take care of it tomorrow."

A beautiful console table stood in the window display at Reid's Furniture. Its ornate trim would blend flawlessly with the rest of the furniture. Moving the portrait didn't make her happy, though. She would have to find somewhere less noticeable to hang it, perhaps the hall leading to the master bedroom.

"No one calls Lostyn Bonin a freeloader at Hendrix Towers. Without my power of persuasion, the company would be floundering in shallow water, and they all know it. It's about time those old men recognized my value. You might not appreciate the gambling industry, but it pays the bills and much more. We aren't hurting for anything this town has to offer." He pulled her up, his tight grip numbing her hand. "You will have the best. Tell me, Linda. Have I taken too long to give you better?"

"Of course not. You've worked hard to build a career. I've been very content. You're an excellent provider." She kissed him on the cheek. "I'm excited for you – I mean us."

He started to kiss her fingertips but stopped. "Your nails are bright."

Her mouth went dry.

"I like it." He laughed and wrapped his brawny arms around her. "If this weekend turns out as I suspect, why don't we buy a ranch near your parents?"

"Really? I've never heard you even hint about living in Nevada."

"Not live there. But I think you might like spending more time with them. The Vegas Group is almost a sure thing. Having a house close to their home base would be beneficial."

"That reminds me. I saw a coyote on our street. I don't believe I've seen any since the last time we were in Nevada. It followed me home." She stopped there, knowing Lostyn would think the rest of her experience nonsense.

"I've been feeding it," he said.

She frowned.

"Not your typical coyote. It has an insatiable appetite – devours anything you give it. Not afraid to milk me for all it's worth, either. No boundaries – like me! See, Linda. Take a lesson from nature. Everything received is simply an invitation to take more." He shrugged. "If you don't get all you want, go for the jugular. That's why I'm so successful."

The only other warning her mother had concerning the coyote was never to feed it. She forced a smile. "Ready to eat?"

"I'll be right there." He picked up the mail and started sorting through the three pieces of correspondence.

"What do you want to drink?"

"Milk."

He dropped the first piece of mail into the trash can.

Junk mail. She headed to the refrigerator and froze. *Milk!* It was still in the back seat. *You never get it right.*

He looked up. "Anything wrong?"

"Oh, no." She flashed him a smile. "I just remembered I need to call Dawn about something. That's all."

He nodded and continued scrutinizing the mail.

She held her breath and opened the refrigerator. Retrieving the gallon carton, she quickly filled a glass and stuck the empty container back inside, out of sight.

Clearing his throat, he held up the last piece of mail. "Why is there a new charge on the Visa?"

"A new charge?" The plate in her hand shook, so she rested her hand on the other side to still it.

Lostyn stepped around the counter. "We discussed closing this account."

"Yes, I remember. It must be a transaction before we talked about it. Maybe, if I look at the date, I can —"

The veins in his neck bulged. "I distinctly remember discussing this before the last statement came." He snapped the piece of correspondence back onto the counter. "My instructions are only meant to protect you. Why can't you understand that? You still cannot think a situation through. Listen to me, Linda. After working seventeen years to earn recognition only to be pushed aside by lackluster freeloaders breaking rank, I am not going to put up with the same behavior at home."

She laid down the plate and covered the potatoes. No matter how hard she tried, she always failed to take the right path with her husband.

Fire red eyes locked on her.

Put the salad up. Letting it wilt would just be another stumble. Linda wobbled toward the refrigerator. With her neck still sore from last night, there was no choice but to face her punishment tonight.

Too late. He was at her back before the next step.

CHAPTER TWO

Friday Morning

The bright morning light caused her head to scream for relief. Wishing she could close the bedroom curtains, Linda slowly raised an arm to adjust the pillow, instead. Feeling around the blanket, she found a soggy Kleenex and patted her raw nostrils.

She'd barely made it to bed last night. But Lostyn? Beat your wife. Then kiss her goodnight and fall asleep. She tossed the tissue back into the pile.

Two nights in a row. After twenty years, the eruptions now came so often, her body didn't have time to heal between the outbursts. She grabbed another pillow before coughing, but pain pierced her side anyway.

Her worn out bandage wrap held its place in the middle drawer of the vanity. After several attempts, she stood, and using the wall to steady herself, shuffled to the bathroom, stepping around the gray and neon orange tennis shoes. There was nowhere to run.

She couldn't just jog to her parent's house in Soquili, Nevada, to let them know the man they didn't want as their son-

25

in-law turned out to be more than a little possessive like they thought. She couldn't go to Bruce either.

Bruce. The only right decision she made while married was sending their son to live with his grandparents. The poor child had just registered for junior high school. The move agonized both her and Bruce but never bothered Lostyn.

The surprise in her mother's voice when she called to say that Bruce needed to move in with them still echoed in her ears. *"He does not need to leave his mother to understand our ways. Such things he can learn as you paint your childhood for him."* But Linda had insisted, saying Lostyn agreed that Bruce should learn farming and experience life near his grandmother's childhood reservation home. The arrangement was supposed to be for one year – eleven years ago.

A sigh slipped out. Perhaps Lostyn felt nothing because he had lived with a court-appointed guardian for most of his childhood. He only spoke with her about those years once, recounting when he was sent home to visit his dying mother.

His drunken father had met him at the door. Lostyn described him as a stiff-backed bag of bones. The man barricaded them inside before staggering to the kitchen to sit with a shotgun to lay across his knees. Staring out the window, his father watched for an imaginary foe while, Lostyn, ten years of age, stood watch over his frail mother until her fatal heart attack.

Lostyn had been drunk the night he relived the childhood memory. As a young Marine, just returning to the States, he told her that he hadn't understood what his father had been watching for until he experienced the enemy firsthand while entangled in the Lebanese Civil War. He said that the only successful rules of engagement were to take control and always be on guard. On point – to death if necessary. It was his responsibility to protect her. The world was dangerous, and women, like her and his mother, were helpless and always prone to go the wrong way.

He came home from service a different man, his once playful personality replaced with somber conversations and intense eyes that watched her like a hawk. Anytime she turned on the radio, he would switch the portable player to the cassette that had the song, *War*, recorded on it multiple times.

She had tried every way to be a good wife and not upset Lostyn. He was right about one thing. Staying in step was impossible.

Bruce could never know the real reason he had to go. The yelling exchanges he witnessed as a new teenager were hurtful enough, but no child needed to know that his mother served as a punching bag while he slept. When X-Men and Band of Thieves video games kept him up later, and his father erupted earlier, it became necessary to protect him. Especially when Lostyn started using the games as excuses to get upset.

Shaking the memories out of her head, she accepted the resulting pain as payment for failing to create a safe environment for her son. Bending over the sink filled with steaming hot water and eucalyptus essential oil, she inhaled. The medicinal odor worked through her sinuses, the coolness momentarily easing nausea caused by the throbbing.

The women at Hope Church could never know her situation. Their marriages were nearly perfect, like her parents'. They wouldn't relate to a woman who knuckled under the explosions of the overbearing man who once tenderly but passionately promised his young bride the world.

The women's shelter wasn't an option for her. It was too close – it would be the first place Lostyn looked if his wife disappeared.

Her hidden stash of money was too pitifully small to support herself.

Besides, it was after 7:00. She didn't have to look out the window to know that the Impala was already parked, positioned to watch her every move – *to protect her* – as Lostyn phrased it.

No one was interested in a loser, anyway. You could only disappoint people so many times until they turned their back. And, as Lostyn beat into her often, she was way past her allotment of missteps. There was no one to help. No one who cared. No winning route.

She pushed the drain button. The oily water surrendered to gravity and swirled down the hole. Freed with just one motion, evidence of its existence vanished. If only it was that simple in real life. Patting her face with a towel, she peered at the reflection in the mirror. Failure stared back.

At least, it was Friday. Lostyn wouldn't return until late, so the entire day was free to get her work done.

A milk-glass vase with three freshly picked day lilies sat in the kitchen on the counter. She grabbed the vase and threw it into the wastebasket, regretting the move immediately. When the cramp in her side eased, she retrieved it and rearranged the flowers, not wanting a black check mark for the third day in a row.

The list lay beside the vase. Lostyn always left a list, rain or shine, fight or not. *Cleaners. Bank. Furniture. I love you.* She crossed out *I love you*, added *milk*, and slid the paper into her purse.

Her phone flashed a text from Bruce. "Going to the ranch 2day. Shh – surprise."

She texted back. "Save some pie for me. Coming soon."

Bruce's image lit up the screen, again. "No promises on the pie. Just letting you know 4 emerg." The image on the screen of her son had the same handsome features as his grandfather's.

Her raw eyes stung as fresh tears formed. Before leaving that morning, Lostyn whispered, *"We'll visit your parents in a few weeks. It always seems to refresh you and get you back on track."* His voice had reminded her of the hiss of the Gila monster she encountered as a child.

She adjusted the Ace bandage. With only two weeks to heal, her father's bear hug was going to hurt, but she wouldn't delay the trip. Being able to see her son was worth any discomfort.

Her phone flashed again. This time, it was Dawn.

"Need help tomorrow! Day trip to Memphis with the youth girls. Leaving at 7. PLZ!!!"

Lostyn encouraged her to help with the youth. Of course,

it was because Brother James always thanked them from the pulpit during the Sunday morning services. Whatever the reason, she cherished the periods of liberation. Being with Dawn lifted her spirits, too. The girl and Bruce had been friends since childhood, and Linda depended on the young woman for updates on his activities, even if they were only on a need-to-know basis.

"Pretty PLZ" popped onto the screen.

The break would do her good. She would complete today's list and ready the house for tomorrow. Lostyn was too organized to assign last-minute duties that might derail such an important day.

"Yes!" she texted back and reached for the herb tea. Her ribs screamed out.

~

Dawn tossed the phone onto the strewn blankets and climbed back in bed. Hands clasped behind her head, she crisscrossed her legs in time with the morning meditations music.

Good! Finally, Linda agreed to do something. No matter how much extra time it took in Memphis tomorrow, she was going to corner Bruce's mom and get some answers.

Like, when was Bruce coming home? The ranch and college used to be his only excuses, but now he had a job there, too. Why couldn't he work here? *Seriously!* Nevada wasn't the only place in the world where people studied cracks in the ground.

What happened to the annoying midnight *"It's a new day so don't sleep it away"* calls? And the *"Mr. Bells sucks at chemistry"* rants between classes? Her lips clamped together. He'd become as evasive as his mother.

The woman was almost invisible these days. Linda and Lostyn had even started slipping out of church during end-of-service announcements. And another headache kept Linda away from the last WECARE charity luncheon.

Her swinging legs paused mid-air. The woman really

needed to see a doctor. She would offer to take her. Stuck in a waiting room seemed like an excellent opportunity to catch up.

Bruce could at least invite her to the ranch. *Seriously!* She'd only been to visit him once, and that was forever ago. The year her parents died, Linda purchased a plane ticket so the two of them could fly to Nevada. They stayed for two weeks while, at home, Granny packed away the remaining evidence of the lives of her parents, George and Dawnita Finley.

She closed her eyes. Bruce only had a driving permit then, but his granddad gave him permission to drive the pickup through the alfalfa fields to show her the wild horse herd that grazed there. Arriving at the lake on the far side, he explained that the dark red-haired horse with the pitch-black mane was called the boss mare and would drink first. Jumping onto the tailgate, his frame stood tall with arms crossed, his gaze fixed on the unfolding scene.

Meanwhile, she soaked in his deep brown irises that used to challenge her pale blue ones to a game of skip rock or dare her to say another word during a Yankees game. That afternoon, his sun-tanned face had glistened under the bearing-down sun.

"Did you see that?" he had whispered excitedly while pointing toward the horses.

When she finally took her gaze off the broad smile stretching across his face, the Mustangs were kicking up a dust storm behind them.

Then, after swearing to secrecy, they pulled onto the highway and drove fifteen miles to the high school. Parked behind the line of buses, they swapped stories. He was mad because no one told him why he had to move across the country. She was mad because her parents died. They decided to run away to the California coast, but it was close to dinner time, and his grandmother had baked bread and pies all day, so after stopping for ice cream, they headed back. She smiled. They never said anything more about leaving.

She looked up and studied the small dream-catcher that his grandmother had given to her the day they left the ranch. Attached to the dangling sets of white and brown plumes were the prettiest strings of turquoise beads she'd ever seen. Gray streaks gave them visual depth, but to the touch, they felt like silk. Rubbing them calmed her spirit just like Wadonii said it would.

Carefully following the Shospokee woman's instructions, she had hung it on the wall over the bed and made sure the earliest morning sun hit the willow circle.

It worked. For the past nine years, only seven nightmares slipped through the round webbed band. All replayed the night her parents died in the car accident. Each time, she repeated Wadonii's words as a prayer. *"Catch the fear and let only bravery slip through."* Then the nightmares stopped, replaced by dreams of her standing in partnership with the dream-catcher, feet planted firmly, and arms crossed.

Like every morning, Dawn reached up, handling each strand of beads as if it were a rosary like she had seen her Catholic friend Mary Elizabeth do. Saying her Protestant prayers, she worked through the beads, first voicing a praise, and ending with a petition.

She dug through the pile of blankets for her phone and pulled up Facebook. Linda's page was old news. Bruce's page was filled with clips of wild horses and links to camping gear, along with Cherise's ridiculous entries.

How did he get tied in with that girl? Seriously, how many color changes could someone do without damaging their hair or having everyone question their sanity? Electric blue today. Burnt red last week. She gasped when the head of tightly curled rainbow-streaked hair appeared further down the feed. *What a clown!* The selfie tagged Bruce and four others. Cherise wrote, "Fun times!" As always, Bruce hit the like button but didn't comment. No one did.

Choosing the right angle, Dawn snapped her own picture to paste on his page and stared at the seized image. An unbraided mass of dirty blond hair fell around the oval face. A small, dark mole on the cheekbone stood out in stark contrast to the ivory skin. *Blah!* She deleted it and jumped up. Jerking the pink bedspread over the blankets, she tossed the round fluffy pillow on top and sat Scorch the Dragon beanie baby in the middle.

They were adults now. Futures were being shaped, and Ozark Ridge wasn't part of Bruce's plan. Why would it be? He'd even encouraged her when she talked about joining the Peace Corps. He managed to counter every objection she voiced.

In the kitchen, she poured granola cereal into a bowl. When Trevor invited her to the junior prom, Bruce had asked, *"Isn't he the dude that scared Amy in seventh grade?"* She didn't go to the dance. The next year, she turned down all three invitations to the senior prom. Then declined every proposition in college. She shoved away her breakfast. No one asked anymore.

Fine! Ozark Ridge offered nothing, but the Peace Corps provided endless opportunities. It was time to shake things up. She called and left a message for the recruiter.

Then she called Cute Cuts. "Hey, Rachel. Can you fit me in next week? Great! Mark me down for short. I'm serious! A color, too."

CHAPTER THREE

Reno, Nevada

Bruce jerked up. His least-favorite song always seemed to be the one blasting from the radio, interrupting a good night's sleep.

He grunted. Mrs. Guild down the hall would grumble about the blaring Country music. The lady was older than dirt, but man, could she hear. His picking up her prescriptions and peanut brittle every month kept her from reporting him to the landlord, though.

"This shot's for you, Mrs. Guild!" He grabbed his rolled-up socks from the floor and threw them at the alarm. The practiced aim hit, sliding the clock off the chest into the laundry basket and burying it deep in yesterday's clothes. "Score!"

He retrieved the clock and turned on the shower. The weather forecast for the next three days was perfect, and today's workday short. The extra work hours were finally paying off.

"Saturday, Sunday, Monday —" The phone's ring interrupted his song. He shook the water from his hair and looked at the wall above the mirror. The Motocross clock read 6:16 am.

33

He hit the phone speaker button. "Hey, Chief!"

Out the window, he watched the Ferrari 458 Italia backing out of its spot. "Man! Who can afford one of those?"

"What?"

"Silver Ferrari with a blond chick behind the wheel." The car accelerated onto the expressway.

"Neither."

"What?"

"You can't afford either."

"Right! What do you need, Chris?"

"The seismometer at Troy Canyon went down last night. Can't have that, especially when our latest player Hawthorne has been recording micro-quakes every hour since the sun went down. Another 4.6 hit around 2 a.m., nine kilometers, if I remember right. So, go to the lab and grab a board. Then meet up with –" Chris shuffled papers. "Troy. No, that's not right." His boss muttered a curse. "Anyway, meet up in Lovelock. There's a Mexican restaurant on the main drag. Yeah – didn't write that down either. But hey, how many taco joints can there be in Lovelock? Be there at 1:00. Then, my man, the rest of Friday is yours."

He changed his mind about the Polo and dug through the pile on the closet floor for his Rocky Mountain T-shirt instead. He chose a pair of camouflaged cargo shorts and gave them a quick fabric-freshener misting.

Field assignments were routine. Most of his colleagues were married, either to a wife or to the golf course, both of which dictated too much of their time. Chris knew it and found it easier to send the young, unattached man to work the remote sites. Bruce grumbled, but secretly enjoyed it, except when he had other plans.

Rubbing the stubble on his chin, he dug in a drawer for his razor and threw it in the duffel bag, along with extra shorts and shirts.

In the hall, Mrs. Guild stood with her hands planted on her hips. Dropping the bag on the ground, Bruce placed his sun-bronzed hands on her shoulders. Her small stature reminded him of Grandmother.

"Ma'am, I'm going to bring you back the best peanut brittle in all of Nevada, guaranteed to pull the fillings right out of your teeth." The elderly woman kept frowning, so he added, "Maybe some pie, too."

"Your grandmother spoils you. That's your problem." Her twinkling winter-gray eyes betrayed the scolding finger.

"I'll be back early Monday night. Have a list ready, and I'll run to the store for you." Tipping his cap, he took off before the little woman remembered why she stepped out of her apartment.

He cranked up the jeep's radio and exited north onto Interstate 80. Who needed a Ferrari? If getting somewhere required wheels, his rattletrap would get him there.

The High Trail of the Sierra Nevada Mountains loomed in front. Only three weeks remained until the annual seven-day hike in his favorite hiking spot. With all hints of snow melted by then, he could travel the way God and nature intended, foot to path just like the Native Americans trekked thousands of years before explorers arrived.

He lifted his cap to run a hand through his thick, sweaty brown hair. Hopefully, he wouldn't encounter a bear like last season. The *Reno Gazette* reported it as the first confrontation in the mountains between the furry beast and man in eight years. Every hike offered insight and leaving food exposed had made an impression on him after facing the hungry omnivore. That, and the value of being in shape. He flexed his right bicep and nodded. Extra workouts made a difference.

Last week, he kept his conversation with Grandmother short to keep from spoiling his surprise visit. When he arrived today, she might curse under her breath in Shospokee while meeting him at the door with a tall glass of tea. If tending to her flower gardens, she might wave him on into the house. Either way, there'd be a delicious meal before sunset.

He dug for his sunglasses. The summer before eighth grade, his mother came into his bedroom to tell him he was moving to the ranch. She said his grandfather needed help on the farm, then hugged him and ran from the room.

His father came in right after that. "Take that nonsense Nintendo with you. There'll be no reason for it to remain here. I'll instruct John Hugh that you are only allowed to play the game thirty minutes in the evening. That is if you've finished your work. And yes, you will work. I'll not have my son being a freeloader." When he asked how long he would be there, Dad said there'd be no further discussion. There wasn't. No one, including his grandparents, ever said what he'd done wrong never to be able to move back home.

He had worked hard on the ranch. In his free time, he watched the wild Mustangs. Not that a lot of downtimes existed. Granddad harvested alfalfa four times each year. Repairing equipment and checking fences filled the long work days between harvests. When Granddad caught up, Bruce always offered to help Grandmother with her garden, but she would send him to another task. *Every time.* He chuckled. Anything to keep him away.

He understood. Alone time equaled freedom. Relationships were necessary, but at a distance was good enough. He preferred connecting with the great outdoors. There, the day changed to night, summer to winter, snow fell, and flowers died. Night gave way to day, the cold weather subsided,, the snow melted, and seedlings grew. The only safe commitment in life was making time to appreciate nature. The monkeyflowers and butterweeds never complained of his presence. As long as he gave the pikas and rattlers their space, they welcomed him, too.

Downtime was this weekend's agenda, and nothing was going to interfere. He looked forward to joining his grandparents on the porch to watch The Annual Great Reno Balloon Race. Granddad would log each balloon that passed over the ranch in his notepad with the time and years in competition. New balloons received an honorable, hand-scratched star by their description. Grandmother always had fresh-baked fruit pies.

When his stomach growled, he pulled a protein bar out of

the console. When the phone rang, he hesitated. Answering guaranteed him another assignment.

~

The probationary lab assistant opened the windowed wooden door and leaned against it.

"Hi, Bruce."

Bruce turned sideways, trying to squeeze through the doorway. The hourglass-shaped body turned to block him. Charise's height matched his, and he squirmed when her giant Venus flytrap lashes fluttered. University of Reno, Seismological Research Lab wasn't prepared for the likes of the oddly dressed creature in front of him.

"What are you doing here so early?"

"There's a clock on every wall in here that reads 8:00," he said with a wry smile.

She stepped back and swooped her hand, motioning him in. "I guess I lost track of time. I've been here since 6:30 for Lab prep, you know. It's been hopping this morning. Eight printouts already. Seven from CERI, Memphis. I put them in the inbox. You want to look at them?"

He glanced at the full tray of paper but shook his head. "It happens. Usually, when a rookie, no offense, gets excited and forgets we know how to read online."

"You don't have to worry about this girl wasting trees. It would take some pretty significant jolts to get me excited this early in the morning."

"What's Hawthorne doing? Chris said data showed micros every hour."

"Three since I've been here. All under magnitude 1.5, southwest toward Mono Lake. Maybe Memphis is trying to outdo us. Either that or Ricky just wants my personal attention again."

"Maybe." He headed to the storeroom. Charise followed, bumping into him when he stopped at the door.

She giggled. "Oops."

He stared straight ahead until she grunted and stepped back.

The electronic boards were stacked behind the Fed-X boxes, and he restacked them to make a path.

"Hey!" The blue-streaked head of hair poked inside the room.

"Yeah?"

"There's another backstage party at the Events Center Saturday – by invitation only. Consider yourself invited."

"I can't."

"You had fun last month. I watched you and that blond. Be my date this time. You like brunettes, don't you?"

"Uh, need a mirror?"

"I could be brunette by the end of the day if I wanted. I was once. Boring, though." She moaned. "Kind of like this job. Oh, come on. No attachments. Just a fun night."

"I'm going to the ranch."

"Oh, well. Your loss." Her high heels clicked away.

He grabbed a toolbox. The board was already intact, regaining him part of the thirty minutes that was lost stuck in traffic. He snuck through the lab, focusing on the exit.

"Come here a minute."

When he groaned, Charise raised her eyebrow. "Too busy to help the newbie? Or are you afraid of me?"

The freshman didn't scare him. Not much more than the plague, anyway.

"What is it?"

"Is this a glitch or something?" She pointed to the computer screen.

"We don't have glitches." He leaned in to examine the reading.

She leaned in too, brushing his shoulder.

He cleared his throat.

She grinned but moved enough for him to type a sequence

on the keyboard.

Nothing. He sat down and tried another sequence. A location popped up on the screen. "There you go. It's the Mongress Fault – southwest of New Madrid, Missouri."

The intern gave him a blank stare.

"Between Memphis, Tennessee, and the Arkansas-Oklahoma border, approximately one hundred miles southwest of the epicenter of the first large earthquake to strike the New Madrid in December of?"

"1811."

"Correct. Which was?"

"Magnitude 7.2 to 8.2."

"Correct. Located?"

Charise threw her hands up. "Northeast Arkansas. Followed by three more of similar magnitudes in a three-month period. Largest recorded in mid-America. The current weakest asperity is eleven miles under the Mississippi River valley. 15,000,000 people live in the zone. When that little patch can't take any more stress – when it reaches its breaking point? Yeah – Hades is coming to visit. I got it." She rolled her eyes. "I mean, isn't that how life works? Everyone has a breaking point, and it's never pretty when somebody reaches it. Anyway, I passed my entrance exam with flying colors. Satisfied?"

He adjusted his cap. The slip rate flashing on the screen was minuscule. "Chris been in yet?"

"Are you kidding? I may be the newcomer, but I knew the answer to that question before I walked in this morning. And, I'm sure Arthur and Brian are chasing golf balls by now." She noted the pile of equipment at his feet. "Looks like you're ditching this place. That's too bad. Maybe we can work together alone another time." She turned back to the computer.

He headed out the door. If his bosses could be no-shows on Friday, him investigating further could wait until Tuesday. "Just copy and paste the findings on the Scroggins Log."

Melissa Kirk

Chapter four

Friday Afternoon

Oxycodone tempered the pain, allowing Linda to get a lot accomplished. She pulled the roast beef out of the oven, put in cornbread tarts, and set the timer. As soon as they finished baking, she'd go to the store and get back before the medicine wore off. With no refills left, it wouldn't be wise to waste any relief they offered. Lostyn's extended list, via text, included bourbon and rum, which meant a trip all the way across town to Sam's Spirits.

He wasn't due home for another four hours, but tangerine and sandalwood oils were already diffusing in the bathroom. The steam from his shower would enhance their soothing effects. There wasn't any reason to worry, though. Because tomorrow was such a big day, he'd be careful to keep the house – and her – in good shape.

She poured a glass of mint-tinged water and went outside. Shoving the deck chair with her foot to position it under the porch fan, she lowered into the seat and stretched out.

A rabbit sat in the yard under the white crepe myrtle. He pulled his ears down to lick them and then started to groom his brown and tan streaked back but stopped and pointed his ears and nose straight up, instead. His black eyes opened wider as he braced on all four legs.

Another rabbit slid under the fence and hopped to him. They both propped on their hind legs, fixating on the wooden slats. Three more hares joined them. When the last one reached the small herd, they bounded across the yard and disappeared under the opposite privacy fence. The rabbits headed toward the afternoon sun like the deer at the playground had.

A stray deer and rabbit or two weren't unusual, but so many groupings of wild animals in town was uncanny. And the aggressive coyote unnerved her.

Lostyn shouldn't have fed it. Mom had always warned not to trust them. *"They will play games with your soul."* The hair on her forearms rose. She wished the fan was on a lower setting, but it would require too much effort, so she lay back and closed her eyes instead.

Images of her childhood home in the Great Basin infiltrated her mind. Bristlecone Pines and Junipers flanked the edges of her imagination while shoulder-high sagebrush and prickly pear cactus invaded its interior. Bighorn sheep stood on the ledges of the Sierra Nevada range, their shadows darkened by a fiery orange sunset that contradicted the scorched but cooling ground.

She wanted to join the journeying animals, heading west and not stopping until they reached the ranch. The hot afternoon sun rebuked her for the thought and slipped behind a dark cloud, veiling the imagery.

Stark reality was the gateless, eight-foot fence that imprisoned the backyard. Along the back, the neighbor's tall crepe myrtles laden with bright pink blooms encroached over the top, lending charm to the immaculate landscape. The only escape from the seemingly beautiful confinement was by way of the front of the house – where the Impala was.

She sipped the water. A second home in Nevada sounded

fantastic. Lostyn never mentioned the fact they would be closer to Bruce. Hopefully, it wasn't an oversight that would later make him change his mind. Their son was older now, though, and busy with his life, so she doubted if he'd spend much time with them, regardless where they lived. He hadn't been home since February.

Her bottom lip protruded. They were growing apart. She had to rely on Dawn for the few details the young girl pulled from him. Like the last, most texts she received only informed of his whereabouts in case of an emergency.

Maybe, it was just as well. With Lostyn's outbursts happening more frequently, it'd be necessary not to encourage the family to visit often, if they did move closer. The miles separating her from the rest of the family was now as much a necessity as a burden.

The indoor clock chimed. Her relaxing muscles begged her to be still, but time was slipping away.

~

"Whoa!" Bruce held the steering wheel tight, his body jerking from side to side as the jeep bounced over the rocky shoulder before coming to a stop on the dirt field road. He put it into park and pulled his upper body through the window to see better. The Mustangs always grazed on Mr. Lomeli's north fields in the afternoons, but they weren't there now. He slumped into the seat and eased back onto the highway.

A crumpled paper fell from the sun guard onto his lap. Scribbled on it was the name of a classmate that Dawn had given him. When he didn't recognize the name, she'd gone into a long story about their grade-school romps. He still drew a blank, but she insisted he make contact, so he promised. *Right.* He'd search through twelve thousand student's names to find some green first-year-student.

He texted with one hand "Hey."

Two minutes later Dawn called.

"That was quick," he answered.

"I'm running errands. What's up?"

"About this Ryan. I need his cell number."

"You haven't been in touch with him yet? Bruce! You promised me you'd take care of him. He's younger, you know. Being a freshman in a strange environment is not a pleasant experience. You remember that feeling, don't you?" She let out an exasperated breath. "Come on. You said you'd do this for me!"

He grunted.

"Well, you remember, don't you? Being a freshman is super intimidating. And he's far away from home. Bruce. You there? Bruce!"

"Sorry. Bad connection here."

She pouted. "Don't you play that game with me! You just don't want to help. You don't even care, anymore."

"Okay. Okay! I called you to get more information, remember?"

She didn't answer.

"What? This dude your new boyfriend or something?"

"Bruce John Hugh Bonin! He is not! He's nothing but a friend. Like you used to be."

"I'm kidding. Cool down. I've been busy. Well, that's not exactly true. I forgot." He scratched his head. "Do you have a number or not?"

"I'll text it to you. Maybe *Charise* can help you find him."

"You know Charise?"

"Not like you do. Just heard of her colorful personality. So, what are you doing?"

"Heading to the ranch." He slowed to check for horses in Mr. Lomeli's south fields. Empty. They must have already moved on toward the lake.

He missed what she said. "What?"

"I said it sounds like fun. I've not been there in a long time, as you well know." She moaned. "I've not been anywhere. But that's going to change. Paul – you remember me telling you about him, right? The guy with the Peace Corps? He's sweet and helpful. Bruce! Are you even listening? I said he's sweet and helpful."

"Yeah?"

"Yeah. And guess where I said I wanted to go. Drum roll, please." She didn't wait for him to answer. "India! Isn't that exciting? I'm supposed to hear something by next week. Honestly, Bruce, they are so slow. But I'll get the assignment. I know I will. Hey, did you even hear what I said?"

"I'm sure you'll hear something soon." The Peace Corps had to be smarter than to send a blond-haired, blue-eyed, too-bold-for-her-own-good girl to India.

"You think they'll let me go?"

"I think so," he lied.

Granddad's west fields came into view.

"I'm taking the youth girls to the Memphis mall. Your mom's going with me."

"Oh, yeah?"

"Eight girls are going. And Miss Connie. I think she'll enjoy it, don't you?"

"Miss Connie?"

"Your mother!"

He couldn't picture his mother with a bunch of squealing girls.

"I think she needs a break. She looks tired all the time. Kind of beat down, you know? Has she said anything to you?"

"Nope."

"Well, maybe you should try talking to her more often! *Seriously!* I know more about your parents than you do."

That's the way they liked it. "I texted her earlier, okay? She's coming in a few weeks. Are you sure she needs to help with a bunch of girls?"

"Good grief. They're girls. Your mother is a girl. She'll have a blast. Now that I think about it, going with us will be the perfect medicine. Agree?"

He lied again. "Sure. Hey, you're breaking up." Tossing the

phone into the console, he cranked up the radio.

Of all people, Dawn should understand. It was plain and simple. You couldn't depend on parents. People don't need people to survive anyway. They need land. Water. The beast of the field. The fruit of the land. That's what it took to survive, and he was mastering all those necessities. Occasionally connecting with his grandparents was enough to prove he wasn't a recluse.

His mother never helped with *his* youth activities. Traveling across six states to be part of his life would have been too much to ask. So, he didn't. Why should she be there to help with his homework? Or to watch him score the winning touchdown for all-conference? Keeping Dad happy was more important. *"We don't want to disturb your father, son. Let's not upset him, okay?"* More like explode. *Yeah, Mom.* Attending graduation was enough. *Not a problem, Dad.* The company golf tournament that kept you away? Paramount.

The front passenger tire blew while veering off the road into Granddad's field. He hit the steering wheel. It was supposed to be a relaxing weekend. Watch the Mustangs and eat Grandmother's pie. Watch Granddad watch balloons.

He chucked the spare tire out of the back of the jeep. It bounced and rolled. Chasing the runaway, he stopped it with his foot right before it reached the road. He shook dust out of his face and spit. Staying home and tormenting Mrs. Guild would have been simpler.

He rolled the tire back, following a long, jagged crack in the earth. It reminded him of the Mongress fault which reminded him of the pile of printouts on Chris's desk. They may have referenced Charise's findings. More than likely, they contained details of increased activity in Memphis. It would have been smart of him to explain to Charise the significance of the asperity they discussed and help her write a response back to Memphis for whatever they were wanting.

His shirt served as a towel to wipe the sweat off his face. *Forget it.* That's what Chris got paid to do.

As he tightened the last lug nut, a foul, musky smell assaulted his nostrils. Bruce raised the lug wrench. Turning his back to the vehicle, he worked to the front and hoisted himself onto the hood.

Other than the flat tire, nothing stood out – except him. He hopped back off before anyone coming down the open stretch of highway thought he was drunk. The putrid odor penetrated the air again, causing him to fight back vomit. He jumped in the jeep and floored it.

~

Linda answered her phone. "Almost home?"

"We're entertaining potential clients on Beale Street tonight. They flew in unexpectedly from Atlanta. I won't be driving in."

"They'll like Beale Street, Lostyn. Maybe you can take them to see –"

"It's not a sightseeing trip. They're not interested in anything but how Hendrix Towers can fatten their pocketbooks."

"Of course."

"You should see these two bozos. One's all teeth. Looks like a young Mickey Rooney. He has no clue that his custom-made suit screams daddy's boy. I wonder how many hard-working men got stomped to make room for that brat to move up? The other – Doyle – is the decision maker of the two. He's on his third Crown and Coke as we speak. His worn-out Bashford jacket tells me the company is tight. But, the bosses think the connection is worth something. They delayed this morning's meeting just so these two could sit in. We're heading into the boardroom soon. I'm pumped. They are getting ready to hear some impressive numbers, thanks to me."

"I'm proud of you."

"You should be." He momentarily muffled the phone, making his words to another person unintelligible.

He continued. "I made reservations at Spilotro's for 8:00. Fine dining with Saltimbocca and a couple of bottles of Barolo – that ought to loosen their wallet. Hey!"

"Yes?"

His voice lowered. "I wish you were going with me instead of them. I'm sorry, Baby. If I didn't spend such an enormous amount of time on the road, I could enjoy you. You'd like that, wouldn't you? I know you can please me when you're on your game. If things were different, I could be there to watch over my beautiful bride, myself. But, if tonight is a success, there's no way that I won't be the next Senior Vice President of Marketing. Lostyn Bonin, SVP. It has a nice ring to it."

"That's wonderful."

"This is our ticket to a new standard of living. We'll be moving to Memphis."

"Memphis?"

"It makes perfect sense. There's no way I can continue to drive back and forth as I do now and carry out my new responsibilities. Next week, I'm going to look at the gated communities north of the city. I've heard that Grandville has some prime homes left."

"Oh."

"You're not expressing concern, are you? You do understand I'm talking about two brand new homes for you, right?"

"It's just that this has been home to us for a long time." Maybe he'd let them keep this house – although the idea of three homes was ludicrous.

He laughed. "Don't worry. I'm doing this all for you, Baby. It's my duty. You'll like the city, I'll make sure of that. Listen, I'm going to stay at the Lucky Draw Casino tonight and be back in town mid-morning. I'll go straight to the golf course. You will be ready for tomorrow night?"

"I will. I'm making a –"

"Just make sure it's good." He hung up.

She covered his meal and poured a cup of hot water infused with chamomile. Everything on her list had been checked three times. Tomorrow evening just needed the final touches. Her body ached too much to lie down, but when the tea settled her, she'd try to rest on the sofa. Not having to remake the bed in the morning was a gift she wouldn't deny herself.

Most women craved the luxuries Lostyn provided. Extravagance wasn't important to her, but her husband decided what was important, and she didn't dare argue. To the contrary. To keep him happy, she always went overboard thanking him for everything.

He never refused her the few things she asked for. That was the key. Never assume anything and always allow him to give. That's what he wanted, and there was no one to blame but herself if she failed.

Being a Senior VP should make him happy. Senior Vice President of – what was it? Oh well, the new position would hopefully relax the pressure he felt.

She yawned. Her social life was practically non-existent. But, there were a few charity activities that Lostyn didn't mind her participating in if everything was in order and he didn't have other plans. There would be opportunities to do charity work in Memphis. She'd give him a list to consider. Asking for his permission always made him happy.

Maybe he'd let her work again if she convinced him it was primarily to make business contacts for him. Finding a nursing position was never a problem, and there'd be plenty of doctors in Memphis willing to invest in gambling. Helping him be successful would make him happy.

Her only course of action was to keep Lostyn content. That required perfection. Her mother was perfect most of the time. Not that Mom had to worry. Her husband treated her like royalty. Linda made a mental note to write down everything her mother excelled at. Then, she resolved to do those things perfectly all the time.

She rewrapped the bandage around her ribs and swallowed

two pain pills before sinking carefully onto the sofa. The Memphis trip hadn't come up during the telephone conversation. Her eyelids grew heavy. He wouldn't mind her checking out their future home. If there were time, she'd even make a point to look at the gated community he mentioned.

The only sound in the house was the ice-maker dropping cubes into the tray. Starting at the top of her head, she worked the tension away by envisioning layers of pressure sliding off her skull. Then, rolled her eyes deep in their sockets before wiggling her fingers and toes and relenting to their heaviness.

She was drifting off when the flower beds came to mind. *Weed-filled beds can be dangerous to one's health,* she thought right before the chamomile and medicine overpowered the need to find her garden gloves.

The phone rang.

Linda pulled herself back up. "Hello?"

"You did it this time."

"What's wrong, Lostyn?"

"Why is it difficult for you to be accountable?"

"I —"

"*I?* That's right. It's always about you. Well, it's not you in the hot seat, is it?"

"I don't understand."

"Bingo! For once, you're right. Let me enlighten you. I pulled Chambers and Associates over to our corner last November. With their recommendations, I streamlined the second and third-floor pits, reducing labor costs twelve percent. Do you know what that means? No, you don't. That's a three-hundred-thousand-dollar savings by the end of the year. Do you think the bozos were impressed? No. They stood up and left before any corrections could be made. Do you know why?"

Lostyn's breaths grew longer.

She cringed. "No."

"Because I forgot a few zeros behind the three in the report. I typed three-thousand! All because you didn't allow me the common courtesy to adequately prepare last night." He growled. "Mr. Gartino yanked his stupid round bifocals off that bubble nose of his and demanded an explanation. I looked like an idiot. Terrance called the meeting short. That has never happened. Never! But, I can't say I blame him. So, because of you, the Hendrix brothers will not be playing golf tomorrow. Instead, I will be in their joint office first thing in the morning trying to explain that oversight. You made me look like a fool! And fools do not become Senior Vice Presidents."

"I'm sorry."

"Not near as sorry as you're going to be. You've pushed me to my breaking point. Are you listening to me? Answer me!"

"I'm listening."

"Do you think the last two nights have been a party? Take my advice. Enjoy your rest because when I get home tomorrow, we are going to dance the night away." His voice dropped to a guttural snarl. "When we're done, you will understand how bad you've messed up. Consider this in that shrinking pea-brain of yours. How often do I operate in the world of uncertainty? You can be certain of this, Linda. You break me, I break you!"

Melissa Kirk

CHAPTER FIVE

The German-made clock on the wall was designed to be wound every week. The next time – Linda tried to think but couldn't recall when it was supposed to be wound again. The calendar on the refrigerator had that information recorded, ensuring she never overlooked the responsibility. How long had the clock been there, its pendulum's constant swing warning her to stay alert?

Her forehead muscles protested as they pulled into a deeper frown. Lostyn received it as a gift to celebrate his fifth anniversary at Hendrix Towers. That was fifteen years ago.

It had been on Bruce's ninth birthday. The den was full of children playing pin-the-tail-on-the-donkey. Mothers stood around, feigning excitement for the game while gossiping about the alleged affair between the senior coach and the new first-grade teacher.

The festivities came to a halt when Lostyn marched in with his gift and began bragging about the quality of a Hermle clock. Everyone dutifully watched while he ceremoniously hammered a nail into the wall and hung it. The children squirmed when he insisted they wait for it to chime at the top of the hour.

When it did, he swung Linda around and danced her through the room, laughing like one of the young party-goers. She tried unsuccessfully to direct his attention to the party. The mothers gathered their kids shortly after that and left, the game not completed and only a handful of gifts opened.

After Bruce had gone to bed, Lostyn confronted her about the lack of excitement over the gift. *"Bruce will have plenty of birthdays. A five-year anniversary only comes once,"* he said before slapping her. That was the first night he worked her whole body over, deciding her ribs were the most convenient landing spot for his fury.

The clock chimed the three-quarter mark of the hour. She lifted a corner of the window blind. The neighbor's vehicles were in their garages, leaving the street void except for the Impala and the steam from the light rain lifting off the pavement.

Before the Impala, a service van had parked for a week by the electrical pole. Before that, a black Dodge Charger sat in the driveway of the vacant house. Wherever she went, the vehicles followed.

None of the neighbors seemed to notice the strange vehicles. But there was always one, watching her every move. Tonight's stalker was parked one house down, across from Brianna's.

She decided long ago that there had to be more than one person assigned to watch her. The vehicle windows were always tinted too dark to tell. But, no one could sit that long without developing a blood clot or begging off from boredom.

She moved to the French doors that lead to the back. No one had ever questioned the fact that the fenced-in yard didn't have a way out. A movement caught her attention. *Tüdampa!*

The coyote sniffed the lingering scent of the rabbits before circling a small spot under the white crepe myrtle. After several turns, he lay down with his head facing the door, unfazed that he was being observed. The outdoor lamp post on the deck automatically came on with the dusk, casting the animal into the shadows. His glowing green eyes fixed on the house's prisoner.

Her back slid down the wall. It didn't matter that she hadn't believed Shospokee superstitions. It didn't matter how *Tüdampa* had gotten into the yard. The coyote was there to remind her that there was no way out.

The ice maker broke the silence to drop more cubes. Being hemmed in proved she didn't deserve freedom. It was true. For every reason Lostyn gave for her being a terrible wife, she could match it with grounds that made her a horrible mother.

The clock chimed the Westminster, followed by seven clear strikes, just like it did the first time Lostyn danced with her – *all night.*

A gasp caught in her throat. Rolling to her knees, she forced herself up and grabbed the suitcase out of the hall closet. After throwing clothes in it, she tossed on top the stash of money that had been hidden in her lingerie drawer.

Through the kitchen window, the Impala's front bumper protruded into the scene from the right. If she dared to talk to the occupant, would the stalker believe Lostyn was going to kill her? A gut feeling said that they didn't care, and her money envelope didn't have enough cash to persuade them otherwise.

Left-over raindrops slipped off the unattended hummingbird feeder. The bully had gone to its nest for the night but would be back tomorrow as aggressive as always.

Next door, the mist formed large water drops on Brianna's bike handles. The young girl never left the bicycle out. Her parents were as protective of their daughter's belongings as they were her. If they ever noticed the strange car –.

Locking the kitchen door, she tossed the luggage into the car and dialed 911.

"911. What is your emergency?"

"There's a strange vehicle sitting across the street in front of my house. It's been there all day. I'm sure whoever is driving it is stalking my daughter. They pulled up while she was practicing cheerleading moves and haven't left. It's an Impala. Gray. I can't see through the tinted windows. Isn't dark tint against the law? Please send someone. I'm terrified. My address is 4442 – I'm sorry – 4444 Wantland Road."

"I'll dispatch an officer to check it out."

"Thank you."

Less than a minute later, a city police car pulled onto the road with its blue lights flashing. It parked diagonally at the rear of the Impala. Two officers got out, their large-brim hats covered with rain protectors.

The car window rolled down. A heavy-set man sat still with his hands on the steering wheel. The officer on the driver side motioned for him to step out. The big man obeyed, the exertion leaving him obviously winded. He looked toward the house, and she leaned back, out of his view. The other officer checked the interior of the car and nodded, before walking up the neighbor's sidewalk.

Linda jumped in her car and opened the garage door. The officer only gave a quick glance her direction, but the heavy-set man stared as she pulled out and drove away from the blue lights, swerving to miss the coyote standing in the middle of the street.

~

Bruce slapped the dust off his cap and sat on the porch glider to unlace his boots. Sweat poured from his brow into small pools of water onto the wooden slats.

The electric-charged atmosphere at the field had made his skin crawl. There had to be a reasonable explanation. He tapped his forefingers together. Based on the evidence . . . Electromagnetic fields presented with weather can manifest biological . . . Blah, blah. He shook the excess sweat from his face and wiped it with his sleeve. Science had an answer for everything.

The wind blew from the southwest and cooled his left cheek. The air stream was perfect. Granddad wouldn't miss any balloons being pushed through the area too early.

When he walked into the house, Grandmother set a big glass of tea on the table. "The work day was long for you."

He bent to kiss her forehead. "I had a flat, or I would have surprised you earlier. Where's Granddad?"

"He is taking a shower before the six o'clock news." Her nose wrinkled. "You will be next."

"I don't stink." He sniffed his armpit and winked. "That's the smell of a working man."

She fan-folded her pink apron hem back and forth.

"Uh-oh. Come on." He led her to the table and pulled out a chair.

The short woman planted herself on it and folded her arms.

He pushed the small step stool over to steady the dangling feet and pulled another chair over for himself. Resting his elbows on his knees, he propped up his chin. Mason jar terrariums filled with different healing herbs and secured to the wall framed her petite figure. "What's wrong?"

Her foot tapped. "Much change has come. Many new people. Modern ways are more important to them than me. Maybe it is time for me to stop."

A veiny hand guided his gaze across the room. Grandmother's prayer shawl lay folded neatly on a wooden bench. The pottery bowls that once belonged to his great, great-grandfather, healer of the Shospokee tribe, were lined up according to size on the table. Next to them, was the battered aluminum ladle wrapped in a sweat cloth. Fresh sage spread across a white tea towel draped over the drying rack.

"The elders depend on you. And what about Granddad? Because of you, his rusty old knees keep moving."

"Do not speak of my John Hugh as rusty. If he hears you, there will be plenty of work for you to do until your knees squeak, too."

He snickered. "Shh. Don't tell on me. I'll claim that your

old ears are rusty."

"I am old."

"So, you're ready to die?"

"No!" She jumped up. "I am not understood. That is what I mean to say." Grandmother went to the sink and stretched to turn on the faucet to rinse the colander of blueberries. Patting them dry, she spread a layer of washed berries on a cookie sheet.

"Let me." He took the pan and carried it to the freezer while she attacked her blue-tipped fingers with a white bristled brush and soap. "Someone say something to you about your medicine?"

"No."

"Then, why are you upset about it?"

Her shoulders squared. "I am not."

"You just said –"

"I know what I said, young man."

He sighed. Granddad's shower was taking too long. He handed her a towel and led her to the work table. "Look. These tools are evidence of your God-given talent to heal people. Don't worry about the doctors in Reno. They won't put you out of business."

"I did not mean to speak of medicine." She held up her prayer shawl. "This is why I am not understood. This is why I am weary, today."

The folded pink and white material was more threadbare than he recalled. One fringe hung from a single thread. The shawl had covered him when he was upset because no one wanted to talk to the new kid at school. When he had pneumonia, she tucked it around him and said a prayer. When Dawn came to visit after her parents died in the accident, Grandmother wrapped herself tightly in it and walked to the prayer rock where she stayed until the next day.

Gently removing the shawl from her hands, he unfolded it and draped it over her shoulders. "You have the special gift of prayer – *Duwaniitehai*. You know that."

58

"You speak truth, Bruce John Hugh. But much makes a soul weary. Trouble approaches us in a thick cloud. It is pushed with a fierce wind. Do you feel it?"

He scratched his grizzled chin. "I don't guess I do."

The corner of her lips turned down. "Your grandfather's showers take too long."

He downed the tea.

She took the empty glass. "I called your mother yesterday. She was weary too."

"Mom didn't say anything to me about it."

Her eyes lit up. "You spoke to her!"

"I texted."

Her eyes narrowed into tiny slits.

His grandparents insisted he respect his elders. Texting was enough.

"I spoke to your father," she said. "He said they will come in two weeks. It will be a good time for you to visit. My *pai'tiompu's* spirit will lift when she is able to see her son. My spirit will be refreshed too."

Whatever. The mountain hike was then. The two women's spirits would have to soar without him. As far as his father was concerned, Grandmother would never understand. She might be able to discern the spirit world but was naïve in the real one.

She poured him another glass of tea. "We are not prepared."

"For what?"

"People we love are –" Her voice cracked.

Granddad walked into the kitchen and gave Bruce a bear hug. *Finally!*

"Good to see you, Son. Didn't know you were coming." He took Grandmother's hands in his. "What about the people we love, my dear Wadonii?"

"People we love are hurting. Their hope is frail, and it will shatter soon. It is because truth hides in the darkness, John Hugh. When the world bows to the trickster –" She lowered her head.

"*Tüdampa* roams with no worry. He has become bold. I fear we are not prepared."

Granddad gently cupped his hands around her face. "Nothing in this world can separate us from the truth. No matter what happens in this old world, together, we will stand strong. Our spirits cannot be broken."

"This is hard for me to believe. You know how *Tüdampa* plays."

"We're prepared for whatever or whoever comes our way. *Tüdampa* will not win." He retrieved his shoes sitting beside extra-small moccasins.

Granddad always patiently allowed his wife to weigh the problems of the world. Then he'd assure her everything was going to be okay. Bruce's answer was much simpler. People care about one thing. Themselves. That was truth. No one had to dig deep to discover that.

Grandmother pulled a brown paper sack and a mason jar of milk out of the refrigerator and sat them on the counter next to two blueberry pies. "You will take these with you, husband."

"Wait." Bruce sniffed the air. There wasn't anything cooking. "You aren't going to Mert's house tonight, are you? It's the balloon races!"

"I'm sorry, Son. The Almighty sets prayer times. Your grandmother walked the path today and discerned it is time to pray. You know I don't disregard a word received."

A bunch of old men was going to meet to pray. At their age, one would think they'd cherish every opportunity to see the annual races. Some of the men didn't have many years left, for Pete's sake. God could wait one more day to hear their petitions. It wasn't like the world was suddenly going to fall apart.

As if Grandmother heard his thoughts, she set her jaw. Balancing the pies on one straightened arm, she opened the back door.

"But the balloons –"

Granddad put the jar of milk in the crook of his arm and

picked up the sack lunch. "Not to worry, Son. You can log the balloons for me when your work is done."

"What work?"

He raised an eyebrow. "The work these old rusty knees didn't get done today. Please sweep the shed and then water the flower beds while we pray. Seize the opportunity to reflect on respecting your elders. You don't mind, do you?"

~

The cracked concrete slab beside the bus garage at the church set under a Maple tree that was trimmed high on one side so that the portable basketball goal would fit under it. The other side was left untouched to block the view from the highway. The rainstorm had shifted the goal sideways, exposing a portion of the net that gapped open where the strands had been torn.

Linda turned off the car, this the third parking spot for the night. She massaged her temples. At her first stop, she searched the web on her phone for women's shelters in Missouri that were far enough away that Lostyn would have trouble finding her. It had taken her an hour to work up the nerve to call one, only to be told they were full.

"Try the Gatehouse. Do you have their number?"

That number was no longer in service. When she called back to get a working number, the line was busy and stayed busy until she finally gave up.

At the second stop, she tried a shelter in Springfield, Missouri. They informed her that residents had to be referred by the Springfield Police Department or the Department of Human Services.

"Go to the police," the woman told her. *"It's the safest way."*

Linda said that wasn't an option.

"Would you be interested in donating to the shelter, then? There are a lot of women in the same position as you, right? I can take your card information over the phone, or you can go to our website..."

61

She turned off the windshield wipers. No one who could help came to mind. Her circle of friends had dwindled to mere acquaintances, none close enough to trust with her secret.

Her money stash totaled only two thousand, twenty-four dollars. A hotel room would eat it up fast. Gas money – to where? Not that she should leave town in the car. Lostyn would report it stolen.

A cynical laugh escaped. The only difference between her and the most desperate woman on earth was a two-week, on-the-run survival fund.

Rain trickled down the windshield. Sporadic lightning flashed horizontally, too far away now to be matched to the low thunder rolls. The storm had passed through, creating power outages and downing tree limbs. Suddenly, she regretted not traveling with the storm. Instead, the torrential downpour and high winds had kept her off the interstate where the semi-trucks went full speed, ignoring the summer disturbance.

A small gnaw encouraged her to go home and try to ride out Lostyn's fury. Perhaps his rage would subside as the storm had. At least food and shelter were there.

Every argument she had in the past for not leaving was proving correct. There was no way to run away from the abuse. Now there wasn't any turning back. She was a colossal failure.

Car lights flickered through the tree. A vehicle passed at a crawl, made what seemed to be a wide half-circle, and stopped. She started the car and left the church without turning on the headlights.

~

Bruce propped up against the headboard and counted the rings until Dawn answered. "Hey! It's a new day so don't sleep it away."

She yawned loud and long. "Bruce John Hugh Bonin. I have to get up early in the morning, goofball. What's up?"

He looked at his half-eaten chicken salad and fry bread sandwich. "Just finishing dinner."

"Baloney."

"Chicken."

"That's not what I meant. Everything all right?"

"Yeah. Just thinking about Ozark Ridge. What's everyone doing?"

"Sleeping. They do that in Nevada?"

"You see much of Mom and Dad? I mean, you said Mom looked rough. Think she's sick or something?"

"She mentioned a few times that she had a headache. Maybe she's stressed about something. As far as your dad, I see him on the sixth pew from the back on the left side of the church on Sunday. That's it."

"Yeah." Why didn't the man get a job closer to home? The long drive made him a tired, grumpy old bear whom Mom had to wait on hand and foot.

"Mom didn't go back to work, did she?"

"Wow, Bruce. Don't you ever talk to your parents? Maybe that's what's wrong. Have you ever thought that your mother might be missing you? Ever heard of love, Bruce? L-O-V-E. Fact is, people miss the people they love." Dawn mumbled something. "No matter what, they're your parents, and Ozark Ridge is your home."

"Stop. I heard enough of that today. Look, go back –"

"Oh, no you don't. Don't wake me up in the middle of the night because you want to catch up on the old home front without asking about me! Remember me? We've only been best friends for how long? Oh yeah, for all of our lives! Here, let me help you. Hey, Dawn, how are you? – Oh, fine. Tell me about the Peace Corps. – I'm really excited. Are you sure that's what you want to do? – Definitely. Now more than ever!"

"I –"

"I'm not done! Hey Dawn, anything else going on with you? – Yeah, I miss my parents. And, oh yeah, I'm going to color my hair on Monday in rainbow colors. There! You're all caught up."

"Go back to bed." He hung up. Who cared? No one in Ozark Ridge was interested in his life. Mom's problem didn't amount to more than just some guilt trip because she didn't please her husband enough.

Light from the TV in the living room flashed odd shapes on the hall wall. He picked up his sandwich. *Sports Highlights* came on in a minute, and his chores were done. The compost pile even got turned and the hoe sharpened.

He paused in the hallway by his grandparents' bedroom and peeked through the cracked door. Grandmother danced, spreading her shawl out like wings, dipping from side to side. Her eyes closed as she bent toward the floor and then opened to search beyond the ceiling as her arms spread out and reached up.

She stopped to open the window. "The full moon will soon grow thin." Turning toward him, the shawl trailed behind before falling still at her sides.

"Sorry. I didn't mean to intrude."

Padding across the room, her chin lifted high to search his eyes. "All is not as it seems. The moon only borrows the light it casts on the earth. Soon, the sun will rise. It is then that everything that appears right will be tested in the true light."

When he didn't respond, she continued, "Dear boy, it is good to learn what truth is. This you have yet to do. Your young mind says many things are certain, but your heart struggles with your thoughts. This makes war. *Gehetmo* will soon come. When you enter the battles, do not seek the wisdom of man. Trust only the Creator of *Amigota*. Do not play with *Tüdampa*."

"Why would I play with the coyote?"

"He will trick you, dear boy. His spirit is not from *Amigota*. As he prowls, evil fills the air with the stench of foul lies."

He flinched.

Her calloused hand reached to caress his cheek. "I pray at the rock every day for you."

Bruce covered the warm hand with his and smiled. "I just came to watch the balloons. I'm sorry you had to pray." He pulled back with the brute honesty, expecting her to slap his arm.

Instead, she pulled the prayer shawl across her chest. "I'm never sorry to pray. I regret I don't make petitions more often. When I walk to the rock, the Creator hears *Duwaniitehai* and promises boldness to face the enemy that can be seen, and my faith remains unbroken. In this room, I pray for the unseen foe that works to deceive our heart."

"I don't understand how you pray and dance at the same time."

"I do not. I make requests on my knees. I celebrate answers in my dance."

"What answer are you celebrating tonight, Grandmother?"

She patted his chest. "Your victory to come." Stepping in rhythm, her actions became light and free again as her arms mimicked the motions of a butterfly.

Soft chanting floated behind him like a haunting ghost as he walked the last stretch of hallway. The only action he had planned was hiking in the mountains with a backpack filled with walnuts, salami, and a water flask. If that was the battle and anticipated victory, Grandmother's dance was welcome, but not necessary.

He plopped down on the sofa. The living room hadn't changed much over the years except for the big-screen TV. He propped his socked feet on the coffee table and turned up the volume.

Granddad's Air Parade log lay next to him. A number six written in red ink marked the front of it. The first five record books stacked on the bookshelf were evidence of how long the races existed.

He understood Granddad's fascination with the balloons. It matched his own preoccupation with the Mustangs. They never failed to come. They never made demands.

While finishing the chores, he'd caught glimpses of the

balloons as they passed over and pulled the log out of his back pocket to make each entry. A new balloon, a gold airship with a French flag had passed over. He had saved the star mark for Granddad to note. But it was late, and Granddad would go straight to bed, so he marked it, imitating the senior man's scratching. *Gehetmo.* He didn't have to fight to know the truth. Dad had never seen the balloons and Mom never mentioned them anymore. Ozark Ridge was a lifetime ago. His mountain hike could not come too soon. Those were the facts. Thinking any coyote could distort that made no sense. Grandmother had already taught him everything he needed to know about *Tüdampa.* Don't feed him.

Swallowing the last of the sandwich, he flipped through the channels until landing on the sports station. The three familiar hosts dressed in suits were already analyzing tomorrow's games.

Did Dawn say she was getting her hair done in rainbow colors? *Huh.* She was going to look like a clown.

CHAPTER SIX

Saturday, 06:30 AM CST

Linda pulled up to the ATM and swallowed four more pain pills before inserting the debit card. The nightmare in the early morning hours was still so fresh, her hand shook as she keyed in the password.

In the dream, a monstrous shadow had chased Bruce.

"Bruce! *Nahuto* – look out!"

He couldn't hear, and the dark shroud overtook him. The shadow arched as a high-pitched bark followed by a lone howl came from within it.

"*Nahuto! It's Tüdampa!*" She ran but didn't gain any ground. "*Nahuto! Nama heganda et'noo – na! Na!*"

Her mother appeared.

"*Koiyah!*" Linda pointed to the shadow.

Wadonii pulled her prayer shawl tight and walked, defiant yelps shrieking in protest as she disappeared into the darkness.

Howling saturated the air. Linda covered her ears and screamed, "*Koiyah!* Bruce! My *nahuto!*" Her feet wouldn't move. "Please, *Tüdampa*, no!"

The words were lost in the chorus of what sounded like a pack of coyotes closing in on her.

"Koiyah! Duwaniitehai!"

Immediately, everything stilled, and the shroud lifted. Bruce stood in the middle of the road. He looked around.

Linda waved.

He turned and ran to hug his grandmother.

"Bruce! *Koiyah!*"

They heard her but walked away.

The gray Impala pulled in front of her. The front doors swung open. Lostyn stepped out of the passenger side. Linda tried to yell for Bruce, but strong hands reached from behind and covered her mouth.

She awoke screaming Bruce's name and grabbed her phone to call but realized the time difference. Two cups of coffee and recalling that she was on the run convinced her not to call at all.

She pulled the money from the ATM slot. The bank's cap for withdrawals per account was three hundred dollars. Withdrawing from both checking accounts and two credit cards yielded an additional twelve hundred to add to the stash.

After looking every direction for the Impala, she pulled away from the bank's service lane. Other than the curious headlights near the church last night, there had been no indication that anyone was following her.

Earlier, while taking a shower at the COMFORT Truck Stop, she had practiced her speech. "I'm sorry, Dawn. I'm sick to my stomach. The ride here about did me in. I can't go and risk infecting these girls with whatever I have, can I?"

Then Linda recognized her error and changed the plan. Busses left Memphis daily that went across the country. Going with Dawn was the best escape route.

She'd even figured out how to make everything work out. Every city begged for Certified Nursing Assistants. She'd find an opening and volunteer for the extended weekend option. That would provide her a place to sleep for at least two nights without having to spend any money. As long as she chose a state that honored Compact Licenses, she could land a registered nursing position in under a week. Her first paycheck would be in three weeks. Surely, an apartment would be available by then.

Arriving at the church, she watched Dawn climb into the van. The blond head soon re-emerged, carrying a small bag of trash. The slim girl walked around the vehicle, lifting her pleated maxi skirt enough to bend and check the condition of the tires.

When Dawn finished the inspection, Linda climbed out of the car and tugged her vest closed, hoping no one questioned the extra layer of clothing on such a warm morning.

The three girls already there chased and grabbed each other. She crossed her arms, relieved the teenagers paid no attention to her.

"Linda!" Dawn came running toward her.

She braced.

"I'm so glad you're here." Dawn hugged her.

Linda drew in a sharp breath.

"Are you okay?"

"I'm fine. I tripped, and the corner of the kitchen chair jabbed me. It happened right before I left."

"I'm sorry! You are so prone to accidents, aren't you? Well, I promise to keep my hugs to myself the rest of the day. You're not going to believe what happened. Miss Connie is sick and can't make it. Can you believe that? It's just you and me with a gang of girls!" She laughed and pulled off the rubber band dangling from her wrist to work the long hair into a side braid. "I'm thankful you're here. I better warn the girls that you're hurt, or you'll be in a world of trouble. Girls! Listen up. Don't hug Mrs. Bonin today." Dawn hurried the preteens into the van and held open the passenger door.

Linda reached into the car to retrieve her purse and suitcase, and crossed her fingers, hoping the rest of the day went as planned. Freedom began today.

Dawn laughed and pointed at the luggage. "Wow, Linda.

Running away from home?"

~

9:00 AM Central Standard Time

"Look! We're in Tennessee!" Lindsey pointed to the sign hanging from the high steel arch of the covered bridge.

Faces covered with masses of curls and big barrettes strained to see out the windows.

"In the middle of the Mississippi River!" one girl exclaimed.

The burst of laughter caused Linda to dig for more pain pills.

They passed the Bass Pro Shop at the Memphis Pyramid. Sunlight bouncing off the glass-covered structure momentarily blinded them. Dawn swerved to miss a pothole. The jerk ripped through Linda's midsection, causing her to groan.

"Sorry," Dawn said.

She straightened slowly. "If you take the next exit, you can turn to the left and be only a couple blocks from parking."

"Great! I'll be glad to be rid of that car behind us. It's been riding our tail for a while."

Linda broke out in a sweat. "A gray car?"

"It's yellow with a bumblebee racing stripe."

"Oh."

She caught a glimpse of Lucy. The teen sat quietly, staring out the window. "Something wrong?"

"No, ma'am."

Lindsey yelled from the back of the van, "She's sad. Her dog ran away yesterday." The chubby girl leaned over the seat. "It's okay, Lucy. Your mom will find him today."

"Sit down and buckle up!" Dawn ordered.

Lindsey fell back into her seat.

"He'll come home soon," Linda said.

"I doubt it," said Lucy. "He ran away with me standing

right next to him. Some dogs I never seen before crossed our yard. There was four of them. Buxley took off. I yelled at him to come back, but he ignored me. I never seen him act that way. He's always minded me before. I watched until I couldn't see him anymore." Her eyes squinted. "The sun was too bright."

"Did he leave with the others in the morning or at night?"

"Right before dinner. I couldn't eat anything. But, Dad didn't get mad at me for wasting food. I guess he was sad too."

She reached back carefully and patted the young girl on the knee. "Let's decide Buxley went visiting and will be home this evening. We'll go to the pet pavilion and buy a bone. My treat! But you must promise me you'll try to have fun today. Deal?"

Lucy smiled, revealing braces sporting neon pink and green bands. "Deal."

Linda turned back around and slipped a hand under her vest to adjust the wrap. Buxley and the pack were on the move the same time as the rabbits and deer.

Crossing into Tennessee with no snags boosted her confidence. Dawn had an itinerary but so did she. First, enjoy the free day with the girls. Then, when the rest of the group climbed into the van to leave for home, she would go to the bus terminal. She fabricated a story about visiting an old school friend, and Dawn hadn't questioned.

The Mega Bus's last outbound was at 10:00 pm. The terminal was four miles from the pyramid – an hour's walk.

Dawn turned up the radio and smiled. Linda smiled back. After reviewing the bus schedule, it was obvious that her new life should begin in Dallas – a large city with a short winter. Her next life wasn't going to have any lists or fancy wall clocks to wind up. Every meal could be made in a crockpot if she wished. And the bandage that was cutting into her skin was going in the trash.

Her phone flashed, and Lostyn's picture popped up. The text read, "Come home."

She shrugged. Her grace period was over, but he was one hundred miles away.

71

"I got the promotion. You are forgiven."

The freedom to not have to answer him was exhilarating.

"I'm tracking you with GPS."

The blood that had just rushed to strengthen her resolve suddenly deflated her heart.

Dawn exited the interstate and slowed. While the youth leader gave her charges safety instructions, Linda took her own precaution. Rolling down the window, she rested her arm on the ledge. When the van eased toward the right, the phone slipped out of her hand and into the greasy water puddle by the yield sign.

∼

07:00 AM Pacific Standard Time

Grandmother was already working in the flower beds. Granddad headed to the shed, leaving Bruce to his thoughts. He leaned forward on the porch swing, causing its hinges to squeak in protest. He'd been awake most of the night replaying Grandmother's words. *"Dear boy, it is good to learn what truth is. Prepare."*

The truth was life had been busy lately. That was the reason for the break this weekend. But prepare for what? He'd studied seismology since high school. He knew as much, if not more than his boss and could tackle any situation that came up on any work site.

Most of his peers struggled with relationships or money. The truth was that he had little of the first and, thanks to the monthly deposits from his parents, plenty of the second. He did a quick calculation. Three more months until he turned twenty-four and the money stopped. It was okay with him – Mom and Dad wouldn't have to feel like they had to make any more guilt offerings.

He clasped his hands behind his head. He was competent. He had money. The truth was that he had a good life and the ability to keep it that way. Grandmother's celebration dance last night was timely – he was coasting in victory lane. The only preparation in store for him was gathering supplies for the hike.

Grandmother joined him on the porch. "How long will you be here?"

"I don't have to be back to work until Tuesday."

"Good." She wiped her forehead, leaving behind a streak of dirt. "You will have time to rest. Did you bring your dirty laundry?"

He smiled. "Nope. Decided to give you a break." Reaching over, he rubbed the smudge away. "Surprised?"

"Yes, I am. It is a good change."

"I'm saving it all up for my next visit."

"Hmm! Your apartment will smell of soiled clothes and friends will stop coming to visit." She put her garden gloves back on and retrieved the basket hat from the hook by the door. Squatting in the next section of flowers, the petite hands began pulling barely visible weeds from around each cluster of tiny pink flowers. The flowerbed ran the entire length of the porch, but no matter how hot it got, the old woman would work until her weekly crusade ended.

Granddad stood by the shed, cleaning each garden tool. The freshly oiled hoe and shovel stood propped against the metal building, while the rake and other tools lined the other side of the door, awaiting their anointing. When finished, Granddad would turn his attention to the crop. The strategic notes the man kept for each farming season matched those of a general preparing the next campaign.

Bruce smiled and checked the field. Round alfalfa bales dotted the land, except for the farthest acres by the tree line which stood ready for harvest. That's where Granddad would begin work Monday.

His smile evaporated. That morning, his grandfather had walked in for breakfast just in time to sit down to two eggs, bacon, and waffles. He didn't say a word about the previous night's meeting or why it lasted until daybreak. That was the man's mantra – quietly do the work of Almighty God. Grandmother had talked her usual chatter, never questioning her husband's long night.

Bruce rolled his eyes. Grandmother spoke practically non-stop in riddles but then become silent when she needed to speak up. Just one question from her might have given insight into his supposed *Gehetmo*.

He'd always made it a point to not dig deep into the mysteries of life and soul, but he had to understand what she meant. Her talk of wolves and coyotes and *Gehetmo* was about God and evil, and the war between the two, but he wanted to be able to relieve her worries.

Only one person around could decipher the Shospokee's peculiar spiritual insight. He grabbed the porch railing and swung his legs over.

He stopped. Granddad wasn't in sight. The shed door was closed and padlocked. Grandmother's hat and gloves hung by the door.

CHAPTER SEVEN

The Riverfront

01:00 PM Central Standard Time

"But Miss Dawn, he's cute!" Lindsey failed in her attempt to whisper. "We saw him outside the window, smiling at us and everything. He stared at you, big time."

"Hush." Dawn's face turned red when the host leading them to their table overheard and winked at her. He passed out the menus and joked with the girls, causing a wave of giggles.

The extra pain pills worked. After massaging out the stiffness in her neck from continually looking back, Linda finally decided no one was trailing her and had walked the entire mall, enjoying the teens' constant chatter and Dawn's admonitions when one strayed too far from the group.

She slid into the booth next to Lindsey and picked up a menu. Her gaze glazed over the options that faded in and out of double vision. She tried to remember how many pills she had taken but it required too much thought.

Some of the girls lay their heads on the table. The busy day was taking its toll on Dawn, too. Her braided hair fell out of its twist, and the long skirt was hiked higher on one side, exposing a tiny cross tattoo above the ankle.

The late lunch and one hour at the Mud Island Museum were the only stops left on the itinerary. Pointing out how tired everyone was might encourage Dawn to cut the museum and head back earlier. Then Linda could join up with her imaginary friend. She preferred to get to the bus station before the early drinkers emerged onto Beale Street.

The teens huddled around the menu Dawn held as she pointed out which meals they could choose from. One girl asked for steak. Another wanted crab legs.

"You're not paying attention," Dawn warned. "We have a budget."

Linda smiled. As kids, Dawn and Bruce laughed and teased like the girls did today. The twosome had spent hours together, either hiking the trails at the park or playing cards on the area rug in the den. Lostyn was much more relaxed back then. Confrontations had been rare. Many Saturday mornings passed while the four of them sat in a circle playing Crazy Eights.

"Have you decided?" Dawn asked.

Everyone at the table stared at her.

"I'll just have a vanilla milkshake." She handed the menu to the waitress.

"Is your side still bothering you?" Dawn asked.

"Huh?"

"Are you still hurting?"

"No. I mean, yes. Well, maybe a little." She changed the subject. "I've never been here before."

"Isn't it wonderful? I googled Beale Street and Mud Island. This spot popped up on both." Dawn lowered her voice. "It may be a little pricey, but the girls are worth it. They've been super great, don't you think?"

"They have." She loosened her vest. "So, have you talked to Bruce lately?"

"I spoke with him yesterday." Dawn groaned. "Do you know he never does anything I ask him to? At least, not until I beg him."

"I can't remember when I heard that last," she teased.

"He's too busy to talk most of the time. What he does and who he hangs with takes priority over everyone back in *Podunk* Ozark Ridge. I bet he's not that way with you."

Linda recognized the sudden set chin and turned down mouth. It was classic Dawn when Bruce refused to concede. She folded her hands on the table. Dawn was right, though. Her son didn't have many connections left in his childhood town. She couldn't remember the last time he had bothered to contact his father.

"Please stay in touch with him. You've been friends too long not to."

Dawn shrugged.

The waitress set drinks on the table, and the girls passed them around. Across the room, a man jumped up, sending his chair airborne to the next table, barely missing the couple eating their meal.

"I said no!" The man yanked the little boy out of the next chair and pulled him toward the back of the restaurant. "I'll teach you to listen."

He glared at the woman who cowered in the seat. "You baby him. It's your fault he's such a brat. I'll deal with you later." He jerked the whimpering boy into the bathroom.

The dining area fell quiet. The woman looked down and pulled her hair forward. Linda's stomach clenched, and she smoothed her own hair into place. A loud wail came from the bathroom. Everyone stared at the woman. Linda knocked over her water glass and jumped up. "Oh my! I can't believe I did that. Waitress!"

Everyone turned to her.

"I'm so sorry! What a mess." She sopped up the water with the stack of napkins. "Oh, my! Can you believe how clumsy I am? I didn't get any of you wet, did I? Thank goodness our meals aren't here yet."

The woman at the other table turned toward the wall.

"There! I think I've got my mess cleaned up."

Lindsey rolled her eyes, and the girls giggled. When Dawn frowned, they covered their mouths, fighting back the laughter.

The other patrons turned back to their meals except for the round-bellied man sitting alone at a window table who had ignored the scene. Undeterred, he continued reading the newspaper that rested high on the fat stomach, shielding his face. The only movement from him was a snap with his chubby hands to straighten the open paper that started to fold down.

"What else did Bruce have to say?" she asked, a little too loudly.

Dawn pouted. "He was going to the ranch this weekend. I wish I could go somewhere. Anywhere!" A huge grin turned her lips back up. "But! I'm expecting a call from the Peace Corps any day now. I'm going to India! It's so exciting! My experience working with the youth has prepared me, don't you think?" Lindsey tugged on her braid. "What, Lindsey?"

Poor Dawn. The Peace Corps would not send the naïve girl to India.

"Are you sure you want to do that?" Linda asked. "It can't be as glamorous as it sounds. In fact, it's probably very dangerous."

"My parents started mission work when they were younger than me. And your mother taught me how to pray for bravery. I do it every morning. I'm ready! Besides, there isn't anything here, anymore. Well, my granny is still living, but you know her memory is gone. I won't be missed between visits. And Bruce isn't interested. I mean, well, you know . . ."

Dawn distracted herself watching shoppers pass by outside the window. The pained look crossing her face was one Linda had never seen before. The lovely young woman had grown from a stick-legged, gawky girl into a stunning likeness of her deceased mother.

Linda sat back. Bruce and his playmate weren't children anymore, and the Peace Corps wasn't the answer Dawn Finley was looking for. Until now, she'd assumed Dawn didn't date because of her busy charity work schedule. Her heart quickened at the thought of not being around to see what kind of relationship developed between the now grown-up friends.

She twirled the silver wedding band on her finger. If only God would rewind time and rewrite history to give Lostyn a decent childhood. Give their marriage the chance it deserved without the life-changing trauma her husband experienced as a Marine. Most of all, she wished all the years that Bruce was gone could be undone, and instead, she able to share every moment of his teen years with him.

"He is just busy, right now, Dawn. Guess what? Lostyn said there's a chance we'll buy a home in Nevada, soon. If we do, you'll have someplace to visit! You two can spend a lot of time together." She bit her lip at the unintended false hope.

Dawn looked down and busied herself with the untidy braid. "That's great, but I doubt I'm on his priority list."

Their food was taking a long time. Linda looked around for the waitress. The woman who sat at the table was gone.

~

04:00 PM Central Standard Time

Linda tapped the pen against the wrought iron fence that ran along the sidewalk overlooking the Mississippi River. While the girls finished touring the museum, she scanned the last list she ever intended to make.

There was enough money for the bus ticket, three nights in a Motel 6, and a cheap phone. She would buy two pairs of scrubs and a good pair of work shoes. Once in Dallas, she could use public transit to find a temporary CNA position while looking for a job and housing. She folded the list and put it in her purse.

Everyone else was gathering at the van, but she wasn't ready yet. Telling Dawn goodbye without displaying any emotion would be almost impossible. Getting her suitcase and walking away – she forced back tears. The day had passed quickly. In less than four hours she'd be on a bus to Dallas. Alone.

Two joggers with elongated shadows passed by on the grassy stretch below. They jumped the stairs two at a time. Once on the sidewalk, they sped up, disappearing around the corner of the museum. It was a perfect day to run. She followed their course to the end of the fence, broadening her steps to match their wet footprints that were drying fast on the hot surface.

Over the river, cotton-ball clouds pushed a dark reflection of the opposite Arkansas shoreline toward her. Mid-river, the sun burst through the clouds, spraying golden rays over the water and up the bank.

She laughed. She wasn't that big of a fool. The sun-kissed portion of the river was as cold and dark beneath the surface as it was under the image of the bank cast in black. The entire Mississippi churned, its currents ready to pull down and swallow any intruders. *You can't have me.*

A woman passing by frowned and pushed her children ahead. They must have heard her laugh, but it didn't matter. They were strangers. She could be anyone here. Liz, maybe. Or Janice. *Hello, I'm Janice – from Memphis.* But, Hendrix Towers was in Memphis, so she couldn't stay. It was Lostyn's territory.

Across the street, tall brick buildings with rows of empty windows faced the riverfront. Monday, the doors to the School of Law would open for hundreds of students to stream in. Some bleary-eyed from late-night partying. Others looking for friends. All with names. Some with secrets.

Hello. I'm Janice.

In the parking lot, all the doors to the van flew open and the girls loaded their newly purchased treasures. Lindsey buckled a stuffed brown bear in a seat and posed for a picture. Lucy climbed in. Dawn opened the passenger door.

"You won't be joining them."

She looked over her shoulder. The big man from the

Impala stood eye to eye with her. His thinning black hair parted on the left. A mole grew in his eyebrow on the same side. When he scratched his cheek, she recognized the chubby hand that belonged to the man who hid behind the newspaper at the restaurant.

"It's time to go. I'm going to be paid handsomely to take you home. Then, I'll be able to go on an extended vacation. I don't believe your husband will worry about you running off again."

She'd been as exposed as the woman at the table, and now felt as helpless as the little boy being dragged to his chastisement.

"The police should have locked you up," she spat out.

"I've got a Private Investigator's license that says otherwise. Brad, the cop, and I caught up on days gone by – had a good laugh about the last call-in on me. That was a long time ago. I've nearly paid my entire mortgage watching you."

He squeezed her arm, sending tingles to the tips of her fingers.

"Ow!"

"Oh, I know you're used to much worse than that. I've watched a few skirmishes through the window. I'm not sure how you were always able to upset your husband before I could even record my hours and leave. But, he tells me you are a master at screw-ups." He gave a small tug. "Let's walk. Mr. Bonin is anxious to have you home."

She jerked away. "I will walk on my own!"

He stopped and cocked his head.

The air stunk like sulfur. The blue herons at the harbor were gone. North of the Pyramid, a barge carrying bulk freight appeared stalled.

The investigator swore.

Linda took off her sunglasses. The buildings reached skyward. No. The ground was moving! She reached for the railing, but it rose above them, pulling the sidewalk with it and throwing them back.

The ground moved in waves underneath her. Thunder from beneath the earth rumbled in sync with the pulse of the earth.

Blood dribbled into her eye. When the motion stopped, she blinked to clear her vision.

The bridge once connecting the two shorelines now ran from the opposite shore into the middle of the river. Beyond the bridge, a train hung from the railway overpass, two of its boxcars swaying like a pendulum. The frame of the Pyramid, stripped of its glass, tilted toward the river.

Noises rushed back in. The Civic Center collapsed, jolting the ground. Pieces of wreckage whizzed through the air. A window pane flew over her and drove itself vertically into the cracked sidewalk. A low growl grew to a roar that dwarfed all the other sounds. Linda looked for its source.

"No!"

The Mississippi River ran backward, creating a dam that rose into the sky. It arced over the flattened law school. She scrambled to wrap her legs around the twisted sidewalk railing where she stood moments ago and brace.

"Pray for me! *Koiyah!*"

Her back took the brunt as the force of the water jerked her away and into the demolished building. The world went black.

"Duwanii – te – hai."

~

Translucent droplets splashed, bouncing white rings onto the black. Each sphere grew, transforming the blackness into rainbow colors.

"Hey, lady."

Linda forced her eyelids open. Clouds of pale green and brown passed in front of the sun. She vomited up gritty water. Hands turned her head to the side, cleared the waste, and turned it back.

A square-jawed man with a bloody scrap covering most of his face knelt in front of her. "You walloped the pavement. Got a cut above your ear – not too bad, though." He tore off the bottom of his t-shirt and wrapped it at an angle around her forehead and over one ear.

She coughed up more grit. "Is this the parking lot?"

"I don't know which lot you're talking about." He helped her stand and held on until her legs steadied. "There. That's good. I'd get away from this building if I were you. And stay away from the river!" he shouted back as he ran off.

She stumbled through the mud-covered brick and glass. In front of her, a hand with long fingers and pale painted nails stuck out of a pile of rubble. Adrenaline surged through her body. "Hold on!" Throwing aside concrete chunks, she shouted, "Can you hear me? I'll get you!" Her hands dug faster. "I'm helping!"

The shoulder wasn't attached to a body. She scrambled back. *Oh, my Lord!* What just happened?

Across the river, fire shot into the sky, followed by an explosion. Like fireworks, smaller flames burst from the ground, spewing material every direction. The blast threw dust into the air that rained back down, coating everything with ash.

A horror movie played in front of her. The river's new course flowed west of its bank. Wild-eyed men holding limp bodies ran, looking for aid. A little boy's face puckered as he cried out. Women staggered, searching for the lost toddler, praying it was theirs.

"Dawn!" Holding a discarded beach towel over her nose and mouth to protect from the fumes penetrating the air, she followed a split in the earth that ran down the middle of Front Street toward the parking lot. Pools of fire dotted the ground, forcing her to detour around them.

A group of men pushed the van to what remained of the street, and the girls climbed in. Lindsey limped, but otherwise, everyone appeared to be okay. Dawn shook the men's hands before moving to the open area and circling.

Linda started to wave but crouched down instead. The P.I. was in the parking lot, standing next to the Impala. He brushed away the broken glass from the passenger window. Pulling a shirt out of the car, he applied pressure to his arm to stop blood flowing from a long gash.

Dawn needed to know that she was all right, but the young girl was heading toward the investigator. Forcing her shaking hands to obey, Linda bound the beach towel around her ribs and raked the mud off her shoes.

"Forgive me!"

She stumbled the opposite direction.

CHAPTER EIGHT

Linda ran, jumping over desks and twisted window frames while praying the shattered glass wouldn't penetrate her shoes. Following the wide gap in the road that ran for blocks along the yellow center lines, she covered her ears to the wails escaping from under the flattened buildings. On the other side of the split, a tract of river-stripped land stretched to the embankment.

Black sludge slid where the river once ran. Large bubbles floated on the surface, ballooning in size until they popped, spewing green gas into the air.

A woman jostling a baby in her arms grabbed her. "Have you seen my husband? He went to get the car. I must find him! Emma's bottle is in the diaper bag – it's time for her to eat." She bounced the ashen-faced baby up and down so hard, the tiny girl's lopsided headband popped off.

Linda swallowed and looked back where the concrete garage once stood.

"Jimmy!" The young mother bolted toward the garage. Emma's lips puckered at the jolt.

"Wait! Don't go in there!"

"Jimmy! I need you!" The child's petrified face disappeared under the only standing support column. The woman's voice hollowed as she repeatedly shouted her husband's name.

Linda dragged a piece of lumber to the gap in the road and shoved it across. A dark-haired man clutching a diaper bag came around the corner of the same building the joggers ran by earlier.

"Are you Jimmy?"

His jittery eyes widened. "Sandra and Emma! Where are they?"

When she pointed to the garage, he threw the bag over his shoulder and sprinted.

Using her arms to balance, she steadied one foot at a time on the board. The earth trembled. A crash rocked the ground, forcing her to jump across the rest of the divide. *Don't look back.*

Next to the old river bank, a group of people was raising a makeshift tent beside an ambulance. A swarm of people flocked toward the already overflowing area. Some were covered with concrete dust while others were soaked from the river's fury. All wore the same stunned look.

Just outside the tent, a young teen in a Memphis Redbirds jersey stood guard in front of three deceased men, dressed in the same top and lying in a row. A tall man in a white shirt with rolled up sleeves was assessing the injuries.

"I can help."

He glanced at her banded head and waist. "Looks like you need help."

"Just a bump and bruised ribs. I'm a nurse –"

"Thank goodness. Here –" He pulled a pair of gloves from his back pocket. "The woman in green shorts has a possible right humeral fracture. Superficial layer of skin gone on the child's right foot, and the senior in the striped dress has a laceration over her left ear. Paramedics are working on two critical."

He inspected the bump on her head. "Not bad. Listen, if you can triage those –"

"On it." She headed to the wounded who were scattered around the perimeter of the tent.

"Hey."

"Yes?"

"I'm Doctor Randall Gipson. What's your name?"

"Janice, from Memphis."

"Thanks, Janice."

Two broken legs and a possible shock victim caught her eye. An elderly man's hands clenched his chest. She guided him to the doctor first.

~

"Hang on!"

Dawn shoved the last girl into the van as it slid backward. She dove into the driver's seat to push on the brake, but the vehicle jerked to a standstill when its tires hit a curb.

"Please make it stop!" Lucy burst out, burying her head into the big stuffed bear. "I want to go home."

"I know you do, honey." Dawn leaned over the driver seat. "Eyes this way. Anyone hurt? Lindsey, what's wrong?"

"I fell." She pointed to a swollen ankle protruding from the hem of her jeans. "I twisted it."

"Lucy, move back and let Lindsey rest her foot on your seat."

Lucy reached to help, but Lindsey cried out.

Her lips quivered. "I'm sorry."

"It's all right," Dawn assured her. "Hey, didn't you bring a camera? Take some pictures for us."

Lucy dug in her purse.

"I'm going to borrow the bear." Dawn lifted Lindsey's leg and set it on top of the stuffed animal. "Anyone else hurt?"

The girls shook their heads.

"Thank goodness. Now, hold hands with the girl next to you and bow your head. Pray silently. Now!"

One girl whimpered, causing a round of sobs from the

others.

She slung open the door. "I need all of you to do me a big, big favor. I'm going to get out and –"

Lindsey's face paled. "Don't leave us."

"I promise I'm not going far. I have to look for Mrs. Linda. She'll be looking for us. I'm just going to step out and wave my arms to help her find us. You'll be able to see me, too." She shut the door before they could object and ran to the open area.

"Linda!"

Scared faces glued to the van windows watched her. Giving them a thumb up, she prayed for the earth to stay still. Vehicles tossed into a heap blocked the sidewalk. She jumped onto the hood of one, but wet muck slid her off. Pulling up a corner of her skirt, she wiped a spot dry and climbed back on.

Fires dotted both shorelines, casting an ominous shadow over distorted bodies lying in piles where the wall of water deposited them. Fighting the impulse to run to the van, she signaled the girls that she'd be back. Sliding off the other side, she choked back her fear and worked through the corpses, pushing aside the top bodies to see if Linda was beneath them.

The earth moved again, sending the partially standing parking garage crashing to the ground. Concrete dust spewed into the air, mingling with the green clouds billowing toward her. She scrambled back over the cars.

The girls were climbing out of the van.

"Get back in!"

Her head whirled. *Think!* The bridge they crossed only a few hours earlier was destroyed. If the one on Interstate 55 still stood, she'd cross the river and find a safe place for the girls. Then come back for Linda.

She rubbed her face. If she could just talk to Bruce, he'd be able to tell her what to do.

"Did she call?" she yelled at the girls.

"Who?"

"Mrs. Linda. I thought she might try to call."

Lindsey started crying.

"Come on, now. Mrs. Linda just can't get to us, but emergency teams will be here soon, and they'll help her." She grabbed her phone and punched in Linda's number, which started a frenzy of girls hunting for their phones. Her call went to voice mail the first attempt. The signal disappeared the next.

Lindsey threw her phone down. "My mom didn't answer."

"The cell towers aren't working. I'm going to get you home, honey, I promise. We're leaving right now. Mrs. Linda will be transported with everyone else who is stranded."

Lucy's camera flashed. "We should wait for her. I'll take lots of pictures. I can show them in Social Studies."

Dawn set her phone where she could watch for a signal and started the van. "Won't we all have a story to tell?"

Emergency crews hadn't arrived yet, but surely, they'd come. She forced her ragged breathing to calm. *I'm sorry, Linda.*

~

Bruce stirred when John Hugh walked into the den and sat down.

"When do the Cubs and Diamondbacks play, Son?"

"At 5 o'clock, I think." He scrolled the channels. "The Padres and Mets game may already be on. Yep. Here it is." He handed the remote to his grandfather. "I'm getting a glass of tea. Want one?"

"Sounds good. While someone I know slept, I worked up a thirst," Granddad grunted. "If you're going to run with the big dogs —"

"I know." He imitated Granddad's voice, "You've got to get off the porch."

The older man laughed.

"It's all Grandmother's fault, you know. She served me two slices of pie for lunch." He patted his stomach. "Not used to that kind of eating at the college cafeteria."

"Please pour your grandmother a glass. I saw her coming this way."

"She been down the path?"

"Yes."

"Granddad, I want to talk about last night."

"Not now, Son. I'm ready for baseball and tea." Granddad's freckled head leaned against the recliner.

In the kitchen, Grandmother was folding her prayer shawl.

"That's still as pretty as the first day I saw it." Bruce pecked her cheek. "Just like you."

She patted his arm. "There is more pie. You do not have to persuade me with your tongue."

"You *are* beautiful. I mean that."

Her eyes sparkled.

"So, I'll take ice cream with that pie." He dodged her playful swing and laughed. "I'm going to pour us some tea. Go and sit with Granddad."

"Do not bring my drink in a Mason jar," she warned.

"I won't." He pulled out her favorite, a frosted glass with painted turquoise tulips, and set it next to two larger quart jars.

Maybe she'd offer to take him down the path this weekend. He'd only been invited to the rock a few times. Grandmother took him there the morning after Granddad disciplined him for fighting at school. There was the time he struggled to decide which college to go to. Oh, yeah, when his granddad had gallbladder surgery, too.

He cut a half lemon into three large slices. It was weird. She'd kneel in front of the rock and spread her shawl over it as if expecting to catch God's answers to her prayers. An unexplainable energy encompassed him during his visits – much different from the incident he experienced in the field yesterday.

He blew out his nostrils at the thought and drew in the scent of fresh-squeezed lemon and blueberry pie.

As soon as the ball game ended, he'd bring up the subject of last night again. Something significant happened to trump the balloon races with a prayer meeting. Something connected to

Grandmother's concerns that she undoubtedly spoke of at the rock.

He wasn't at war with anyone, although he did feel a tug between needing to know why his mother would be hurting and not caring if she did. She wasn't there when he hurt. His grandparents had carried that burden. Grandmother should be perturbed instead of worried.

He respected the culture his Shospokee grandmother grew up in and admired her regard for nature. He appreciated the status elders still held in their tribe, especially when compared to the attitudes many fellow students had at the college. But, Granddad was the one who understood all the talk about moons and coyotes – not him.

Crud! They were just old folks who worried too much. It didn't take a lot to shake them up. That was the truth.

The volume on the television increased. He chuckled. Grandmother always stood during the National Anthem. The dear lady couldn't keep up with the fast-changing world, but she stood rock-solid, unwavering in her convictions.

That's why the woman was really *Mom* to him, although he would never be free to call her that. She wouldn't tolerate the disrespect. But, they all knew that his birth mother gave him up a long time ago.

His grandparents both stood in front of the TV when he returned. He set the drink tray down. "What is it?"

The evening news anchor said, "We hand it over to Glen Stone. Tell us what you know, Glen."

The news field reporter shook his bangs from in front of his glasses and nodded to the cameraman. "Information is just coming in of an earthquake, Julia. Right now, the closest reporting we have available is from Topeka. Our affiliate there is reporting that all traffic east of Kansas City on Interstate 70 has come to a complete halt. We've heard similar reports for Interstate 40 near the Little Rock area in Arkansas."

Someone handed the reporter a note and his eyebrows

furrowed. "One moment." He muffled his microphone and stepped out of camera range.

Bruce felt his pocket and ran to the bedroom where his phone was charging. There were five missed calls from work.

"What is it?" Granddad called out.

"Turn the sound up!" He hit the call button. *Come on, Chris!* He tried again, but the circuit lines were jammed.

The reporter's voice shook through the house. "The preliminary report is a 7.2 magnitude earthquake along the New Madrid Fault line."

He bolted to the television. "7.2!"

"John Hugh." Grandmother fell to her knees.

Bruce picked her up and carried her to the chair.

"Calm down." Granddad rubbed her hands.

She pulled them away and grabbed his shirt collar. "My *pai'tiompu!*"

"I've got to go," Bruce said. "Chris has been trying to call. They'll send me there – I'm sure of it. I'll find Mom, Grandmother. I promise I will."

Granddad stood. "You've been called."

He tried the number again. "I know. If I can't get a signal by –"

"That's not what I mean."

He looked up.

"You have been called to help, Son. God has prepared you for this time. The Almighty set our hearts to intercede on your behalf last night. We will continue to pray for you as we did until dawn – for protection and discernment until we hear from you." Granddad walked to the door and opened it. "Go with God."

CHAPTER NINE

After four days, the air still hung heavy with gray smog. Linda repulsed the sickeningly sweet smell of death encompassing her. As of yesterday, she'd narrowed her view to the immediate surroundings, refusing to look west. In that direction, hundreds of corpses were lined up with the few survivors still in the area walking single file past them, searching for loved ones.

A steady flow had passed through the tent for medical attention, but only a handful waited now. The critical had died. The slightly injured realized they would live and climbed on buses rerouted to transport out of the city. Everyone left looked like either the destitute or predators preying on them.

Emergency teams combined forces two days ago, moving further into the business district, where generators provided much-needed power. Her teammates had decided to disband in the morning. Tomorrow night, the makeshift first-aid station would succumb to the darkness.

Anyone staying in the private residences bordering the blocks of former quick-service stores, cafes, and small offices were being encouraged to leave immediately.

Lack of sleep pulled Linda into the metal folding chair. She wished she could crawl into a corner and pass out until the withdrawals from the oxycodone wore off. The sweating was still profuse, but at least the hand tremors had stopped.

A stout woman in a torn high-waist dress sat down in front of her. Blood seeped out of a u-shaped laceration and onto the lady's rolled-down knee-high sock.

She patted the woman's knee. "In ordinary circumstances, stitches would be in order. But, I believe we can get you fixed up."

An old, dull blue Chrysler bounced over the cracked road and jerked to a stop too close to the tent. People waiting for the next transport bus scurried out of the way. A man got out and hobbled toward her.

"My leg is broke. You gonna have to help. Oh, it hurts." He made it to the chair and pushed the elderly woman. "Move over. I gotta be seen now."

Linda grabbed the chair to keep it from overturning with the woman in it. "What do you think you're doing?"

He swung at the flustered woman and missed, toppling him into Linda. His breath stunk of booze.

"Sit down." She pushed him into the next chair.

A lanky woman with tangled hair jogged over and dropped her backpack to the ground. Her chest sucked in, begging for more air. When her breathing evened, she said, "I have to get to St Jude Hospital. Will you help me, please?"

"Are you hurt?"

"No. I've been trying to get there since the earthquake. When the aftershock hit, it messed up my car. I've walked from Batesville."

"You can't walk that far."

"Well, I did. Took me two days, but I'm here. The children need me." She held out her lanyard. *Volunteer* was typed under her name. "Please. I can't walk any further."

Linda stared at the name. "Reports I heard indicated most

of the children have been transported out."

"But they love for me to play games with them. It takes their mind off the pain." The volunteer teared up. "They've suffered enough."

Linda agreed. If there were any children still there, they needed their dedicated play companion. She grabbed the man's keys. "Here."

"Wait. You ain't taking my car."

The elderly woman kicked his foot. "Oh, shut up, old man. The children need her."

"Why, you old biddy. I'll –"

Linda stood. "You want that leg treated or not?"

"You can't refuse me service." He belched. "You gotta fi— fix it."

She put her hands on her hips. "Do you see anyone that's going to make me help you?"

The volunteer got on her knees and folded her hands together. "Mister, I'll bring it back. I swear."

"No."

The female patient grabbed his coat and pulled out a flask. "Just as I thought. What were you saying?" She started pouring its contents on the ground.

"Stop! Here." He threw the keys. "But you bring it back tonight."

The volunteer ran to the car.

He swung for the flask. "Give me that, you heifer."

"I oughtta knock you over the head with it. You sit there and behave, or that's just what I'll do." The female patient shoved it into his chest. "I'm going to tell the doctor on you."

Linda bandaged the woman's leg and helped her to the transport section. Grabbing the volunteer's abandoned backpack, Linda pointed to the man, "You stay right there."

"Ah. Sticky fingers." He waved a finger in the air and muttered.

She snatched the scissors and ducked behind the toppled

neon business sign. Digging through the pack, Linda found the woman's driver license stuck to the bottom. Using the sharp scissors, she cut through the laminated I.D. without effort. The picture fell off to the ground. *There!* Her full name was now *Janice Mitchell.*

"Anyone know where your nurse went?" the doctor asked.

"Sorry, Doctor." She ran back and glared at the drunk, who slipped his hand up to cover the hidden flask in his shirt.

~

Doctor Gipson dropped a pair of scrubs beside Linda. "These are the last ones. Found them in a box someone dug out of Regional Medical's storage facility." He pointed to her clothes.

"I'm sorry, Doctor."

"No apologies. You've worked harder than anyone." He held out his hand to shake hers. "Things are about to finish up here. In case I don't see you after we leave, I want to thank you, Janice.

"You're welcome."

She slipped behind the sign and changed, shoving the dirty clothes into the backpack. The driver license picture on the ground with the real Janice Mitchell's face stared up at her. She pushed rubble over it with her foot. The volunteer had no idea how helpful she had been.

The rest of the team had joined the exodus of people hours earlier. First responders made rounds the night of the earthquake, distributing snacks and water. After that, the medical teams scrounged for food, managing to feed everyone who came through until yesterday, when all resources were depleted.

The days since the earthquake were a blur, but what stood out was the calm, focused doctor she worked beside. During her career, she'd witnessed more than one doctor crack under less pressure. The hundreds of people treated by Doctor Gipson were fortunate.

Only two male patients remained. After them, the doctor and *Janice* could gather up the remaining supplies and get out, too.

"Janice," the doctor said in a hushed voice.

She glanced around the sign. Across the street, a gang of men ran into the only store still standing.

"Get our patients out of sight."

With a quick motion, the patients joined her. They peered through gaps in the broken plastic. The gang reappeared, their arms overloaded with plunder. Two shouted obscenities at each other. One hooked his arm around the other's neck, and they fell, scuffling in the dirt. The rest laughed and broke them up.

Randall knelt on one knee.

"I can't see. Why did he kneel down?" Linda asked.

"I can see," the older patient whispered. "Things are going to get tense, I'm afraid."

The doctor stood again and adjusted his belt. The movement caught the group's attention. One by one, they set their merchandise down.

The shortest man in the group stepped out. "What are you looking at?"

Randall tightened his stance, his right hand by his waist.

"What's the matter? Cat got your tongue?"

"I'm a doctor. Out of patients and out of supplies. I'm getting ready to move on."

The leader crossed his arms. "What if you got something we need?"

"I told you. I'm out of supplies. Already been stripped of food and money. There's nothing here for you."

"No worries, Doc. We're just going to mosey over. See? We won't —"

A jeep careened around the corner and screeched to a halt. Soldiers piled out, guns trained on the gang of men who froze.

Instinctively, Linda stepped between her young patient and the scene unfolding. Her heart skipped a beat

The leader bolted toward the store. A gunshot split the air.

The runner stopped and thrust his hands up. He gave the doctor a lopsided smile. "Almost had you a new patient, Doc."

After the gang was loaded into the back of the vehicle, the driver circled and stopped by Randall. She didn't understand the language he spoke. After a short exchange, he tossed a box on the ground and drove off.

Randall held his arm up to stop them from joining him. He walked across the street and went inside the building. After a minute, he reappeared and yelled, "All clear."

They met him at the tent.

"Wow," she said. "That was too close."

"Shake it off. It wasn't our first encounter, but hopefully the last." He opened the box and counted. "Six cartons of rations and bottled water. We will feast tonight."

Her growling stomach squashed what had just happened to a mere annoyance. "I'm starved."

They tore open two packs. Randall formed the heat tray and started the small burner. The younger patient shook his head when offered the first warmed meal.

"You need to eat to regain some strength so you can get out of here and meet up with your family." She handed it to him.

"My family is under twenty feet of concrete." He threw the meal and hobbled off.

The other man took the next portion and gobbled it down. He thanked the doctor for a second ration pack and followed the jeep tracks out of the area.

The doctor heated their meals and sat down. "I'm fluent in three languages. He spoke French. We are dining on French combat rations. *Ceci est delicious, oui?*"

"I can guess what that means, but I don't know French. What did he say?"

"He told me to finish our business and get out by noon tomorrow. They're pulling out. The next team isn't scheduled to be here for at least a week."

"I can't believe we haven't seen the American Red Cross."

"The talk is that numerous refugee camps set up outside the city and north along the river. Maybe they're focusing on those sites." He used his finger to claim the can's remaining contents. "I'm afraid FEMA wasn't prepared for a disaster of this magnitude."

"I wasn't, either." Thinking ahead had saved her from Lostyn's wrath many times, but she never fathomed being rescued by an earthquake.

He handed her a fruit bar. "No one imagined anything like this."

Bruce and his colleagues did. They talked a lot about the New Madrid fault and the destruction it could cause. By now, all seismologists were probably buried deep in their work. Except for Bruce. No doubt he was helping her parents look for her and missing valuable work experience.

How typical for her to fail even in a humanitarian crisis. It was just another reason to start a new life. No one would miss her mess-ups in the old one.

The doctor covered the box of rations and pointed down the street. A weary-looking group of people walked toward the tent.

She massaged her neck. *Janice* had more patients.

~

Bruce helped Lostyn to the chair.

"You need to see the doctor with that leg, Dad."

"I did if that's what you can call the addle-brained old geezer." He growled. "You'd think there'd be someone capable of dealing with a broken leg. Idiots! Typical small-town incompetence. I sat in the ER for over twelve hours. By the time the doctor examined me, they were out of the basics."

"Man, that's terrible! I'm glad it wasn't worse. I've been trying to call but couldn't get through. Sheesh! I never imagined it'd take half a week to get here. They grounded our helicopter in

Wichita, Kansas because air traffic over the seismic zone is so heavy. We waited two days for the work jeeps to relocate. Bumper to bumper traffic both ways! Chris went to Cape Girardeau, Missouri and assigned me Marion, Arkansas. We can't work Memphis until we get the okay."

"Bring me a drink of water. Do you think you can handle that?"

Bruce gritted his teeth. Other than the few extra pounds, Dad was the same obnoxious jerk. As soon as he talked to Mom, he was out of there. Mission accomplished. Grandmother could rest, and he could get to his job.

He rubbed his hands together. Hikes in the mountain paled in comparison to the investigative work waiting on him. Plotting maps of reasonable test areas in his mind while traveling had been like shots of epinephrine that warded off a headache caused by lack of caffeine.

Pulling out a bottle of water from the cooler, he grabbed a carton of juice for himself.

"Put that back," Lostyn barked. "The stores are out of everything but water."

"Sorry." He tossed it back in and walked around the room. Other than the busted flat-screen television face down on the floor, everything appeared to be in good shape. "It's hot in here. Doesn't surprise me about the electricity. I didn't see one line up as I came through town. Have you heard when the power will be restored?"

"No."

"Where's Mom?"

"Not where she is supposed to be."

Bruce rolled his eyes. "How are supplies getting in? Semi-trucks aren't allowed to cross the bridge. They're backed up for miles on the other side."

"Hand me that pillow."

He retrieved the pillow from the floor and tossed it to his dad.

"I started seeing damage around Springfield, Missouri. The post-quake images of the plateau are incredible. And the stats coming in? Unbelievable! Measurable damage begins in northern Illinois and runs all the way through Louisiana. You know, our seminar last semester focused on the possible devastation from a six-point magnitude. This blows those projections out of the water." He straightened the wall clock. "Can you imagine what Memphis looks like? I've heard there are several thousand dead."

His dad stared straight ahead.

"I don't guess you've heard any official reports with the power down. The quake was a 7.2. Aftershocks have varied from 4 to 5.5. That's a real blessing. Often, they're just as intense as the initial shock and sometimes worse. Here, let me see if I can make your leg more com –"

"Don't touch me!"

Bruce stepped back. "Not a problem." He inhaled and blew out frustration. In a similar circumstance, he might have the same demonic scowl on his own face. "I bet Hendrix Towers took a catastrophic hit. But, hey, I'm sure they'll be able to move their operations to Las Vegas. Does Hendrix have any casinos there?"

"No."

"Well, I'm sure there's going to be options, Dad. You've been with them a long time. What about Mom? She at the church? I figured they'd set up a crisis center there."

"Your mother is in Memphis."

Last week's conversation with Dawn hit him like a truck. He'd been too busy searching for the Mustangs to pay much attention to when Dawn said the trip was.

"She didn't bother to inform me." Lostyn braced his hands on the chair to stand.

Bruce held out his arm to steady him, but his dad slung it aside and hopped on one leg out of the room. The bedroom door slammed shut, sending the wall clock airborne.

He snatched the keys to the jeep and ran out the door, colliding with Dawn, who was climbing the stairs. He grabbed her to keep her from tumbling back down.

"Bruce!"

Her clothes stunk, and her blond hair was a tangled mess. He helped her into the house. "Are you okay?"

"I couldn't find your mom!" she cried. "It was horrible. There were fires everywhere, and the ground kept moving. The river changed directions! I looked for her. I promise I did." She fell onto the sofa.

He yanked her back up. "What do you mean you couldn't find her?"

Her blue eyes grew big.

"Stop crying and talk to me!"

"I saw her near the law school. Then it hit. The girls were scared. There were bodies everywhere. The river rose straight into the air before –" She gasped. "The water!" She buried her head in his chest and sobbed. "I didn't know what to do."

Dawn's shoulders heaved in agony. His heart raced but not just because of Mom. The last time he and Dawn's bodies were that close was when she visited the ranch. He had given her a friendly hug that shot his mind into unfamiliar territory.

They were just teenagers back then. Now, more acquainted with the feelings, he squirmed. The miles between Nevada and Arkansas that had kept him free from the snare of emotions with his grown-up friend was suddenly reduced to tiny pulsations between them.

In her unkempt state, Dawn was more beautiful than the pictures they exchanged on social media. Past the stench of unwashed clothes was the smell of a woman. He needed to pull away and catch his breath but couldn't.

Instead, he wrapped his arms around his frightened friend and stroked the mane of thick, silky hair. "It's okay. I'll find her."

~

The full moon illuminated the broken advertisement

billboard in front of the parked jeep. The green road sign leaning against it read: *Memphis 40 miles.* Bruce was slumped behind the steering wheel with his cap pulled down over his eyes. The shock of the news had finally worn off enough for him to sleep.

Dawn muffled a yawn and massaged the cramp out of her leg. She had fought sleep all night. Every time she drifted, the concrete parking garage crashed to the ground, sending the green cloud to pounce on her.

Linda wasn't near the buildings when they fell. That's what Dawn kept telling herself, even when more busloads of locals arrived from Memphis with no Linda aboard.

Lostyn accused her of lying and consorting with his wife. *The man was nuts!* Even if Linda had decided to stay to help the injured, she would have let her know. *Seriously!*

Dawn wanted Bruce to help explain how hard she had tried to find Linda, but he barely spoke to his dad. He wasn't saying much to her either.

She insisted on going to Memphis with him and had squelched his protest by promising to show him the exact spot where they were when the world went berserk. She sniffled and pulled the blanket higher.

"India may be delayed," Bruce said.

"I thought you were asleep."

"I was until you woke me up thinking." He reached under the seat and pulled out a bottle of water. "Want some?"

"No thanks. And I can't wake you up just thinking."

"You kept bumping me with your elbow. I knew before opening my eyes you were braiding your hair again. You always do that when you're deep in thought."

She let go of the braid. "Sorry."

"You remember when I cut your hair?"

"How could I forget, Bruce John Hugh Bonin? You practically left me bald!"

"I did not."

"Yes, you did. It was way too short. I couldn't even start a braid."

"Yeah, well, I didn't have to worry about you bumping me with your elbow then, did I?"

"You were mean to me."

"I was just playing around."

"My parents didn't think so. Neither did your mom."

He adjusted his cap.

It had taken twenty-six hours and four detours to get where they were. The idea of getting to New York to catch a flight halfway around the world wasn't imaginable. Finding Linda seemed just as impossible, but she couldn't let Bruce down. She wouldn't.

"We'll find her, Bruce."

"Maybe."

Clouds passed in front of the moon, plunging them into blackness. She didn't have to see through the darkness to know Bruce's forehead was creased with concern. "Bruce —"

He draped his arm over the back of the seat and leaned close just as the grey-blue cloud slipped by, exposing their faces within inches of each other. Tiny creases stretched from the corner of his eyes. His bronzed features were more chiseled than they used to be, but if she touched his skin, it would be soft.

"What do you want, Dawn?"

She wanted his eyes to light up when he looked at her as they did when he watched the Mustangs. She wanted to tell him everything would be okay — for him to say that she didn't have to be afraid because he would never leave her like her parents did. "Please believe me when I say I looked for her."

"I believe you."

The slight pullback of his mouth told her Bruce wasn't mad at her. But the troubled downward draw of one eyebrow said he wasn't comfortable. Coming back to Ozark Ridge disturbed him.

Nevada had won the tug-of-war between his two homes sometime before they had even graduated high school. Maybe it was the mountains. Or maybe it was having grandparents who cared. Whichever, he was staring at her and not seeing a single reason to come back.

"I would never hurt you, Bruce – not in a million years."

"I know. It's all good."

"Things happened so fast. Lucy was hurt and I –"

He pulled away. "Stop it. I would have done the same."

She crossed her arms. *Lie!* He didn't have to patronize her. He would have refused to leave without his mother.

"We better head out." He started the vehicle.

"Yeah. It's time for your mother to get home." Dawn wadded up the blanket and threw it in the back seat. India might have to wait, but somehow God had to clear up the mayhem. Somewhere there was mission work waiting for her. It was *all* that mattered.

Bruce squinted at the fog. "Man, I can hardly see."

She huffed. "Well, that's because you're apparently as blind as a bat."

~

The sun dipped in the west as Linda packed the last of the medical supplies. "That's it. This box is ready, Doctor."

He tossed her another fruit bar.

"Thanks." She opened it and took a bite. "I'll be glad to move on."

"Gee, thanks." He teased, sticking out his lower lip. "I didn't know I was that hard to work with."

Her cheeks warmed. "I didn't mean it that way. I'm glad we were able to help, but I'm ready to leave. It's the ones we couldn't help –"

"I know what you mean."

His sorrowful brown eyes were a stark contrast to the sharp jawline and prominent Adam's apple.

"I'm sure your family is worried about you," she said.

"I doubt that. Both my parents are gone. My brother and I

parted ways shortly after they died. My ex, who swears she can't get far enough away from me to suit her, is probably in a tropical paradise somewhere oblivious to world events." He shrugged. "What about your family?"

Linda turned up her water bottle and drank it all. Panicked parents, aggravated son, and a furious husband. Tossing the bottle into the trash heap, she wiped her mouth with the back of her arm. "I don't have any family either." She smiled apologetically and leaned against the dilapidated building. "I need to rest a bit."

Grabbing his pack, he sat beside her. "Me too. Sorry to intrude on your space, but it's best if we stay close."

He raised his pant leg, revealing an ankle holster with gun. "Thirty-two caliber. There could be more looters around. There are the coyotes we've been hearing, too. I believe they sounded closer last night. We better leave first thing in the morning." He yawned. "Which direction will you head?"

The pistol's gray on gray finish matched her dulled thoughts. "East, I guess. Maybe Nashville."

"It's south for me, as far from this pandemonium as I can get. I'm exhausted. Let the young deal with it." He stretched his legs out and crossed them at the ankle. "You get the day watch. I'll take the night. Wake me up before dark."

He closed his eyes, and the broad chest immediately moved in and out in a steady rhythm. The shirt, sleeves rolled up past his elbows, was one of the dozens he had changed into, dropped off by a volunteer who lived in the area. The dirty blond hair sticking to his forehead would look thick and wavy when clean.

He peeked out of one eye. "Something wrong?"

"No." She turned her head to hide the red creeping back into her cheeks. "I've got first watch. No problem."

It was too still. No aftershocks or explosions had rocked the area in the past two days. Or was it three? How many days had passed? Six. Maybe. It didn't matter. The fires burned out. No cries came from the debris anymore. It had been long enough for the trapped to die of thirst and the first of the dead to rot.

A white van emblazoned with *TAXI* in bold, black letters maneuvered down the side street. The engine noise broke through Randall's snoring, and he jumped to his feet. When it stopped, a soldier with thick sideburns hopped out and opened the passenger door.

"You're my last stop. Climb in."

Randall pulled her to her feet. "Looks like we've got an early ride."

They squeezed into the crowded vehicle.

"Okay, folks. That's everyone. I'll drop half of you off in quadrant one and the rest of you off in two."

Randall leaned over the seat. "Quadrant? Is that what the exit points are called?"

"No. That's your next assignment." The driver swerved to miss a downed pole, sending Linda into Randall's lap.

"Sorry." She righted herself. "I don't understand."

A deep voice behind her grunted. "Welcome aboard. No rights afforded. Better get your rest. This is your escort service to the next stop in hell."

The driver eyed the man through his rearview mirror. "Your President activated the Health Care Personnel Delivery System at 0800 this morning. All medical personnel is being assigned to four quadrants to assist the wounded. No one is allowed to leave the city. From what I hear from the refugee camps, you'll thank us for that."

She muttered, "What does that mean?"

Randall glowered at the back of the driver's head. "It means you won't make it to Nashville anytime soon. We've been drafted."

Melissa Kirk

CHAPTER TEN

Bruce pulled in behind the line of vehicles.

"What is he doing?" Dawn pointed to the uniformed man wearing a beret who was making most of the cars ahead of them turn around.

"He's allowing only emergency vehicles through."

"Well, don't stop. When we get there, you just drive on. There, like that truck."

The semi-truck with Wal-Mart painted on it took a wide turn around the barricade. The back of the trailer slid off the road, metal grinding metal until the back wheels jumped the street curb, and the truck righted itself back onto the pavement.

The next car in line backed up and swung around. The man behind the wheel stuck his head out the window and yelled profanities at the guard, whose attention had already turned to them.

"This *is* an emergency. You tell him your mother is in there, and we have to find her." She rolled down her window. "Never mind. I'll tell him."

He pulled her arm back in. "I'll do the talking."

Edging up, he showed his ID. "Bruce Bonin, ANSS engineer."

"Sorry. Emergency personnel only. Turn around."

"We are emergency personnel."

The guard bent down to look at Dawn and shook his head. "Turn around."

She started to speak, but Bruce interrupted. "I am with ANSS. NEIC Branch, Reno. This is my assistant. Show them your badge, Dawn."

"Um." She patted her pocket. "It's here somewhere. It must be in the back. It was an early morning, you know."

Bruce tapped his watch. "I'm supposed to be at the work site at 0900. That's less than an hour. How far am I from the bridge?"

"Everything past this point is designated ground-zero disaster. See the orange netted fence ahead? That means emergency personnel only. Turn around, before I have you arrested."

"Right. Arrest me." Bruce leaned to read the name on the badge. "Go ahead, Soldat Friar. Then you can explain to Commander Obright why the USGS emergency team is not intact." He showed his watch again. "At 0900. He'll be there, waiting for us."

The guard took the identification and examined the front and back of it before stepping back. "Stay to the left of the road. Three kilometers ahead, turn left. The next stop point will be five hundred meters."

Bruce tossed his ID on the dash and rounded the barricade.

"Well, I'm impressed. I don't know what all those abbreviations mean, but they must be significant.

"The only thing that impressed him was the name Obright."

"Obright must be an important man, then." Her hands

gripped the dash as the jeep climbed over chunks of road. "I didn't realize you knew famous people like that."

"I just know the name."

They passed the second stop point and wove their way through a narrow strip being cleared by heavy machinery.

"I don't know where we are. I mean, in relationship to where I was when the earthquake struck. If you can find the bridge, maybe I can figure it out."

"Maybe?"

"I'm just saying that they've been pushing stuff around." She gagged. "What's that smell?"

He glanced up the road. "Don't get sick on me now, girl."

"It's horrible."

"I know." He slowed down. "Where's my backpack?"

"It's covered up with all that equipment in the back. Why?"

"Get back there and see if you can find it. There's a map in the side pocket."

She climbed over the seat and began digging.

Speeding up, he passed the line of bodies haphazardly pushed to the side of the road. The back of the vehicle bounced hard.

"Ouch!"

"I hope there isn't much of that."

"What'd you say?" She said over her shoulder.

"Dig till you find it." He drove until the smell cleared and stopped.

"Found it." Long legs led the slim body back into the front seat. "Hey – the Pyramid! I know where I'm at now. Can you get closer?"

"Sorry. We walk from here."

She handed him the map, and they got out. A group of men was removing debris from the top of the remains of the Walcott building. One man bent and put his ear to the mound. He held up his hand, and everyone fell silent. When he shook his head, they resumed digging.

She pulled Bruce in the opposite direction. "Come on. We parked close to the School of Law. It wouldn't surprise me if we found your mother over there helping just like those people are."

He jumped over a deep crevice and helped her across. They followed the crumbled pathway to the riverfront. The river's new path ran rapids through a field of tumbled trees and disappearing behind a line of barges marooned in mire where the opposite shore once ran.

"Unbelievable."

"I'll never forget it. The river rose into the sky and just hung there. When it came down – *oh my goodness* – people ran everywhere! They screamed out names, and I called out for your mom." Her face went pale. "I can't lose anyone else. Do you understand, Bruce? I cannot lose anyone else." She began sobbing.

He wrapped his arms around her trembling body and stroked her back. "It's over, Blue."

Water-wells of sadness looked up. "You haven't called me that in forever."

He wiped the tear streams away. The crest of her damp cheeks glistened like morning's dew. Her nose sloped toward delicate, blush lips. The quivering mouth drew him closer. Just a touch from him would soften her pain. He inhaled the hint of her breath.

He was here to find his mother. Collect data. Dig into the mysteries of the earth. Nothing else. He dismissed the groaning inside and, instead, tugged on her braid. "Yeah, not since your mom threatened me with a switch for picking all her Blue Dawns. Let's find my mom, so I can get you home."

She double blinked. "Um, yes, that's what we came to do." She turned away and spread her arms both directions, pointing with each. "We were over there, and your mom was by that railing. I'm going to check where I parked the van. Maybe she left a note or something. You follow the sidewalk."

"Wait. We don't need to get separated."

Keeping her back to him, she waved and ran to the parking

lot.

He jerked his cap off. It was time to get back to Nevada where his only commitment was the hiking trip.

The path, strewn with chairs and lumber led him by the demolished parking garage to an ambulance parked two football field lengths ahead. There, the bloody clothes, bottles, and food wrappers gave no evidence of their owners.

First-aid stations would have located closer to a hospital, making use of equipment and supplies. Finding the nearest one on the map, he jogged the half mile to where it once stood. A deserted tent flapped in the sweltering breeze. The map showed another facility east of his location.

The earth rolled. A jolt threw him to the ground. When the shaking stopped, he jumped up. New debris blocked the road to the parking lot.

"Blue! I'm coming!"

~

The noon sun filtered through the mix of bumpers and caved-in hoods, giving Bruce enough light to see that Dawn wasn't pinned between any of them. He scooted back out and ran to a red pickup flipped on its side. The cab and bed were clear.

He kicked a tire, landing it in a sand pit and spewing putrid gray powder up.

"He will trick you, dear boy. As he prowls, rank consumes the air."

Bruce ran back to the jeep. An elderly man and woman were helping each other across the street.

"Have you seen a girl my age with blond hair?"

They both shook their heads.

A thick-framed man sat at the edge of the road, resting his head of curly gray hair on his hands.

"Have you seen a girl? Blond hair?"

He didn't look up.

"Sir." Bruce tapped the shoulder. The body fell backward,

113

revealing a metal rod that pierced the broad chest.

Walking toward the business district, he found himself tiptoeing to the mound where the searchers had been. No one pleaded for help and never would. Circling back to the vehicle, he scratched a note on a dirty paper napkin and secured it under the windshield wipers. When he plugged his phone up to charge, the display lit up a missed call from Dawn. Relief mixed with frustration rushed out of his lungs.

A police car with flashing red lights pulled up.

Bruce showed his ID. "I have permission to be here."

"Sorry, sir. We have orders to clear all civilians out of the area. You can leave the way you came, or I can provide transportation."

"I told you. I'm –"

"You'll have to take it up with the officials on the other side of the security fence."

"I can't leave my assistant here. Or my mother."

The officer stepped out. "If they're alive, they'll be escorted out of the city. This entire quadrant is to be cleared by 2100 hours. Are you leaving on your own?" He put his hand on his belt near the holster.

"I'm going." Bruce snatched the note off the dash and drove back to the barricade.

The officer pulled beside him. "Keep going."

"You said on this side of the security fence."

"Not this one. The fence is fifty kilometers further down. Registration centers are set up in Collierville."

"That's thirty miles away!"

"They'll assist you there. Move on."

Bruce cursed and peeled out. One lousy cop wasn't going to stop him from doing what he came to do.

~

Randall grabbed Linda's backpack, and they got in line.

"Where are we?" she asked.

"A processing site."

Soldiers wearing black uniforms and berets were emptying supplies from the bellies of red and yellow airplanes that bordered the edge of the field. The skids were set on the ground where other soldiers separated the boxes with red crosses into several stacks.

"Is that the American Red Cross?" she asked.

"Those are medical supplies, but not the Red Cross's."

"Who are all these soldiers?"

"French – looks like the *Sécurité Civile.*" He pointed to the round emblem on the planes. "They helped with Hurricane Katrina."

"Are they the UN?"

"Maybe. I'm not sure. I thought the UN would have identification – tee-shirts or vests. We'll know soon enough."

"They can't force us to stay here, can they? I didn't sign up for anything."

He lowered his voice. "Do you see what they're doing?"

The soldier at a long white table handed the first man in line papers while another searched his belongings.

"Hey! Stay out of my stuff!"

The soldier slid the bag to the end of the table and pointed to the paperwork. The irate man scribbled something down and shoved the paper back. When he was instructed to stretch out his arms, he threw a punch. A pair of guards rushed over and pushed him to the ground, holding him down until he stopped resisting. They searched him, pulled a knife out of his pocket, and tossed it into a cardboard box.

"Did you see that?" She turned.

The doctor zipped up her backpack.

"What are you doing?"

He pulled her closer. "Pay close attention to what I say. Do you see the cards?"

Four stacks of different-colored cards lined the front of the folding table.

"Yes."

"I believe those are the different assignments. If they do as I think, they'll pull a card from the stacks in order, assigning each person a different destination. I'll go first. You make sure to get the same color card as mine. When you get to the table, I'm going to come back and, well, just follow my lead."

"Huh?"

He motioned her to move. Stepping back, she stopped in front of a puffy-faced man with a teardrop tattoo under his eye.

A coarse whisper grated over her shoulder. "I can show you a sweet time later. Want me to tuck you in tonight, doll?"

She stiffened.

The whisper changed to a hum and grew louder. She positioned the backpack between her and the man and recounted to make sure she had moved back enough places.

Randall glanced back and nodded.

The soldier alternated assignments, handing the next person in line a different colored card.

When Randall reached the table, he filled out the paperwork and reclaimed his bag after it was searched. The soldier pointed to the line forming by the green marker, and he jogged that direction.

All three people ahead of her were required to toss pocket knives into the box.

"Name, please."

"Uh —"

"Your name please."

"It's Janice, from Memphis."

The soldier sneered. "Do you have a last name, Janice from Memphis?"

"Yes, I'm sorry. It's Janice Mitchell."

Randall ran over and threw his backpack on the table just as the soldier picked up her bag. "You took my wallet!"

The soldier set down her pack. "I took nothing. Go back to your assignment."

"Are you sure?" Randall picked up her bag and shook it. "Because it's not here."

"You are making a grave mistake. Are you going to move on, or am I going to have to help you?"

Randall cleared his throat and tossed her pack over his shoulder. "I'm moving, but don't let me find out you took my wallet." He ran back to the green marker.

"*Très courageux!*" one guard called out, and the rest of the soldiers laughed.

The soldier handed her a green card. She retrieved Randall's pack from the inspector and ran to the marker. She tossed it to him and reclaimed hers.

"What was that all about? Trying to get yourself shot?"

He turned his back to the soldiers. "Be careful, Janice. My gun is in your bag."

Melissa Kirk

CHAPTER ELEVEN

"Wow." Linda circled, taking in the massive field hospital operation. Long, inflated structures lined the dirt runway. Doctors and nurses scurried from building to building.

"Pretty impressive." Randall pointed to a truck. "Finally. The American Red Cross."

A bold red cross and the words, Disaster Relief, identified the utility truck parked between the buildings.

"Thank goodness. I wondered if we'd ever see any U.S. relief teams."

"We're the minority. Look over there."

Two rows of planes with French flags painted on them flanked the right side of the base. A helicopter drowned out Randall's voice as it flew overhead and landed inside a big white circle. Crew members dressed in blue and neon-green protective suits jumped out and unloaded gurneys with patients. Medical personnel ran to claim the arrivals. The team jumped back in, and the aircraft lifted, circling around to go back the way it came.

"– like a war zone out here," he said.

"This is crazy. Do you see anything that looks like an administration building? I'm making arrangements to get out of here."

"It's not that easy. You heard the driver. I wasn't joking when I said we've been drafted. We are here until further notice."

"I don't even know what that means." She rubbed her temple. "This is like a nightmare that won't stop. Nothing feels real."

"It's real, all right." He said as he took her arm. "Come on. We aren't going to find out anything standing here."

They went inside the closest building where a cadet officer held out his hand. "Show me your identification, please."

Linda pulled out the cut-up driver's license and quickly zipped up the backpack.

"Profession?"

"What?"

"Are you a nurse? Doctor?"

"Registered nurse."

He handed back the license. "You will report to Pediatrics. 0600 hours." He looked at Randall. "You?"

"Randall Gipson, MD. Pulmonology."

"Report to ICU. Same. 0600."

"Excuse me," she said.

"*Oui?*"

"Have many patients been brought here?"

"*Mille* – one thousand since we set up three days ago. Is that enough for you?" He pointed. "Living quarters are on the north end. Report there next."

Randall held the tent flap open for her. "They aren't going to hurt us. Just do the job they give you. When the crisis is over, we can get on with our lives." He stepped so close she could hear slight hesitations in his breathing that contradicted the air of confidence. "Give me the gun. You don't need to get caught with that."

She slipped it into his pack. "Please be careful."

His brown eyes gazed at her until they exposed her fear.

Her throat tightened. "Don't take this wrong, but you're all I've got."

He winked. "Always do as I say, and you will be okay. I'll check on you as soon as I can. For now, let's see if we can get some sleep."

They crossed the smoothed dirt field where another officer directed them to different shelters.

When she finally arrived at the barracks, it was vacant, but scattered personal items hinted it would be full later. She found an empty cot and sprawled the contents of the assigned plastic bag across the bed. A blanket, fitted sheet, scrubs two sizes too big, toothbrush, paste, comb, soap, shower shoes, and a claim check for her dirty clothes. She picked up the name badge. She was officially Janice Mitchell.

The last two hours had been spent filling out paperwork before being stripped down, showered, deloused, and inoculated. It had been embarrassing and intrusive, but after a week among filth and parasitic decay, she felt clean.

Linda lay back and pulled the pillow over her head. Her last thought before drifting asleep was wondering where Randall hid his pistol.

～

Dawn touched her scalp. "Ow."

"She's awake, Miss Maude!"

"Praise be! Move over, child." A dark-complexioned woman with short hair stood over her. "Careful. That's a nasty knot on your head."

"Where am I?"

A chubby-faced boy peeked around the woman. "You're at Miss Maude's. Your bump is purple."

"Go on, Carter. Leave her alone. I'm Maude Davis, owner, and curator of Assurance Home. Josiah brought you here."

"Josiah? I'm sorry. I don't remember."

121

Maude helped her sit up. "Get a bottle of water for the lady, please."

The young boy ran into another room.

"You were hurt in the aftershock. What's your name?"

"Dawn. Where's Bruce?"

"I don't know where your Bruce is. You were alone when Josiah found you." She handed Dawn her phone. "His name appeared last on your log, so I tried calling him, but service went down again before I could leave a message."

"I have to find him. He'll be beside himself." She swayed when she tried to stand.

"Don't get up. You can't go anywhere with that bump. It's dark outside anyway."

The oil lamp on the table beside her illuminated a large room with a sitting area on one side and scaled down tables and chairs on the other. Bright bulletin boards with artwork lined the walls. Children of different ages stood in a semi-circle, staring at her.

Carter returned with the bottle of water, and Maude opened it. "Slowly, now."

"Thank you." She took a sip. "My head does hurt. But I have to find him. He's looking for his mother and now me. If he isn't hurt, that is."

"Is Bruce your husband?"

"He's my best friend. His mother and I were in Memphis when the earthquake hit. We came to find her." Tears streamed down. "I left her."

"Please try not to cry. It'll only make your head hurt worse. You did what you had to do, child. That's what we're all doing. They will do the same." She smiled. "Are you hungry?"

"I can't eat. Where did you say I am?"

"Assurance Home. I help children find a suitable place to live." She pulled a tall boy toward her. "This is Josiah, the one who helped you. He found you this afternoon, walking in circles and blubbering."

The boy squirmed when the woman's dark eyes narrowed.

"He was much farther from home than he should have been," she said. "But he found you, so I'm thankful. You were in shock. We tried to keep you still and alert, but you wouldn't cooperate. Bless the Lord, you seem much better now, except for that nasty goose egg."

She leaned close to inspect. "The swelling is down a little. We can thank the Lord for that. If it's safe tomorrow, I'll send the older children out to see if they can find anyone looking for you over in that area. For now, though, we'll all try to relax."

The children groaned when the sturdy-built woman began lowering the windows.

"I won't listen to the grumbling. It might get hot, but I will not take any chances. Window and door bars are designed to keep us safe. I will do my part, and God will see to the rest."

"How did this place survive the earthquake?"

"Only by the mercy of God, child. He protected the children. That's all I know to say. The back corner of the home suffered damage. It didn't affect the rest of the house, so I closed that part off. Now, the children will get their duties done while I prepare a small meal."

"You have electricity?"

"A canned meal, I'm afraid. I stay stocked in case of emergencies. We have a generator, but it's loud. I'm only running it when necessary." She whispered, "No one needs to know we're here. The children are my first concern. And now you, of course."

The children went about their chores. Maude seemed to be taking every precaution. Maybe Linda found a safe place like this. Dawn checked her phone. Low battery. No service. No missed call.

~

Dawn's head still throbbed when she woke up.

Carter's face hovered above her. "She's awake again!"

She cringed. "Hey, Carter. Can you do me a favor, please?"

Before he could speak, she whispered, "Talk a little softer, okay?"

He nodded. "Miss Maude! Oops." He held his finger to his mouth. "Sorry."

Maude came into the room. "Thank you, Carter. Now, please leave our guest alone for a while."

He started to protest, but she looked over her reading glasses and pointed to the doorway. Putting a chubby finger to his cupid-like lips, he tiptoed backward out of the room.

Dawn eased into a sitting position. "Thank you. The nap helped."

Maude smiled. "That was a long nap. You've been asleep for over twenty-four hours."

"Oh, no!" She reached for her shoes. "I've got to find Bruce!"

"Slow down, child. You can't go anywhere. It's night again." Maude held up the board she'd carried into the room. "Looters," she explained. "They're getting closer." She laid the wood across one of the front windows and chose a nail from the pile on the sill.

The hammering set off explosions inside Dawn's head.

"They've been transporting people out all day. I bet your friend got on the bus, expecting you to do the same. When you're well enough, I'll help you get to the busing zone."

"He wouldn't leave without me. But, you and the children need to go, Miss Maude."

"Just Maude to you, dear. No, I can't do that. I'm their only family. They might be separated, and it's a dark place out there." Her shoulders shuddered. "No. They'll stay here as long as I have the supplies to care for them."

"How do you care for all these children by yourself?"

Carter tiptoed over and propped up on the sofa cushion. He put his finger to his lip and whispered, "She don't. Miss Kay helps. She lives here, too. Do you know Miss Kay?"

She glanced at Maude. "No, I haven't met her yet."

"That's cuz she ain't here. Miss Kay was at the store when

the shaking started. Miss Maude said she'd be home as soon as it's safe."

"I think so, too."

"That's enough for now, Carter. Please get me another board. They're leaning against the wall by the back door."

He grinned and tiptoed out.

"Kay went to the business district the afternoon of the earthquake. I've been waiting for the opportunity to ask what you saw while you were out there." Her hands wrung nervously. "A lot of damage in that area?"

She dropped her gaze. "Pretty bad."

Maude covered her mouth. "That's what I was afraid of. There are so many tall buildings."

"Maybe Kay caught a bus."

"No. She wouldn't leave the children. She's a dear friend, like your Bruce."

Carter returned and handed a board to Maude.

Dawn winked at him and covered her ears. He squeezed his eyes shut and did the same.

Assurance Home needed more than one adult to take care of the children. Linda, Bruce, and now Miss Kay. Her list of people to find was growing.

Melissa Kirk

CHAPTER TWELVE

Linda carried the tray of hot food to a table occupied by nurses and sat down. "I'm famished, and this meal smells wonderful." She split open the roll and dunked it in the stew.

"You act like it's your first hot meal." The spindly LPN across the table moaned. "I would give anything for some of my dad's BBQ ribs with potato salad."

"Oh, Molly! With baked beans and slaw, too," the nurse named Christy added.

"Stop. I can't take it." Molly shoved her plate toward Linda. "Here. Enjoy."

"Thank you! First time since I've been here I get to eat a full meal without rushing. I'm going to relish every bite. I'll sneak my apple out for later."

"Still in pediatrics?" Molly asked.

"Four new admits already today. It's been three weeks, and they're still finding kids." Linda lay down the spoon. "Most don't know where their parents are or if they're still alive."

"Chin up, buttercup," Christy said. "This can't last

forever."

"It's got to end soon. Dealing with this day after day is like taking a beating that never lets up. I'm exhausted."

"I understand. It makes a person want to run away, doesn't it?" Molly commented.

Christy agreed as they gathered their plates and left to finish their shifts.

Linda rubbed her eyes. Some of the children were treated and released the same day, but most of her patients were mangled. Once stable, their name went on waiting lists for transfer to the overflowing post-surgery therapy centers. Mild doses of sedatives were administered to decrease their anxiety. A hefty dose of *don't care* would do her good right now.

"As Christy said, chin up." Randall sat down across from her. "I'd ask how it's going, but I can tell by the fancy hairdo. Great, huh?"

She chuckled. "It's the best I can manage with that flimsy comb they issued me." She held up the apple. "I'm looking to trade this beautiful, shiny, delicious fruit for a good hairbrush. How about it? Sounds fair to me."

"Fresh out of brushes." He dug into his pocket and pulled out a tube of lip balm. "But, I might trade you this."

"Done! My lips are so dry, they bled earlier." She coated them, delighted with the instant soothing. "I don't know how you got your hands on this. Thanks."

"We played poker last night. A lucky draw won me that."

"Oh." Lostyn spent the night before the earthquake at the Lucky Draw Casino. Before coming home – *to dance*. She tried to hand the tube back.

"Keep it. Something to remember me by." He tapped his spoon on the plastic plate. "They're sending me to the east quadrant this afternoon. There's an influx of patients with lung problems from the poor air quality after all the gas explosions."

"You're leaving."

"I don't want to go." His voice softened. "That first night,

I pleaded for someone with experience to help. Providence sent you to me, Janice." He wrapped her hands around the balm and covered them with his. "So, thank you."

The orderly at the next table coughed. She blushed and pulled her hands away.

Every day since they arrived at the hospital, they had met after hours by the only tree on the grounds. In four hours, she'd be free to share the day's craziness with someone who cared. But, there would be no one there to greet her.

As if reading her mind, he said, "I wish I could stay and take care of you. They didn't give me a choice."

She bit her chapped lips. "I wish you well, Doctor. Thank you for all you've done."

"I told you to call me Randall!" His eyes narrowed. "You're going to be fine." He shoved away from the table and threw the meal tray down at the drop-off station, earning a curse from the buser.

A second wave of nurses joined her, but her thoughts kept drifting from the conversation.

During their talks, Randall always insisted on hearing every detail of her day. He'd demand to know if she was being treated okay. Paranoid about the UN, he warned her to stay out of their way. Their conversations usually ended like this one had, with an admonishment from him. The intensity of his voice sometimes unnerved her, but at least someone was trying to protect her.

The table emptied. She was alone again – something she hadn't been since joining Randall under the emergency tent by the river.

The cook emptied a fresh pan of stew into the serving pan. "You look a little green. I sure hope it's not my cooking."

She offered a half-smile. "I hope not, too."

"Janice Mitchell. Report to A building. Janice Mitchell. Report to A building."

"They're calling you. You're Janice, right?" The elderly janitor wiping the tables scraped crumbs onto the floor. "Report to A building."

"Thanks."

"What did you do wrong?"

"Why would I be in trouble?"

"That's for you to answer." He tossed the dirty towel over his sloped shoulder. "People don't get called to A building that much."

"The watch I requested must be in. Nothing wrong with that, is there?"

She pretended not to notice his shrug and left to make a pit stop on the way to A Building. Lunch was coming up.

~

The sun slipped closer to the horizon. Bruce rested by the busted retaining wall, the sign lying by his feet the only proof that a Holiday Inn once stood there. Gulping down his last drink of water, he stuffed the flask in one pocket while digging in the other for his knife to trim a broken fingernail.

The butt of a pistol jabbed his side. One heck of a find, especially after three weeks of scavengers in the zone. He had pulled it from a poor chump sprawled near the service door to the hotel. The bloated body lay as if running inside the building while everyone else ran out. There must have been something important to make a man run into danger's way.

The soldiers had confiscated Bruce's vehicle when they caught him trying to re-enter the city. Not that it mattered. It wasn't as if any gas stations still existed in the zone. Besides, the work tools in it were pointless right now.

He picked up a small stick and whittled it into the shape of a spear. In high school, he'd learned what the New Madrid earthquakes did to the landscape in the 1800s. That tragic time in history didn't touch what he was seeing. The entire terrain looked like scenes from post-war-zone, apocalypse movies – *Gehetmo*. After being accosted the first night, he decided to treat it like one, too.

Granddad told him that he was prepared. No one was ready for this. Food and water were depleted the first week for most. Anyone with anything left was keeping their mouth shut to stay alive.

FEMA wasn't prepared. Period. And, the Reno University Seismology Lab just needed to record Charise's summary – New Madrid Fault zone – Hades arrived.

Dad wasn't prepared. The man couldn't do anything without his wife. Not that she could ever do enough to suit him. *Crud!* They probably still fought as much as when he was a kid.

That morning, he'd let his nose guide him, traveling as close to rotting bodies as his gut allowed, causing the soldier pursuing him on foot to retreat when Bruce ran past the first pile of corpses.

But, he hadn't traveled alone. "I know you're there. You can't trick me!"

Pitching the knife toward the unwanted guest, it landed point down in the roots of a toppled tree. The lean, buff-gray animal with big ears and a narrow muzzle slunk from behind the log. The canid shook its upper body and sat on its hind legs.

"You don't fool me, chump. Too much to feast on here for you to need my bones. You'll just have to feed on someone's else's misery. Better yet, take your howling buddies and go back to the abyss where you came from."

Grandmother's lessons to always be on the lookout for danger had not gone unheeded. The skills she taught helped him to spot the coyote tracking him almost immediately. She was particularly leery of the animal, but as long as he didn't feed him, he knew the four-foot was harmless.

The scrawny, dog-like creature rose and crouching every few steps, crept closer.

Regretting throwing the knife, Bruce slowly drew the pistol out of his waistband. "You've followed me long enough. Don't try to prove my instincts wrong and make me waste a bullet on you."

131

The coyote stopped.

He bolted toward it.

The animal scampered across the ground, not stopping until its frame disappeared in the glaring sunset. The stench it left behind convinced him that it had frolicked with the dead. Unlike in Granddad's field, this same foul-smelling predator had exposed himself – *Tüdampa.*

He put the gun away. Bold, but barking up the wrong tree. After adjusting the camouflage cap higher on his forehead, he sat cross-legged.

Mom had to be helping in one of the field hospitals. She'd be safe in the compound until he caught up with her. Dawn was a different story. She was too stubborn to leave, but, man, her survival skills were iffy. Every hike they'd ever been on, she spent her time smelling flowers while he spent the day keeping her away from poison oak. Hopefully, she at least remembered his lesson on filtering water.

Crud! Dawn needed to forget the Peace Corps and stay in Ozark Ridge where it was safe. Just teach the girls there about life-stuff like God and hair color.

He poured a collection of cell phones out of a plastic grocery sack, an added benefit of being friendly with the dead. Periodically, there would be enough of a signal to try to make a call, but every attempt so far failed. The first phone he picked up showed two bars, so he punched in a number. The phone rang several times before his dad answered.

"Hey, Dad. I'm just checking to see if you've heard from Mom."

"No."

"It's insane around here, but I'm working on some positive leads," he lied.

"I want her home."

What, no one there bending to your every demand? "There are logistical problems, but I hope it won't be long." He scratched his grizzly chin. "How about refugees? There aren't any trying to settle in town, are there?"

"The county is in the middle of a disaster, and you're interested in demographics. Is that on your priority list?"

"I'm just hoping no riff-raff moves in. Another thing. I got separated from Dawn."

"The girl's a dimwit. Concentrate on your mother. It's our duty to protect her. You understand that, don't you? Prove me wrong and show me that unlike her, you can do something right." Lostyn hung up.

He wrung the sweat out of his tee shirt and put it back on. He was going to take Mom to Nevada until Dad cooled off. Dawn, too. If his father thought he would leave her behind, the narcissist was dead wrong.

The tip of the pyramid was barely visible, but it couldn't be over ten miles away. The nearest field hospital to the riverfront was close to it.

It was time to show Lostyn Bonin what real success looked like. It had nothing to do with casinos and everything to do with overcoming the enemy. He hadn't discerned who that was just yet. It was a toss-up between a ghost land with few walking dead and parents he didn't even know anymore. Either way, it was a battle. Yeah, *Gehetmo*.

He jumped over the retaining wall. His left ankle twisted, slipping under the wall, and wedging between two concrete blocks.

~

The front door knob rattled.

Dawn shooed the children into the kitchen. She sat Serene on Carter's lap and popped the pacifier in her mouth. Josiah kept his back against the wall between the window and door. With a ball bat in her hand, Maude posted herself in the office doorway.

The steel door stood firm against the kicking on the other side. Dawn couldn't understand what the outside voices said, but when Josiah jumped in front of the door to brace it, the women ran to add their weight. Footsteps walked back down the stairs.

"Press hard!" Josiah muttered. The three braced their legs. The prowlers ran up the stairs in unison and rammed the door. The bolt lock held.

"How dare they," Maude growled.

There was a shout, followed by shuffling as the intruders ran off.

Josiah peeped through the boarded window. "The police are after them."

Maude propped the bat in the corner. "That's the sixth attempted break-in."

"But the first in over a week," Dawn said. "The police will catch them. I bet that's the last of the holdouts. Which way did they go, Josiah?"

"Toward Third Street."

"Good! I'm going the other way."

"Oh no, you're not," Maude said.

"I'll be careful. I'll go down the alley, again."

Maude stepped in front of the door. "After what just happened? There are dangerous people out there. Do you know where they walk? The alleys. No, ma'am. You're going to stay right here."

"I have to go. Those thugs were the last, Maude. I'm sure of it."

"We're under martial law for a reason, young lady."

"Tell me Miss Kay's last name again."

Maude sighed. She pulled a picture out of her pocket. "Fisk. I've been praying over her picture. This might help you if the poor girl can't speak for herself." She wrung her hands. "I don't like this at all. Please be careful. Be back before the sun gets low. Do you hear me?"

"Yes, ma'am. Lock the door." Dawn slipped out, and after checking both ways for soldiers, hurried to the alley.

EVACUATE NOW notices were posted on every street corner. As far as she could tell, everyone had complied except for the residents of Assurance Home and a few crooks. Maude Davis was stubborn. If the police discovered they hadn't left voluntarily, it might not end well. The children that the woman was desperately trying to keep together could be separated. *Good grief.* Just something else to deal with.

No matter what, all three of the missing needed to be found today. Miss Kay's picture revealed a beautiful woman wearing bright orange shorts that complemented her bright green eyes. She and Bruce's whereabouts were unknown. But, Josiah had discovered the field hospital near the medical district. Surely, Linda was there.

A helicopter flew over. Dawn ducked behind a garbage can, sticking her head out after it passed to see which way it went. Several flew over daily, heading the direction Josiah said the hospital was.

A hand touched her. She jumped.

"Please, miss. Do you have water?" A senior man leaned against a door frame. "I'm thirsty." His legs buckled.

She grabbed him around the waist to slow his descent. "Here." Reaching into her shoulder bag, she pulled out a bottle of water and a pack of crackers.

He reached up, but his arm fell back down.

"Let me help."

His parched lips opened for a sip of water.

"You're burning up with fever."

"I don't feel good. Maybe you can find a doctor and bring him here."

"I'll try." She placed the bottle in his hands and offered him a cracker, but he opted for another drink.

"Can I help you inside? You shouldn't be out here alone."

"I'll be okay. You go on and find a doctor."

"Okay. Don't stay out here long."

Another helicopter circled before descending and disappearing behind a row of battered buildings. At the end of the alley, she waited until a soldier passed before crossing the street to the parking lot, hoping to find evidence that Bruce had been there.

Footsteps crunched across the gravel, sending her scampering behind a pickup to hide.

"*Américains ignorants.* I despise them all." Spit landed by the front tire.

"We are here to do a job, Matthieu. It is only a means to an end."

"What end is that? This is a game. A game that means nothing – *zéro.*"

"Matthieu, I did not know you to be down. *Ceci est pour le bien commun, mon ami.* That is what I remind myself. *Pour le bien commun.*"

They walked on.

Pour le bien commun. She repeated it aloud several times. Maybe Maude knew what that meant.

The massive field hospital came into view. Planes and inflated buildings were lined in rows inside the fenced area. The guard at the gate held his weapon in front of him, the butt of it on the ground.

She nodded a greeting and started inside.

"Stop."

"I'm looking for a friend. Well, a few. Three to be exact. I'll just be a minute."

"*Papiers, s'il vous plaît.*"

"I don't have *papiers*, sir. I told you that I'm just looking for friends."

"There is a posting area at the end of the road. You can add the names of your friends with contact information. If you have lost friends, then you are perhaps missing to them."

"I don't want to go look. I want to go in. My friend is a nurse."

"Move on."

Her hands went to her hips. "Did you just tell me to move on?"

A man in scrubs came into view. She coughed loudly. He

walked toward the gate.

"See." She bent over and coughed harder. "I need to see a doctor."

"What's going on?" the man asked.

"This woman is —"

Her coughing interrupted the soldier. "Please, sir."

"Let her in."

"*Non!* She is not sick."

"I'm the doctor here, and I'll decide that. Now, let her in."

Once inside the inflated tent, she stopped coughing. "I'm fine. I need to find a nurse friend of mine."

He gave her a stern look. "This is not the time or place to play games. You could get into serious trouble." He sighed. "Who's your nurse friend?"

"She has a natural tan and black hair." She held up her hand. "Stands about this tall."

His eyebrows raised. "Really? What's her name?"

"Linda Bonin."

His shoulders slumped. "I thought I knew her from your description, but I'm sorry."

"Maybe it's her. What's her name?"

"Janice. And I'm sure it isn't who you're looking for. The nurse I know doesn't have any family and hasn't mentioned any friends."

"Oh." She described Bruce and showed him the picture of Miss Kay.

"I'm sorry. I haven't seen any of your friends. Have you been in this area since the earthquake?"

"Most of the time."

"There's a lot of lung problems popping up. If you have real symptoms develop and need inside the gate, ask for me, and they'll let you in." He handed her a card. "I'm Doctor Gipson."

"Thank you, Doctor. I'm Dawn Finley."

"I don't know where you're staying, but if you go out the gate and to the right, you'll see a posting area just down the road.

Look for your friends there. After that, get somewhere safe before dark. Then, I highly recommend you catch a ride on the transport bus tomorrow."

Looking away from the guard, she exited and hurried to the posting area. Names and pictures were tacked in several layers, but none were her missing.

"Where are you going?"

She swung around.

Two officers walked toward her.

"Um, I've been to the hospital. I'm just returning home. I'll be inside before nightfall. I promise."

"There isn't supposed to be anyone staying in shelters this side of the roadblock."

"I'm staying at the Assurance Home." Startled at the admission, she took off running.

One officer started after her, but stopped his pursuit when the other one yelled, "Come back! We'll find her in the morning."

She ran around the corner before stopping to catch her breath. She remembered the man in the alley and stomped her foot in disgust. She wouldn't be able to help him, now. Today had been a disaster.

Maude was going to be very upset.

CHAPTER THIRTEEN

Randall signed the papers and handed off the patient to an orderly. "I've sent a dozen to ICU for respiratory failure this morning. All from the west part of the city."

Linda stripped the bed. "The air was horrible. Your expertise helped a lot of people. Remember how green the sky looked?" She stared at him. "By the way, how did you manage to stay here?"

"I convinced them the need would be greater here within the week. I was right, as usual. Then I said that you've assisted me for years, and I wanted you on my team."

"I'm glad they didn't ask me any questions."

"What does one lie matter in this environment? I feel better with you in the same building with me." He patted his leg. "I have our extra protection right here."

"They've blocked people from coming into Memphis, which makes sense," she said. "But they're not letting anyone out, now. I have no idea where the patients go when they leave here."

"Janice. They've set up refugee camps near the borders.

Remember?"

She diverted her eyes. "Yesterday, I passed by the main gate a little too close, and the soldier ordered me to step back. I don't understand why security is tighter."

"It's tightened everywhere. The UN Systems Coordinator told me the logistics of moving goods from coast to coast was mute. There are too many people to focus on. Anyway, here're my concerns." He counted on his fingers. "One, we were drafted by the President. Two, the UN oversees operations. Three, there's no communication coming in on our level. They seized our phones when we arrived. I haven't seen anyone other than the soldiers with a phone or radio."

She couldn't argue. Blue helmets and black berets were everywhere. The only American forces on the grounds the last three weeks were National Guard convoys bringing in supplies bi-weekly. In her view, that didn't mean the US wasn't in charge. Field hospital operations probably weren't priority as long as they were functioning adequately. Lack of communication was an issue, though. She'd struck up a conversation with the admissions soldier, but he only said they were here for the common good.

"What does *for the common good* mean?"

He waved off the question. "Listen, if it's as bad outside as we hear, staying put is to our advantage for now. It's not like anyone is looking for us, right?"

She ran a hand through her hair.

"Keep your eyes and ears open. If someone starts trouble, find me. Be on the lookout for areas where security might be lax, in case we do have to leave." He downed his nose at her. "I hope you realize that until communication is restored, this should be considered an unstable environment. Do exactly what I say, Janice, and don't cause any problems. Understand?"

The frame towering over her didn't know how vulnerable *Janice* was to mess-ups.

Squealing brakes announced another bus arriving in front of A Building. The scratchy speaker followed. "Doctor Randall

Gipson. Report to Ambulatory. Doctor Randall Gipson. Report to Ambulatory."

"We know the drill. A bus equals a full load. Here we go."

She followed him to Ambulatory. Staying put was her best option. Anyone looking for her wouldn't arrive by bus.

~

It had been a madhouse all day. People arrived from the inner city with broken limbs, infections, and diarrhea. Dehydration topped the list. Linda rubbed her feet. She would give anything for her broken-in Merrell runners instead of the flats with zero support that she'd been issued.

Randall indicated he had news when they passed in the hall, but he had been incognito since then. He must have either gone to Cardiac ICU or the barracks for a nap.

She had information too. The tarmac guards passed each other in the tent hall every four hours, leaving the planes unattended for two minutes. The cluster of trees creating a border behind the aircraft was worth investigating.

"Hi." The young orderly gathered the used bed linens and shoved them into the bin.

"Hi, Jeremy." She pushed the monitor out of the way and hung the clipboard at the foot of the empty bed. "It looks like we may catch up."

"Starting to slow down, huh."

"Thank goodness."

"Quick," he warned. "Don't jinx us. Knock on wood!"

She laughed. "Sorry. No wood in here. Wait!" She reached over and knocked on a wood carton filled with cleaning supplies.

"Whew." He exaggerated the wipe across his brow. "Don't know why I care, though. I ain't interested in leaving."

"I thought everyone wanted out of here."

"What for? It's not paradise, but when your home is gone like mine, this will do." He flipped the mattress. "Out there is bad

141

news. A friend came through yesterday. He was beaten black and blue – over a meal bar! Told me there's nothing out there. Nothing but trouble. Said the only things left are graveyards and pitch-black nights. Trouble served up with a bottle of water and a meal bar – if no one grabs it from you."

"I'm sorry about your home."

Jeremy sent the cart rolling to the next bed. "Ain't no changing it. My friend kept asking if I could get him a job here. Said his next stop was some kind of holding place. You can't even get out of the city, now. The processing areas are full. I ain't interested in going where people are tripping over each other. Muggers and murderers love those places. I hear the closest safe place to be is on the other side of Nashville." He shook the long red dreadlocks behind his shoulders and pushed the cart toward the hall. "Nope. I'm fine right here, emptying bed pots and getting fed twice a day."

The military didn't tolerate trouble at the field hospital, not that it was a problem. Workers were too busy to think and the patients too sick to care. Jeremy was right. Everyone ate well, and the sleeping arrangements were sufficient.

Plus, co-workers liked Janice. She and Molly shared laughs and swapped stories every night. Doctors requesting her for specific tasks made it obvious they appreciated her efforts. Of course, Randall didn't like any of it. He hovered over her like – well it didn't matter. She was used to it.

The workload was taking its toll on the doctor. When she asked where they would go if they left, he flared up and demanded to know why she was questioning his ability to make decisions. After apologizing, he calmed down, and they laughed it off.

Asking Randall to check the area beyond the planes was an extra strain the doctor didn't need, right now. It was probably best to keep that potential escape route to herself for a while. She rubbed her side and wondered whatever happened to her wrap.

She counted eighteen patients under her care. Fifteen were being dismissed today back to the inner city. The puny man in the next bed moaned. She reassured him with a hand squeeze and glanced around. Picking up the clipboard hanging at the foot of his bed, she changed the notation. *There.* That reduced the dismissals to fourteen.

The group at the central station smiled in greeting when she joined them.

"Anyone else needing supplies from B building? I'm heading that way, hoping my aching feet will hold me up long enough to get there and back."

"I hear you. Mine are screaming for relief, but that jerk over there says I have another four hours." Pauline glared at the administrator stationed at the desk. "Look at him. His size thirteens have been propped up since he came on duty."

The male nurse jabbed her. "Don't make waves. You don't want him piling more hours on any of us, do you? The lazy bones loaded me down last week. Let's not give him reason to place us on an extended stay list." He stuck out his hand to Linda. "We haven't met. Todd Bishop, Auxiliary Nurse *Extraordinaire.*"

"Hey, Bishop." The administrator interlocked his fingers behind his head. "Aren't you supposed to be in C ward?"

"Doc caught up, so I'm going to the lab. It seems they're overwhelmed with blood. Go figure, huh." He muttered to the group, "See? I swear me and that dude are going to lock horns sooner than later."

"Meh. Doesn't matter." Pauline waved off Todd's concern. "They'll keep us here until the crowd thins and then ship us off somewhere else. Anyway, the shelf is low on Betadine. If you can get that for me, Janice, I'd appreciate it. The only thing worse than aching feet is cramping fingers from filling out a load of paperwork explaining why I ran out of something. I swear, if life ever gets back to normal, I'll never complain again about computers."

The administrator sat his chair on all fours, and the group scurried in separate directions.

Molly winked as she shuffled by. "Wait till Pauline tells you her story. You'll just die. That girl is a hoot."

"Janice, let me check your list," Pauline said. She scanned the front and back of the long sheet of paper. "Good grief, girl. This looks like you've already been given the *what-for* for running out. What did you do wrong?"

"Nothing. Just been ingrained in me to stay on top of things, I guess."

"Well, it's not like we're going to be called to the principal's office to be disciplined if we screw up. Take it easy. There's enough to worry about around here. Don't stress over this kind of stuff. No one around here expects perfection. Besides, you'll make the rest of us look bad." She handed back the list.

"Where did you work before getting stuck here?"

"Oh, wow. You'd love it, Janice. It's a beautiful building overlooking the Tennessee River in Huntsville, Alabama. I miss it. I was in Memphis because the hospital is an affiliate of St. Jude. The doctor I work with is opening an oncology unit off-site for children. Our whole team came to tour the facility. Doctor Chan is committed to his work and wants his crew fully engaged. He's here now, going nonstop in surgery."

"I was near St Jude when the quake hit," Linda said. "I lost count of the planes that airlifted from there. Do you think they sent patients to your hospital?"

"I imagine so. The new extension at the hospital opened just before we came. A huge new Urgent Care Center opened next door, too. I bet they're overrun with patients now."

"I've never been to Huntsville. Sounds like it's booming. Well, I better get the supplies before shift change. I'll bring back the Betadine."

Outside, she walked the area between A and B Building that was barely wider than an alley. The fetid air made the heat that much more miserable. She pulled her scrub top up to wipe the perspiration beading on her nose and froze.

A sickly-looking coyote crossed the path ahead and paused, sniffing the ground around the trash bins, before rummaging behind them.

A sudden gust of wind roiled his stench toward her, and she turned away.

"Hey!"

Linda jerked back around. "Where'd you come from?"

His eyes flashed. "I've been tracking you," he said. "Are you avoiding me?"

She rubbed away the quickly forming frown on her brow. "It's been wild around here."

"I am well aware of that." He lowered his voice. "The department heads have met daily with the German team that arrived this week. I've been positioning myself near the conference room to listen. They talk about the *common good*, but I've caught enough to know that our best interest isn't what they have in mind."

"Surely not."

His Adam's apple locked in place. "I know what I heard, Janice."

"I'm sorry. I didn't mean anything. I just don't understand, that's all."

"Have you seen anything?"

The steel look twisted her stomach. "Not really."

"Stay alert. I've decided that you and I are getting out of here. Soon!" He strode to the building.

Todd walked out the door and did a quick sidestep to get out of the doctor's way.

His lower lip jutted out. "I sure hate that you got stuck working with him. He's a gasket about to blow."

Before she could respond, he picked up his pace and hurried by. "Hey, Molly, wait up!"

The door slammed shut behind Randall. The doctor *was* really uptight. He had dropped some weight, and his skin had an unhealthy pallor. How much could the man take until he blew?

She rubbed her neck. Todd seemed like a nice person. Molly and Pauline were great women to work with. It took a lot of time to plan for the future, and building a circle of close contacts was imperative. Leaving wasn't the best course of action for her. She stuck the list in her pocket and headed to Surgery. Pauline had said the doctor's name was Chan.

CHAPTER FOURTEEN

Linda shook the doctor's hand. "I'm Janice Mitchell."

Doctor Chan had the slimmest hands she'd ever seen on a man, but they fit his short, dark frame with graying sideburns.

"Hello. You are assigned to me today, is this correct?"

Below the tired eyes rested a pleasant smile which made her relax. "Yes, sir."

"Do you have experience with Pediatric Surgery and Oncology?"

"I worked three years in a neonatal unit, and part-time for a year at a Hematology Clinic – uh – several years ago."

"I see. We have five scheduled surgeries. I hope you woke refreshed. It will be a long and challenging day." He handed her the files. "Please be familiar with each case before the hour is over."

"Yes, sir."

She grimaced. She had plenty of nursing experience, but referring to transferring patients from ER to the birthing room as neonatal work was a long stretch by any standard. The part-time job in Hematology wasn't really a lie. There was no need for him to know her duty was setting appointments. But, working with a reputable doctor in the present surroundings opened the door to working with them later. Performing well in his operating room would be better than any resume. *Don't fail.*

She studied the notes. Under normal circumstances, cases like these were transferred to a specialty hospital. Today, a surgeon who was accustomed to removing tumors would, instead, extract various types of foreign matter from children with compromised immune systems. These were young cancer patients with treatment plans on hold because the medicines weren't deemed essential in the crisis. Children separated from parents who were assumed deceased. She wrapped her arms around the files and hugged them tightly.

Today marked three weeks since the earthquake. By now, everyone at home assumed she was dead. No longer having to deal with his wife's constant fumbles, Lostyn would have plenty of free time to build his career. He'd be an asset in starting Hendrix Towers back up after such a disaster.

Her parents were better off. How difficult it must have been for them to explain that they were raising their grandson because their daughter dumped him on their doorstep. Chastising looks would now be replaced with sympathetic gestures for their loss.

Of course, it was better for Bruce, too. Experiencing the death of a mother had to be a relief after being the recipient of her botched parenting.

No matter what, she owed it to everyone she was leaving behind to become an honorable person who did things right. She already felt different. *Janice* was an excellent, personable nurse whom people called their friend.

"Nurse Mitchell!"

The doctor's stern voice startled her.

"I'm sorry, Doctor. I just finished reviewing the last case. I'm ready."

~

Doctor Chan didn't lie. The day was grueling. But, in a field hospital with minimal supplies, Linda knew the children were benefiting under the care of a skilled surgeon. Conversation limited to only instructions, his hands moved with precision. When they finished, he commended her for an excellent job.

He said *excellent*. She squelched an overly proud smile and headed to the chow hall. She had to remember to thank Pauline for the referral. They might be working side by side in Huntsville soon.

The new soldier at the security gate gave a slight nod in greeting as she passed.

"Many people come through today?" she asked.

"It is slow compared to the north quadrant."

"Great! I bet you'll be glad when you're able to go home."

"It will not be soon."

"Well, if we don't have any patients, we won't need to be here. The city will be empty."

He twirled a long key chain, wrapping it around his fingers and off again. "You would not know."

"I'm sorry?"

"We will be here for a long time. Reconstruction plans for the city are already in motion. *Regarder!* Thousands of contractors will be here soon to begin the work. Work-related injuries and illness will require a hospital."

Heavy equipment that moved in last week dotted the hospital grounds behind him.

She frowned. "But, there aren't even the necessities. There's no infrastructure to support thousands."

"We have the resources. Memphis will be *l'exemple première* for the United States to admire.

"I'm sure in time it will be a thriving city again. That will be many years from now, though. These tents make up a field hospital. This is just a temporary site in the middle of nothing."

149

"You will see. *Oui*, it will be many months – but not years. The IMF is prepared, The UN is prepared. As is WHO." He stood taller. "All will appreciate the good that will come."

"I haven't a clue what you're talking about."

"Americans are clueless, as you say. So, I believe you." He looked at his watch. "My relief will be here soon. *Bonne journée.*"

The chow hall staff was already putting away the clean serving trays when Linda arrived. Randall was eating and didn't look up. She sat at the opposite end of the table. "Long day for you, too?"

"I have very few lung patients left."

"Pediatrics has little room to spare, but Doctor Chan is quite efficient."

"Your transfer surprised me."

She wiped away an imaginary crumb from the table. "They didn't give me a choice." As he said earlier, what did one lie matter in this environment?

"Tomorrow, I'm demanding you be re-assigned to me." he glared at her. "You know they will transfer you back."

What Dr. Gipson wanted, he got. She was at his mercy. Her every move scrutinized.

The day she arrived at the hospital, the confines seemed like a huge space where people's lives were being saved. Now, the prison walls were squeezing the life from her.

"We will be leaving soon, Janice. The situation here is too volatile."

"I –" She bit her lip. The soldier at the gate was new. His information might not be reliable.

He crossed his arms. "What? Are you mistakenly keeping something from me? Tell me."

"Maybe you need a break," she blurted out, regretting it immediately.

He hit the table so hard with his fist, his cup bounced, sloshing coffee all over the food tray. "The only way to do that is to get out of here. It wouldn't be chivalrous of me to leave you behind, would it?"

"I have to go back to work."

"Your shift ended thirty minutes ago."

"I'm pulling extra hours." Her pant leg caught on the chair when she stood, causing her to trip. "Yikes! Okay, so, I have to leave." She ran to the barracks and fell across her bunk.

Sorting through the sick and dying with someone while in the middle of a disaster didn't constitute a relationship. Neither did sharing a day-old bologna sandwich delivered from a neighborhood survivor.

The muscles in her neck tightened. The situation *was* volatile. Randall was going to erupt, and *Janice Mitchell* was too close to be unscathed.

Just yesterday, Molly had confronted her. "He watches over you like a pet project. How much do you know about him?"

Randall was a good doctor. He was estranged from his brother. His ex-wife wanted nothing to do with him. He was paranoid. He was pushing her into a dark place she had been before.

She pulled her wedding band out of the backpack and whispered aloud the inscription. "Linda. Forever cared for."

Her knees pulled tightly to her chest.

～

Pus oozed out the cut on the senior man's swollen arm. He couldn't remember his name, so Dawn nicknamed him.

"Come on, Fred. I'm taking you to the hospital. That infection is spreading, and I'm not going to be able to bring someone here to help you. Let's get you to a doctor."

When he resisted, she shook her finger. "Don't give me any grief about it. I'm not going to have another dead body cluttering this alley." She helped him up. "It's not too far."

He leaned on her as they walked. "You are a fine lady. Ain't had nobody care like you do in a long time. Back in the day, people were nicer than they be now. I stay away from most folks, on account of my condition. I thank you for your mercy, ma'am."

Fred's condition became evident that morning when he begged her to find him a drink. She declined to help at first, but the old man was in pitiful shape, so she followed his directions to a nearby house and managed to dig some bottles out of the debris. He felt better after that.

"Why are you staying around these parts? It ain't no place for a lady."

"I'm looking for friends. And helping some children. Trust me. After they are all safe, I'm out of here."

"This ain't no place for kids."

"And it's no place for you. You must promise me you will leave as soon as you are well."

When they arrived at the hospital gate, the soldier radioed for assistance, but no one came.

"I'll take him in," she said.

"You aren't allowed."

"That's the most ridiculous thing I've ever heard. Look at him! You think he's just going to walk in there on his own?"

"We have rules –"

"I'm not interested in your rules. This man needs help. Look, Doctor Randall Gipson told me he'd help me anytime I needed him to. I need him now! You don't want this man to drop at your feet, do you?"

He scowled but pushed open the gate. "Go to the first building and have them notify the doctor. You have ten minutes to take care of business before I send someone to escort you out. I'm not losing my gate position because of you."

"Come on, Fred. Let's find someone who cares."

Inside, Fred sat in the nearest chair while she went to the desk attendant.

When her phone buzzed, she jumped. Maude let her charge it with the car battery, but there hadn't been a signal until now.

"Hello?"

"Hey, Dawn."

Her heart did a flip. "Bruce!"

"Where are you?"

"I'm looking for you, that's where! I've been so frightened. Where on earth are you?"

"Listen, I've got a problem. I tripped, and my foot is stuck."

The phone crackled. She banged it in her hand.

"– by a Holiday Inn along what used to be Interstate 240."

"Oh, no! I'm at a hospital now. I'll get the military –"

"No! Do not do that."

"They can help you. I don't have anything –"

"If you can find someone else, that'd be great. I'm going to need help." He grunted.

"Bruce John Hugh Bonin! You're hurt badly. I can tell by your voice. Now, I'm really scared."

"Look, it's not safe for you to come, but maybe you can find a man you trust."

"I'll find someone. I promise. Bruce. Are you there?"

"I needed to hear your voice – to know you were safe."

Her voice quivered. "Me too."

The connection died.

Don't you die on me! Doctor Gipson had to help her. She turned back toward the attendant's desk. A nurse was helping Fred into a wheelchair.

Dawn dropped the phone.

~

Linda examined the man's arm. "We'll have a doctor to look at that right away."

"It's sore, ma'am."

"We're going to take care of you," she assured him. "What's your name?"

153

He frowned. "Fred, I think."

"Okay, Fred." She filled out the top form, leaving a question mark by the name. Despite his confusion, the man appeared to be well hydrated.

He was only her second patient that morning. New admits were sharply down, which she convinced herself was good, refusing to think about the injured who died while waiting for help. She unlocked Fred's wheelchair brakes and turned him around.

Randall jumped to keep the chair's footrest from hitting his shin. "Snuck up on you, didn't I?" He smiled a boyish grin. His curls had grown, and he pushed them off his face. "You look shocked to see me."

"You didn't make your rounds earlier."

"No, I needed to check out some things."

"Of course."

"Are you okay?"

"Sure." She reexamined Fred's arm and made a notation on his chart.

Randall cleared his throat. "Nurse Mitchell, step over here, please."

Her lips pursed. "Fine." She retrieved the chart from the back of the chair and marched to the corner. "Should I take notes?"

He grabbed her arm and pulled her closer. "I just wanted some privacy. Do you have a problem with that?"

She yanked her arm away, refusing to show any hint of the pain pulsating where his fingers had dug in. The cocky smile he wore was the same one that made everyone else avoid him.

"I struck up a conversation with the tarmac guard this morning. When his shift ended, he left me standing there alone." He raised an eyebrow. "I'm surprised you didn't notice a breach there. Especially since we agreed to be alert."

Diverting her gaze, she rubbed off an ink mark on her hand. "I'm not back there much."

"The tree line on the other side is about thirty yards deep.

Beyond that is the riverfront."

Bile rose in her throat. "That's where all the bodies were."

He waited until an orderly passed. "They're all gone. The area is stripped clean. Who knows how Mortuary Operational Teams dealt with all the bodies? Who cares? It's our way out."

"What are you going to do now?"

"I was awake all night deciding what to do. We leave tomorrow."

Her mother's face replaced his in her mind, but it was Molly's voice that resonated. *"He watches over you like a pet project."*

Her voice broke under the intense stare. "Be safe."

"Are you saying you aren't going with me?" He rolled his neck. "Do I need to remind you how much I've helped you?"

The pounding of her heart muffled the sounds in the busy lobby. "I'm not as – uh – stealthy as you. Maybe it would be better if I stayed here while you found somewhere safe to go."

He sneered. "I knew you wouldn't be able to keep up. All right. I'll get word to you on where to meet me. I'll use the name RG Stone."

"Who?"

"You really aren't that sharp, are you? If you don't understand anything else, know this – I will be back." He kissed her on the cheek. "I have no intention of letting go of something as beautiful as you."

Workers cleared the hallway as the doctor walked the length of the building.

Linda hoped the soldier was wrong, and the hospital closed before the ticking time bomb, RG returned. She smeared off the kiss with the back of her hand and looked to see if anyone had noticed the exchange.

Dawn stood by the desk, gaping at her. "Linda? It is you."

Melissa Kirk

CHAPTER FIFTEEN

"Whoa lady." Fred grabbed the arms of the bouncing wheelchair as Linda took a shortcut across the field.

Dawn dodged past them and planted her feet, forcing Linda to turn the chair sideways to keep from plowing into her young friend, whose eyes were wide with shock.

"Oh, Linda! I'm so sorry I left you. The girls were scared, and I didn't know what else to do. I promise I came back as soon as I could."

Fighting the churn in her stomach, she hugged Dawn. "It's all right. Why are you still here?"

They both stopped and looked at Fred.

He offered a drained smile. "Good to see a reunion for you ladies."

"Fred! Look at his arm, Linda. He needs help. I have to find Doctor Gipson! I promised Bruce! I can't believe he didn't recognize you!"

"You're not making any sense. Is Bruce in trouble? How do you know the doctor?"

"He's hurt! Bruce, that is. I don't even know where to find him!"

"What! Tell me –"

A soldier walked around the corner. "Time is up." He motioned for Dawn to follow him.

She snarled and turned her back to him. "Linda, find the doctor and meet me out front. Hurry! Oh, I can't wait to tell Maude."

"Move it!" The soldier tapped his holster. "Now."

"I can't leave, but I'll find the doctor. Hang on, Fred." Linda pushed the wheelchair at a jog.

He grabbed the chair arms. "You're a lucky lady to have someone come looking for you. Sure do hope that Bruce fellow is okay."

"He's my son."

"Best be getting to him before his luck runs out, then."

Luck never sided with her. She was supposed to be dead.

"Does Dawn stay with you?"

"No, ma'am. But the mighty fine lady been checking on me. I been in some pretty rough shape."

"Where's she staying?"

"Don't know. Just comes up the alley. She's my guardian angel, that's for sure."

"Please. I have to help my son."

He looked down.

She patted his knee. "It's time to see about that arm."

At the nurse's station, Pauline took charge of the patient.

"Where's Doctor Gipson?" Linda asked.

"Serious problems in Pulmonology. Want to leave a note for him?"

"No." She hurried to the ward. What could she say? *Have I mentioned my name is really Linda? By the way, I'm married, and I need you to rescue my son.*

She rushed through the patients' vitals and ran back to Pauline. "Assessments are done. Fred finished?"

"Slow down, girl. You act like someone's after you. He was sent to Ward C. Looks like he's going to stay for a while."

Doctor Chan scurried past her. "Nurse Mitchell, come with me."

Linda didn't know which way to run.

"Now, Nurse Mitchell."

~

Bruce was *out there* somewhere hurt. Linda was *in there*, refusing to come out. Dawn marched back to the security gate. "Let me back in, please. I have to speak to Doctor Gipson."

"I gave you time."

"Well, it wasn't enough! You saw me helping a wounded man, didn't you? I couldn't just drop him off unattended, could I? Besides, the doctor told me I could talk to him anytime I wanted."

He strode toward the gatehouse.

"It's up to you!" she yelled. "But I'm just telling you that your day will go easier if I'm not standing here telling you over and over again that I need to talk to the doctor. I *will* see him, and I'll stand right here and keep telling you that until your shift ends. It could make for a very long day." She tapped her foot. "I'll just keep knocking!"

He turned a one-eighty. "You shouldn't be that brave, miss."

"Not brave. Persistent! I need the doctor." She crossed her arms. "I'm not leaving."

His eyes narrowed into slits. "I'll page him. Name."

"Dawn Finley."

He smirked.

"Oh, not me. The patient's name is Fred – I mean the doctor is Doctor Gipson." Her cheeks warmed.

He made a call. "Your patient has been admitted."

"When will he be released?"

"Ask the doctor," he said dryly.

"*You* spoke to him."

He threw his head back. "*Non!*"

"I'm waiting."

"Stand across the road while you do. I won't assist any further unless you move back."

"Fine. But page his nurse for me first. Linda Bonin."

"I do not page nurses." He slammed the gatehouse door shut.

Dawn spun on her heels. Linda better have a good reason for not leaving. *Seriously!* She acted like her nursing responsibilities were more important than her son.

She twisted her braid. Bruce was right. They shouldn't have separated. Why didn't he insist and stop her?

Some things never changed.

When they were eight years old, she told him she'd thrown the biggest sticks she could find into the pond. If he had bothered to ask why, he would have learned that it was to stop the turtle from crossing to the opposite bank. She grunted. He'd probably seen the turtle and knew it'd still be there the next day.

Then, the day after her parents' funeral, she told him that her tummy-ache would never go away. He didn't say anything and never asked about it. Of course, it was because he knew there wasn't a cure.

Bruce had no clue how many dates she'd turned down. He never asked. Shaking back tears, she wiped the dust off the toes of her shoes on her calves. No matter what, she'd find him. He knew that, didn't he?

She glared over her shoulder. "I'm still waiting!"

The gatehouse was closed tight.

~

After surgery, Linda ran to the gate. "I need to speak to a caregiver on the other side, please."

The guard tipped his head toward the road. "Are you

looking for him?"

A skinny man swaggered toward them.

"No, I'm looking for a young woman. I'm sure she's just down the street. I'll only be a minute."

"You aren't allowed outside."

"But I –"

"Not on my shift." He pulled out a notepad. "What's the patient's name?"

"Fred. No last name."

"Show me your name band."

She held out her arm.

He scribbled down her name. "A woman named Finley asked about him. If she returns, I'll page you." He held up a single finger. "One time only, Nurse Mitchell."

Dawn didn't know a Nurse Mitchell.

The man reached the gate. He stuck his hands in his ragged jean pockets. "I'm looking for someone."

His gravelly voice sounded like the patients' in the pulmonary unit.

The guard's face remained a stone. "Who isn't?"

"A woman named Bonin." The man coughed profusely, the exertion bending him over. He placed his hands on his knees.

Linda struggled to keep her legs from buckling. She crossed the staging area and slipped behind a delivery truck.

The guard's voice remained monotone. "Is Bonin a patient here?"

"Couldn't tell you. Her old man sent me to find her."

"This is a hospital. You need to go to *Le Camp Des Refugies.*"

"I ain't interested in going there if she's here, you know what I mean? She's a nurse."

He scanned the grounds, his gaze meeting hers through the truck window. He grinned.

"Just open the gate. I think I can find her real quick like."

The soldier's voice edged up a notch. "Nurses are not permitted to leave."

"Her husband isn't going to be happy, you know what I mean? Let me in."

The soldier reached for his SIG. "Move on."

The man threw an obscene hand gesture but complied.

The guard flicked his chin in response.

The stranger walked the fence line, stretching to get a better look at her. He didn't look like anyone Lostyn would walk the same side of the street with. That didn't matter. Whoever he was, he'd report in soon. As adamant as the guard was about not letting people in, his resolve to keep the rules wouldn't be a match for her husband and his wallet if he came.

She ran inside and past the nurse's station.

"I see you're still on the run," Pauline joked.

If her friend only knew. There was only one shift change left at the airstrip before dark. It was her only chance.

Out the back, a large plane coasted to a stop, blocking the row of parked aircraft. Its belly opened, and soldiers emerged. A loaded forklift backed down the ramp.

The adrenaline rush evaporated. Darkness would set in long before they finished and unblocked her only escape route.

~

Dawn bolted past the children and into the office. "Maude, it's awful!"

Maude pushed the chair back. "Have mercy, child! You're shaking."

"I found Linda."

Maude's hands flew to her heart. "I'm sorry." She jumped up and wrapped her arms around Dawn. "It's hard to understand, but God set his time for each of us."

"It's not that." She broke loose and paced.

"My goodness. She's hurt! Did you find her at the hospital?"

"No! I mean, yes!"

Maude's brow furrowed. "Sit down and tell me what's going on."

"She's at the hospital but not hurt. Traumatized, maybe. Oh, I don't know! I'm so confused. Fred's arm was much worse, so I took him to the hospital. He's really, really ill, Maude. While I waited, I got a call from Bruce."

"Praise be!"

"No! You don't understand. He's hurt and needs help! While I was talking to him, the phone circuits went down again. Can you believe it? The most important call of my life! Remember the doctor I told you about? I wanted to ask him to help, but then I saw Linda – Fred's nurse! Do you think she was glad to see me? No! Then that dumb guard made me leave. He's so rude, Maude!"

"Calm down. Let's work through this. One thing at a time, okay?" Maude nodded for her to sit. "Linda is well and at the hospital, right?"

"Yes, but she refused to leave."

"Well, maybe she's in shock. But she's where she can receive help. Now, tell me everything Bruce said."

"He's near a Holiday Inn on Interstate 240. His foot is stuck! How on earth did that happen? He made it clear not to get the police." Dawn sniffled. "He played it down, but I know he's in trouble."

Maude took her turn pacing. "There *is* a Holiday Inn on the highway. It's much too far for you and me to walk. Oh dear. I wish the car wasn't disabled. We'll find someone to help, but I'm afraid it'll have to be tomorrow. It's already getting dark outside."

The tears wouldn't hold back any longer. Maude handed her a Kleenex.

Carter and Josiah stood in the doorway.

"What is it, boys?" Maude asked.

The youngest tiptoed over and sat next to her. "Is Miss Dawn's boyfriend going to be okay?"

"He isn't my boyfriend, Carter. Bruce is a boy I grew up with."

163

He fidgeted. "You sure are crying a lot for him, like he was your boyfriend or something. That's what my momma did when she talked about my dad. She cried just like you cuz he left. She loved him a bunch. They weren't married or nothing, so he was her boyfriend." His lips quivered. "Then she went away, too."

Dawn hugged him. "I'm sorry, Carter. That's a sad story."

"Come on, Carter." Josiah took his hand. "Let's go. Sorry, Miss Maude."

"What do you need?"

"It can wait." They left the room.

Dawn frowned. "I had no idea."

"They all have heart-breaking stories. Parents separate from their children for many reasons."

"No reason is good enough! I would never leave my child. She flipped her hair back. "Linda did."

"I've been privy to some tragic situations. There were some where the parent's actions were justified."

"Well, that's just wrong. No matter what, it's very wrong."

Maude's gaze held steady until Dawn relented under the stare and looked away.

"We can't help tonight, child. Say your prayers. Then try to rest."

"I can't sleep. I'm going to charge my phone. Maybe he'll call again."

"I'm sorry, but the car battery is dead."

Dawn found a pen and wrote down the number Bruce had called from. Then, she called it back.

The answering machine came on. "It's Ethan. Can't get to the phone but I'll get back to you."

"It's me, Bruce. I'm getting help. I promise."

Chapter sixteen

The dew steaming off the planes added to the stifling haze. Linda smiled at the tarmac guard and strolled past him to the long stretch between two planes. The tree line was just beyond them– seconds away in a sprint.

The guard followed her. "This is a restricted area."

"I'm admiring the airplanes." She moistened her lips and pasted on a smile. "You must be important to be assigned to protect this area. I can see why. You look very strong."

His gaze moved down her body and back up to her lips. He grinned, revealing top teeth that crowded his mouth so badly that the center ones faced each other.

"What's your name?" she asked.

"Dominique."

"You must be from France."

"Marseille."

"Marseille sounds romantic, and very far away. I bet you miss your wife terribly."

He stepped closer, his stale breath invading her space.

With a slight sway in her step, she ran a finger along the stripe on the plane all the way to the tail. She glanced both ways. The narrow service path was clear. One direction led to a building with no windows. Barriers blocked the other end.

She fluttered her eyes. "Can you tell me what countries these beautiful planes are from, Dominique?"

"France and Germany."

"And that one?"

"Turkey." His voice grew husky. "I must ask you to please return to your duties and leave me to mine. But later –"

"I shouldn't interfere with your job." Fanning her hand kept his approach at bay. "Hot out here, isn't it? Is it almost your break time?"

He pointed to the building and winked. "I'll be in there."

She winked back and squeezed past him.

Back at the barracks, she shoved only necessities into the backpack, leaving behind a few things to make it appear someone still occupied the space. *Janice's* life was supposed to be different. No games. No regrets.

Back at the hospital, the nurses' station was unattended. She grabbed first-aid items from the supply shelves and crammed them and Pauline's snack cake into the pack before propping it against a wall where it wouldn't be conspicuous.

Pauline returned, carrying a tall stack of paperwork. "What can I help you with?"

She relieved her of half the stack and set them on the counter. "I'm checking on Fred."

"He's gone."

"They just admitted him yesterday."

Pauline shrugged.

"Do you know where he went?"

"Transported or home, I guess."

"Where is that?"

"I don't know! All I know is that the powers that be said to dismiss him. His chart is over there."

Linda dug through the files. Fred's was at the bottom. He hadn't given an address.

"Got to go."

Pauline shook her head. "Always on the run."

She jogged to the gate. "I'm looking for Fred."

The guard cracked open a sleepy eye.

"You took my name. I'm Fred's nurse, Janice Mitchell." She planted her hands on her hips. "How many senior men have left in the last hour?"

"One."

"Anyone waiting for him?"

"No."

"So, you let an elderly man walk out of here, probably *limp* out, with no assistance?"

"That's my assignment."

She wanted to slap him. "Can you tell me which way he went?"

"North."

Back inside, the nurse teased as Linda ran back by, slowing just long enough to grab the pack on her way out the back door.

Dominique was leaving his post, headed toward a hopeful rendezvous in the windowless building.

As soon as the guard shut the door behind him, Randall walked out of Building A and crossed the runway. He disappeared into the tree line.

She cringed. Counting down the remaining minute before the next guard came on duty, she inhaled and sprinted to the opposite end of the tree line.

Randall had told her, "I'm heading south, as far from this pandemonium as I can get."

He was heading south. She was going north. The field hospital had its first two AWOL.

~

Dawn fell asleep on the sofa sometime after the clock chimed 2 AM. When she awoke, morning rays poured through the barred windows, painting stripes of light on the floor. Edging her feet into the sunbeams, she leaned in to warm the back of her neck. A figure shadowed one of the windows.

"Good morning, Maude." She crossed the room. The dear woman had paced the floor with her until midnight before locking herself in the office.

The sound of heavy equipment moving debris and clanging metal signaled the work was closer to their street than last week.

"What are you looking at?"

"Josiah and Kelsey are gone."

"How do you know?"

"I'm in charge of these children, young lady," Maude snapped. "I know when someone is missing." She cleaned her glasses with a handkerchief. "They are going to be disciplined when they return."

"They can't be far. I'll check the backyard."

"Don't bother. I've searched the entire block."

"Where on earth would they have gone?"

Maude's tone sliced through her. "They went to find your Bruce, that's where!"

"They don't even know where he is."

"Josiah heard our conversation last night. He's the one who found you, remember? He's my risk taker, and Kelsey hangs on his every word." She moaned. "Those children will be the death of me."

"Well then, he heard you say that the Holiday Inn was too far."

"What he heard was that we needed someone to help," Maude retorted. "He decided that was him."

"How far is it?

"Miles!"

"Oh no! I'll give them a piece of my mind, too."

"I think you've done enough!" Maude stormed into the

kitchen.

"I'm going after them!" Dawn called out. It hadn't been daylight long. She'd catch up with the kids. Before sending them back, Josiah could direct her toward the highway.

Maude burst back into the room. "I said you aren't going anywhere."

"I can't let them get too far ahead of me."

"For once, you need to sit up and pay attention, child. You're less prepared than they are. They have some street smarts – unlike you! You'd be worthless out there, and guards would wind up following you back here. I don't need that! I just hope Josiah turns around when he realizes how much trouble they're in. What a mess!"

"If you will just –"

"Don't tell me what to do, young lady! *You* help Serene and Abay get dressed. Then do Kelsey and Josiah's chores."

A sofa pillow went airborne as Maude cleared a path back to the kitchen.

Dawn dressed the toddlers and made the teens' beds. A scrap of paper with a map drawn on it lay on Kelsey's nightstand. Red ink circled the spot where four lines intercepted. It made no sense to her. Straightening the array of perfumes and makeup on the dresser, she worked into the next room, stopping every few minutes trying to call Bruce.

He was the only person she'd ever been able to depend on. After her parents died, he gave her pointers on what he learned from living with his grandparents. He told her that elderly people were different. Just accept it as normal. The best thing to do was to meet her grandmother on her turf, and sooner or later, the older woman would meet her halfway back.

So, she began reading the Bible to Grandmother. They discovered Dawn had a natural gift for storytelling, and the spry eighty-one-year-old encouraged her to practice. Before long, they were sharing popcorn and watching movies together. Whenever Grandmother didn't understand something, Dawn picked a Bible story to relate it to. Other than the zombie movie, they had a great time.

Maybe she wasn't the smartest person in the world, but no one told a story as animated as her. She could make a dismal meal portion seem like a gourmet feast while telling the story of manna. Teenagers and old people loved to listen to her.

She threw a pile of shoes into the closet. It was time to go where she could be useful. Find Bruce and leave! Linda could stay and play nurse if she wanted.

"Come on, kids." She shuffled the toddlers to the kitchen table and gave them a snack. "Maude, if you still refuse to tell me how to get to the interstate, I'll have to go ask one of the soldiers. I'm not going to sit here and wait any longer."

"Is that right? Well, I'd appreciate it if you didn't bring trouble to this home. If Bruce is out there, the kids will find him if they don't run into danger first." Maude glared over her glasses. "You've done enough."

There was a commotion outside. Maude grabbed the children's ball bat while Dawn ran to the window.

"It's them!" She flew out the front door.

Bruce's body lay sprawled face down on the ground, his foot wrapped in a bloody shirt. She kneeled next to him.

Josiah gently pushed her aside. "Clear a path. He's hurt bad."

~

"He's waking up." Carter tiptoed to the kitchen to tell Maude.

Dawn rubbed Bruce's hands. "Can you hear me? Wake up, Bruce. It's me. You're safe now."

His eyes fluttered open. Pain distorted his face as he pushed to sit up.

"Don't move. Maude is finding a clean cloth to wash your foot."

"Leave it alone."

"It'll get infected."

"It's okay. Where am I?"

"It's a children's home."

Maude came in with water. A white shirt torn in strips draped over her arm. "I'm glad to see you sitting up, child. Although, I wish you had waited a moment so I could have sneaked a peek at your foot." She set the pan on the small table. "Let's take a look."

"Thank you, ma'am, but better not."

"Nonsense. I've tended to many injuries."

He laid back. "I cut my toe off."

Maude patted her chest and swallowed. "I would have never dreamed."

Dawn soaked a strip of the cloth and patted his forehead. He felt feverish.

"What time is it?" Maude demanded.

Carter ran to the kitchen. "It's Six-Thirty-Five O'clock!"

"Josiah, get the utility wagon from the backyard. Kelsey, find two blankets to line it. Carter, bring a board from the storeroom – the size I secured the windows with. We need to stabilize his foot. Dawn, you'll have –"

"I know! If Josiah helps me pull the cart, we can get him to the hospital. I'll have Josiah back by dark. I promise to keep him safe."

Bruce mumbled as they all struggled to put him in the wagon.

"Don't talk. Save your strength." Dawn shared the wagon handle with Josiah as they pulled it off the porch.

Bruce cried out at the jolt. "You're killing me here." He tried to climb out. "They'll arrest me."

"Stop it. Just stop! We're trying to help."

"Didn't you hear me?"

"I heard you. But I'm not going to let you die." She burst out crying.

"I'm not dying. Just let me stay here."

"No way," Maude said. "Now hurry! I'll be praying for you."

"Thanks, but no thanks. Prayers are what got me here."

"Bruce John Hugh Bonin! You listen to me. You are going with Maude's prayers whether you like it or not!"

He growled but repositioned his leg on the board. "I couldn't have gone another step without those kids."

"They're good kids. Now be quiet. We don't want to draw any attention to us." She cut her eyes to Maude. "You'll find excellent help at the hospital. I promise."

Josiah pulled the wagon, and she got behind to push. Kelsey started to follow, but Maude pulled her back in.

"No way, young lady. You've got some explaining to do."

CHAPTER SEVENTEEN

After discovering Randall had kept going instead of stopping in the patch of trees, Linda breathed a sigh of relief. But, by the time she worked up the nerve to move on, a work crew had arrived and began leveling the road, forcing her to stay hidden. When they finally pulled out, the sun was almost touching the horizon. With no streetlights to stop the thick shadows creeping across the wasteland, dusk was settling in fast.

Staying out of traffic's view, she followed the storefronts, running across each intersection for cover until coming to the cobblestone street at the end of the strip.

Climbing over the row of blocks once supporting a café, she propped a table up against the 50's mural on the back wall and scooted behind it only to jump back up when a fat rat ran over her feet. She bolted out of the dining room and didn't stop until she reached the residential district.

Apartments lined both sides of the first street that was the width of an alley. Garbage cans were strewn about, their spilled contents picked clean of food scraps. She walked around the back steps of each unit, looking for a place to take cover.

"Are you lost?"

She jumped.

Fred sat on a short stool, beside a tall stack of pallets. A dangling plaque with Apt 28 B painted on it hung above the dilapidated entrance to the sun-faded-brown dwelling.

"You scared me! Is this your home?"

"Not much left to call it home."

"You are my Godsend. Can you tell me where Dawn is staying?"

He wobbled to his feet. "My angel lady come from down there." A shaky finger pointed to the opposite end of the alley. "I sure would have died without her. Course, there ain't much living to do here, now."

"I have to find her."

"You can't be roaming around on these here streets. If the police don't catch you, the hoodlums will."

"I can't go back to the hospital."

"I figure not. I guess I'll be taking care of you till morning."

He stepped behind the pallets and stuck his head back around. "It ain't much, but you be okay here. Except if you don't think you can keep quiet. Then you have to move along. I got to protect what's left."

"You won't hear a peep from me. Thank you."

A wooden gate nailed to a splintered door covered the entrance. He shoved it aside with his good arm. "Come on in. Like I said, it ain't much."

Noise floated down the alley.

She dove into the opening. Fred pulled the gate back in place, pitching them into blackness.

~

Someone threw the garbage cans around and muttered.

Linda and Fred froze.

The intruder broke into a coughing fit as they came closer to Fred's apartment.

They leaned back when the gate moved.

"*Arrêtez!* Stop!"

The gate fell back into place, and footsteps pounded the ground, followed by more in pursuit.

"Sounded like Barber. I seen him a while back. That soldier there will catch him, I figure. Oh, well. Maybe he get fed." Fred stood. "Keep your seat. I'm getting something for us." He shuffled in the dark and returned, grunting as he sat on the floor next to her.

"Here." He held a bottle in front of her face."

"What is it?"

"Rye Whiskey."

"No, thank you."

"Take a drink. It'll ward off the chill that's fixing to hit." He tapped her with the bottle until she took it. "Just a swallow. That's all you need. Trust me. No one here gonna judge you."

"It's not that. I don't like the taste."

"Suit yourself." He felt for the bottle and gurgled a long drink.

"What does Barber look like?"

"Bald as a cue ball." He took another swig. "You're lost ain't you?"

"Kind of. I left the hospital to look for my son."

"He lived over here? Cuz if he did, he don't no more. Me and Barber is all that's left in this neck of the woods except for some strays looking for trouble."

"He lives in Arkansas."

"Like, I said then. You're lost."

Her eyesight adjusted to the darkness. In front of her, a broken tabletop rested on four coffee cans where an upside-down crate served as a chair. A tin coffee pot sat in the middle. Behind that, two wall cabinets once mounted to the wall now sat, one on each side of the kitchen sink. The window between them was boarded up.

"Is there someplace you can go that is structurally sound?" she asked.

"I feel better here."

"How's your arm?"

"It still hurts, but they gave me some pills and said it's gonna get better."

"You should have taken the transport bus out of this area."

"I ain't leaving." He retrieved a plastic sack from the table and pulled out a rectangular box. "Here."

She recognized the French rations. "Thank you, but I'm not hungry."

"Suit yourself." His hands trembled as he gnawed on the biscuit. "Lady, you need to get back to the hospital first thing. It ain't safe out this way. Your son ain't here. I ain't lying on either account."

"Dawn knows where to find him."

"That's one good lady. Your kin?"

She chuckled. "Feels like it sometimes. She mentioned the name, Maude. Know anyone by that name?"

"My memory ain't so good so can't say I do. I guess she lives down that road. Not too far, I don't reckon – just not my roaming parts. Like I said, you should go as soon as the sun wakes us up."

"I can't. I left without permission." The temperature in the room was dropping, and she wished she had packed another shirt to layer up with.

"I didn't mean that. You get on home. I heard you talking to my angel and the doctor." He patted both ears. "I got good hearing. Got good eyes too. I could see you was scared."

"Can I tell you something in confidence?"

"Who am I gonna tell?"

"I ran away from home." It sounded childish.

"No, you didn't."

"When the quake hit, I ran away."

"You took a break is all. I got eyes inside of me, too. Good people don't run away. They take breaks to figure things out."

Handing her a blanket, he put on a torn, cotton coat and pulled a piece of cardboard over his legs. "I know my name now. It's Thomas – since the day I was born. I figured I needed to tell you. Ain't no sense in going by another name. I am who I am."

"Do you have a family, Thomas?"

"Ain't had no family in many years."

"My name is really Linda."

"I heard Dawn call you that. It's a good name, and it's real. It's harder to get lost in what's real, you know."

Dawn had managed to find an old man in need of help in a deserted alley. Bruce's playmate had always sought out and championed for the underdog. She wrapped up in the threadbare blanket. She sometimes felt like the underdog – a whipped pup most of the time. If Dawn ever discovered the truth, she'd try to have Lostyn locked up. But that would only humiliate Bruce.

When she caught up with Dawn, she'd be back in the real world where everyone thought they knew her. But, there would be a hidden side-note to her life. *Janice – the failed attempt at freedom.*

Night stole the last of the room's light.

"Hey, Thomas?"

"Yes, ma'am?"

"I'll take that whiskey now."

~

Linda woke up when Thomas opened the gate and went outside. She laced up her shoes and stood to stretch, accidentally tapping the hanging ceiling tiles.

Pictures were thumbtacked in a neat line on the living room wall. In one, a much younger Thomas leaned against a shiny, cream-colored Cadillac. He wore a smile so broad, his eyes squinted. A small boy with the same smile stood in front of him. One of his hands rested on the youth's shoulders, and the other draped around a pleasant looking woman.

He returned, carrying a jug of water. "Those police are pretty reliable on their passing by. You got time if you need to relieve yourself." He picked up the coffee pot. "Been thinning the morning mud to make it last. It'll wash your belly, though."

"Where is your water supply?"

"I don't think I be saying, but it ain't gonna hurt you."

She slipped out, and when she returned, Thomas secured the opening behind her. He lifted a small board, allowing light to filter through the slit. A screen door hook held it open.

"Don't dare much more light than that. The patrollers don't come close, but I won't chance nothing, especially since I have company." He smiled and handed her a cup with a broken handle.

The ice-cold coffee was bitter, but the caffeine would get her moving. Too much precious time had already been wasted. Bruce needed her. She pulled out a meal bar and halved it. "I'll share, Fred."

"Thomas."

"Yes, Thomas." She sat on the overturned crate. Playing cards lay scattered on the floor. "What's your game? Poker? Or is it Solitaire?"

"I used to play Go Fish some, but I didn't like it much. I used them there to build a card house. It stood real big too, till the quake shook it down."

"Seems like a fun way to pass the time."

"I used to think so, but I just see it as a waste of time now."

"I don't know about that. Someday, the madness will be over, and you can build the biggest house ever. I bet you're good at it."

"Too good. When I was sitting here last week and hurting real bad, I decided too much time can be squandered on stuff that don't last, like card houses. Feels like pure old nonsense, now."

"Is that your family in the picture?"

He finished his coffee before answering. "I sent them

away."

"Want to talk about it?"

His shoulders heaved high and then fell. "Nora had her inner monsters, you know. One day, I couldn't take no more, and I told her to get on out. It was the last time I seen my boy."

"I'm sorry."

"Me too." He poured more coffee. "I had my own monsters –just weren't ready to admit it. I wound up at the mission down the street for a spell. Sure was a bad time. My inside eyes weren't near as good back then. I was living a lie and didn't even know it."

"No one is immune to problems that can distort the truth."

"Lies never done nobody good." His fingers drummed around the cup. "The preacher came to the mission on Tuesday nights. Every week, he talked about the same things – mercy and grace. It sure made me mad. One night, I walked up to him right in the middle of his sermon. I told him I didn't want to hear no more about all that. I needed an answer. He looked at me direct and said, *They's the only things that matter, sir.'*

"I guess the preacher knew I didn't know what he was meaning so he told me they be like the flip sides of a coin. Well, that didn't make no sense to me neither and I told him so. He challenged me to do something to help explain it to me and the rest of the menfolk. Told me that every time I heard him say mercy, I should say grace. The other men egged me on, so I took the challenge. He fired the word mercy almost every sentence, and I fired right back. Mercy! Grace! Mercy! Grace! We battled it out.

"When the war ended, Preacher didn't say nothing, but his face carried a look like my grandpappy's did when he hoped I heard down deep what he said. That's when I realized I'd been the only one in a fight. Them monsters inside me didn't want no talk about such things."

He sat down. "I went home and let my heart study on it. I didn't like the feeling that come over me. It was like everything was stuck but getting ready to pop right out of place. Kind of like the quake did, you know. It took a long time before I finally worked out the mercy and grace business. When I figured it out, the biggest weight of the world fell off these shoulders. It was the most freeing thing I ever felt in all my years on this here earth. I walked up and down that alley out there telling the neighbors how good I felt."

He laughed. "I even took off running sometimes. Barber bought a stopwatch at the flea market just so he could time me. I could move pretty fast. You can, too. You sent me and that wheelchair flying."

She smiled. "We'll race sometime."

He blew over the cup as if the coffee was hot. "After all that, a heaviness started coming to rest on my chest. I couldn't sleep. Even though the wife and boy were long gone, I knew I needed to go tell her how to get rid of *her* monsters. Didn't have no business not sharing how to get rid of such evil things. So, I found out where they lived. But it was too late."

"She wouldn't listen, huh."

"Never got the chance to help her. She done killed herself."

"Oh, Thomas."

"I never looked at Nora as having an end." He shook his head. "Time goes by fast. People don't need to go wasting life figuring out their monsters. They just need to know they got some and that mercy and grace can take care of them."

He stood and set their cups in the sink. "As soon as the police pass by, you get on the road. Time's wasting away."

Thomas didn't know how big her monster was, but he was right. Today seemed to be the beginning of the end.

Chapter eighteen

Maude trimmed the artwork with scissors. "You're going to wear a hole in the floor, child."

"Sorry. I was just thinking about Bruce. Can you believe what he did?" Dawn's toes curled at the thought, and she sent a silent prayer for his foot to completely heal. He'd be devastated if his hiking days were over.

"People will often do the unimaginable to be free," Maude said.

"I guess so. I hope you weren't too hard on the kids for leaving without permission."

"I couldn't make myself punish them. They saved that young man's life. My, how I want to protect them. But I can't keep them under my wing forever. Did you know that Kelsey's been with me the longest?"

"Really?"

"Twelve years. She came to me the day before her fourth birthday. I didn't think she'd be with me long. She was such a sweet child – not difficult at all. I've never understood why no one agreed to give her a home. With things the way they are now, I'm afraid she'll never find a family."

"Maybe this is where she's supposed to stay. She seems very content here."

"I would miss her. But every child deserves their own roots – a history with family."

Maude padded to the bulletin board and tacked up brightly colored laminated leaves that the younger children had first traced from real ones. With great care, she arranged them around the tree branches. Each leaf bore the name of a child.

Dawn handed her the nameless leaves to tack on the green construction paper grass stapled along the bottom. It reminded her of her storytelling days with her grandmother in children's church services. "If you would like, I can tell a Labor Day story to the children tonight. It's one my grandmother taught me."

"That would be wonderful."

"How many children have come to Assurance Home?"

Maude stopped. "I have all their names recorded, but I refuse to add them up. I'll not have myself thinking of any of the children as a number. Each one stole a piece of my heart. Love is what they needed, and I needed to give it." She closed the decoration box. "How does it look?"

"I love it!"

"So, do you think Linda and Bruce have seen each other yet?"

"They must have by now."

"Good."

"I hope it's good. Linda acted crazy. She kept saying she couldn't leave. Why wouldn't she want to find Bruce? Good grief! I mean, he has been through enough, don't you think? Do you know that they sent him all the way to Nevada to live with his grandparents? How could parents do that to their own child? I don't get it."

"We never know what goes on behind the scenes. I can't answer that."

"Well, I think she's selfish. Maybe she didn't want to give him any attention. Or maybe she didn't want to share her husband. I've heard of people like that. I think his dad has gone crazy, too. Do you see him here looking for her? Nope. He's just sitting at home, mad as a hornet. He has his issues, for sure."

Maude busied herself preparing meals while Dawn swept the kitchen floor. Linda sure had fooled her, sending Bruce away and never letting him come home. A parent was supposed to love and protect their children. *Seriously!* The woman needed to take a lesson from the administrator of Assurance Home.

She paused at the open shelves. The food supply had looked slim when she arrived, but all the essentials were still there, including cleaning supplies. The coming months would get tough, though. Memphis winters were cold, and there wasn't any heat source. Maude insisted she wouldn't risk losing the children. She was the opposite of Linda.

Miss Kay was still missing, and no one dared speak the obvious. None of the kids had mentioned her in several days, and the youngest ones seemed to have already forgotten the assistant.

Later, she would ask permission to adjust Kelsey's bedtime, so the girl could stay up and be part of the nightly planning and prep work. The void left by Miss Kay needed to be filled.

Surely Maude had noticed how much slack Kelsey picked up. No matter what the Director of Assurance Home thought, the teenager claimed Maude as her mother and was following in her footsteps.

She put the broom away. "I'll get the little ones ready to eat."

"Make sure Carter changes his shirt. I swear that child dirties up more clothes than all the others combined."

There was a knock at the front door. Dawn picked up Serene and headed to the bedroom, motioning for Abay and Carter to join her. "Shh," she whispered. "Let's sit quietly for a minute, okay?"

Carter held his finger to his lips, and Serene mimicked him. Abay stuck his thumb in his mouth.

Maude opened the door. "May I help you?"

"I'm looking for a young woman –"

Dawn ran out. "Linda!"

~

Children surrounded Linda when Dawn pulled her into the room. A stout woman cut through the crowd of children.

"So, this is your Linda. She looks just like you described her." She shook her hand. "I'm Maude. It's nice to meet you finally. I've heard a lot about you."

"Nice to meet you, too."

Everyone stared, and Linda suddenly felt light-headed.

Maude scolded the children. "Step back and give her some air. Let's not scare her away."

In unison, the children took one step back.

"More than that. Sit in your assigned places, please. You'll have plenty of time to visit our new friend. Carter!"

A stocky young boy jumped up. "Yes, ma'am. I'll get some water." He ran to the other room but stuck his head back in the doorway. "Sorry, Miss Dawn. I forgot to tiptoe."

Maude directed her to sit.

Dawn dropped to Linda's feet and sat cross-legged. "Tell me everything! Like where have you been all this time? I mean, I know you've been at the hospital, but where were you before that? One minute I saw you by the School of Law, and the next you were gone."

"Slow down, child," Maude said. "Give her a chance to catch her breath." She looked Linda in the eye. "Did anyone see you come here?"

"No."

"Good! We must be careful. I'm sure you understand. Are you hurt? Oh, I suppose not, since you worked at the hospital. I

184

guess it would be better to ask if you *were* injured."

"That's right!" Dawn smacked her forehead. "You were hurt before we even left Memphis. The jolt from the quake must have been terrible. Are you okay, now? I mean, really, really okay?

Linda smiled at Carter when he offered her the bottle of water. "Thank you. The first several days are a blur."

"Bruce said you would be helping people."

"You found him!" A burden like the kind Thomas described fell from her shoulders.

"You didn't see him? Unbelievable!" Dawn's face contorted. "He cut his toe off."

"What!"

She pointed to the older children, "These two found him."

Linda looked from Dawn to Maude, and back. "I'm confused."

"It's too much for me to explain right now. What matters is that you're both safe."

"I'm going to set an extra place at the table for lunch," Maude said. "Then you two can go check on Bruce together."

"I can't go."

Dawn threw her hands in the air. "There you go again. First, you couldn't leave. Now you can't go back. I don't get it. Don't you want to see your son?"

"Of course, I do. But, I guess I'm what you call AWOL."

~

Linda sipped the steamy herb tea prepared on Maude's camping stove. She inhaled its citrus fragrance until moisture formed on the tip of her nose. Maybe someday, she'd have an herb garden, smaller than her mother's, but just as lovely and aromatic. Friends could come to visit and drink fresh herb tea while fruit pies baked in the oven. They could laugh together, writing off mistakes as life lessons. She winced. Achieving all that was beyond her capabilities.

Dawn walked in, her arms full of clothes that had hung to dry under the back-porch cover, and the three women began folding the assortment of shorts and tee shirts.

Maude was the no-nonsense type. The home was clean, organized, and secure. The children behaved well. Linda wanted to ask why Assurance Home still tried to operate in Memphis but couldn't because she was the one under scrutiny.

Dawn was angry at her because she refused to be interrogated. But, Bruce would expect the same answers, and he deserved to hear them first – which she would have to give to him if they were able to speak to one another before Lostyn caught up with her. A moan slipped out.

Maude glanced up. "You okay?"

She nodded. Other than wondering why God hadn't put her out her misery by dying in the quake, she was fine.

Maude asked her something.

"Sorry?"

"How long do you think it will take Bruce's foot to heal?"

"Since it has been over a week, and we haven't heard from him, I think he must have an infection. Thank goodness there's no shortage of antibiotics. I don't know how much damage his foot suffered, but they'll release him as soon the infection clears, whether he can walk well or not. Most of the patients board the transport buses. If he doesn't, he'll have the police to deal with."

"They're strict about the curfews," Maude said. "They've started stopping people walking down the street and hauling them off. I don't know where they are taking them now that the borders are closed."

"Did he say why he didn't want the police?"

"No."

"Why are you and the children still here, Maude?"

"She cares about *her* kids," Dawn spat out. "and isn't about to put them in jeopardy."

Maude cleared her throat. "There aren't any good options. As long as the children are together, I can watch over them. If we left, I'm afraid they might be taken from me. While I have the resources and can care for them, we will stay here."

"I don't know how you've managed. The supplies needed to keep this home going is no small amount."

"I believe in being prepared."

Dawn whipped a small shirt in the air to straighten it.

"Dawn, it must have been terrifying for you, trying to get the girls home safe. Were things okay in Ozark Ridge?"

"I managed. Home isn't bad compared to here. Of course, your husband is understandably upset." She marched out of the room with an armful of clothes.

"I'm sure you had reasons to stay in Memphis," Maude stated it more like a question.

Linda picked up the rest of the laundry. As she turned, her arms passed over the corner of the countertop, knocking over the porcelain Humpty Dumpty cookie jar. It crashed to the floor, strewing tiny, odd-shaped pieces onto the tile.

Maude's face knotted in disbelief. Kelsey and Carter ran into the room. Their mouths fell open. Dawn followed behind.

"Someone's in trouble," Carter said.

"Carter," Maude warned.

"But you said if we ever touched your cookie jar, we would be in big trouble."

"I asked you to be quiet, Carter. It was an accident. Miss Linda didn't mean to break it."

Kelsey scowled at Linda. "Miss Maude kept our Easter sugar cookies in it."

"I'm sorry, Maude. I'll replace it."

The young girl slung her palms up. "You can't get another one. It was specially made. She's had it ever since Assurance Home started. It was a gift from her favorite aunt."

"Kelsey," Maude said. "We will graciously accept Miss Linda's apology. It was just a cookie jar. She is our friend. Friends forgive one another. There is absolutely nothing more important than looking past the mishaps of others to love and accept them."

Carter matched Kelsey's stance and glared.

Linda's emotions rolled, threatening to empty her tea onto the broken pieces. "Excuse me." She went to the back room. There wasn't any reason they should forgive her. Maude successfully managed an entire home of children in a calamity rivaled only by war. Bruce and Dawn defied the odds and found her. Her only clumsy claim to fame was missing in action.

She hung her head over the wastebasket. MIA. Something Lostyn wouldn't accept, either.

CHAPTER NINETEEN

"I am *Officier* Rosier, and this is my deputy, *Adjoint* Gray."
The broad-shouldered man at the door walked in without an
invitation. The shorter, uniformed man thrust a clipboard in
Maude's hand and brushed past her. They stopped in the center of
the room and turned full circle in opposite directions. The men
wore different identity badges than the soldiers at the hospital.

The children had been noisily playing when the officers
knocked, and Carter answered the door, giving Linda no time to
hide. She sat beside Dawn on the sofa.

Serene balanced with one hand on the entry table leg. The
head covered with beaded braids bounced off Linda's knee, and
she hoisted her onto her lap. Abay pushed a toy car in circles,
making motor noises.

"What is your name, please?" The senior-ranking officer's
voice overfilled the room.

"What is your business with me, please?" Maude echoed
his tone.

"We are conducting a census." Pushing a toy truck aside

with his boot, the deputy cleared a path to the play table covered with crayon scribbled pages and puzzles.

Dawn straightened, and Linda gave a tiny shake of her head in warning.

Maude motioned to the two boys sitting at the table. Their gazes were locked on the soldiers. "Boys!" She got their attention and motioned again. "Clear the breakfast table, please."

They left the room, the older boy jerking his companion into compliance when he paused in the doorway.

Deputy Gray guffawed. "What is your enterprise?"

"My name is Maude Davis," she said evenly. "I am the director here. I'm quite sure you saw the sign by the front door, which said as much. Assurance Home is a residential home for displaced children."

She glared at Dawn and shoved the clipboard back at him before directing her attention to the taller man. "Who wants this information and what are they going to do with it, Mr. Rosier?"

"He is *Officier* Rosier to you."

The officer raised his hand to quiet his partner. "We have been dispatched by the Logistics Support Division of the UN to gather necessary information from establishments that are attempting to continue operations since the earthquake. This business route was cleared last week. How your institution was missed is uncertain. Since the borders are now closed, we must assess your situation. Our assessments ensure survivors in this area receive the help they need."

"The borders are closed?" Dawn asked. "When? What does that mean?"

Deputy Gray stepped in front of her. "The census will be forwarded to the *Agence de Disposition*, who will arrange for provisions to be delivered here." He looked back at Maude. "You want the help, don't you? For the children?"

Dawn sat back, accidentally leaning on a talking doll. Squeaky laughter mocked the tenseness in the room. She pulled it from behind her and handed it to Serene. The toddler giggled and pulled the doll tightly to her, setting off another round of laughter. Maude redirected the attention back to herself. "I would never turn down help for the children."

The deputy laughed. "I didn't think so."

"I don't release information frivolously. As director, I take the privacy and care of these children seriously. I am the only one advocating for their safety and well-being." She moved forward, this time trying to direct the man's attention from Dawn. "I don't know anything about the agency you're talking about," she continued. "What kind of help? Where is your headquarters? Who's your supervisor? And when can I expect to receive your assistance?"

Deputy Gray ignored Maude's attempt at diversion and spoke to Dawn, "Your director considers her work necessary. You must be beneficial to her, or she would not have hired you." He glanced at Linda.

"Yes!" Maude said. "Now, tell me what you plan to do, and how long I can expect the assistance to last."

"It appears you are secure at this time," Officer Rosier said. "Tell me about your food and water supply. How urgent is your need?"

"I keep an emergency supply of food and water. We have enough for the immediate future."

"Be more specific, please."

She huffed. "I keep a six-week supply on hand at all times, which I will emphasize, is for the needs of this facility only."

"Some might call that admirable. It is unfortunate that your supply gave you a foolish sense of security." He shrugged. "This crisis will outlast your supply. These conditions will not improve in the next three weeks."

The deputy stepped sideways to keep from stepping on a toy car and bumped into the small table. Cursing, he caught the wobbly lamp setting on it before it fell.

"I'll ask you to please watch your language in front of the children. What is *Le Programme De Coupons?*"

The flustered man patted his jacket pocket and muttered, "I left the packets outside." He attempted to retrace his steps, but Abay had moved and blocked him.

"Abay, come here, sweetie." Dawn moved the little boy. "There's an opening for you, Mr. Gray."

"It is *Adjoint* Gray." He righted his cap and stormed out the door.

Maude crossed her arms and stared straight ahead until he returned. She examined the contents of the packet he handed her. "This means nothing to me. I don't recognize the name of this organization, and your credentials look foreign." She handed it back. "You'll have to explain."

Officer Rosier cocked an eye. "We are from the Logistics Support Division, *Le Brigade Français*. We are directing emergency operations in Memphis."

"Ridiculous! The United States doesn't put foreigners in charge. What do you make me out to be, a fool? I don't know what you're trying to pull, but I'll not have any of it on my property. I would turn you over to the real police if they didn't already have their hands full."

"I am sorry that you do not understand. The United States does seek aid during this time. The damage extends 300 Kilometers from the epic center. The earth under your nation's capital moved. The United States of America's resources are strained. You should not worry. We are not taking over. We are overseeing most operations in Memphis until further notice. I'm sorry this information disturbs you, but I assure you we are here to help."

He took a coupon-style book out of the packet and handed it to Maude. "These are your assistance *chèques*. You will find there are allotments for food, medical necessities, and other essentials. Each resident is allotted one *chèques* book per month unless otherwise noted. Have you taken in any children normally not under your care? If so, we will escort them to the east gate, where every effort will be made to reunite them with family."

Deputy Gray's smile exposed crusty yellow teeth. "They

will be taken care of there."

Dawn pulled Abay closer to her.

He leaned over the child. "This one must be missing his mother. *Voulez-vous venir avec moi petit homme?*"

Abay whimpered.

"Enough!" Officer Rosier commanded. His voice softened. "We are not here to create confusion."

Deputy Gray took the packet from the officer and pulled all but one additional coupon book. "This will be your allotment for the month."

"The officer said one per person."

He sealed the envelope and tucked it under his arm. "I am in charge of *chèques* and not required to give you any. Do not concern yourself with this. Your orphanage will not be approved to stay much longer. *Au revoir!*"

Maude snapped the door shut behind them.

Dawn dropped her head. "I'm sorry."

She ignored the apology and crossed her arms. "We get a grand total of two of these coupon books. And I suppose they think they are doing a good thing. Phooey!"

The east side of the city is the worst hit," Dawn said. "I don't know why they would take kids there."

"I'll be in my office." Maude closed the door.

Dawn scowled. "She should have left the first day. But, oh no, some people just want to hang around. Isn't that right, Linda?"

~

"I'm sure Maude felt she made the right decision," Linda said.

"I wanted to go home as soon as Bruce was able, but I can't leave here now," said Dawn. "This is too much for Maude to handle. I'll have to find food and supplies for the children. Kelsey needs to be taught how to prepare lessons –" She moved shoes from the doorway. "– and how to stay on the others about keeping

193

the entry area clear. Goodness – and the door locked! They need to learn to be more alert to emergency measures. That's going to be the next lesson plan."

"Their motto is for the common good."

"Yeah, right. Deputy Gary is a creep. A creepy creep. He's evil."

The children had gathered in the room.

"Is he really evil, Miss Dawn?" Carter voiced the concern etched on the long faces. "Are we going to run out of food?"

"It's just a misunderstanding, Carter. I will get it all straightened out. I promise. Now, begin your chores, everyone. Kelsey, take Abay and Serene to the kitchen. I'll be there shortly." She turned back to Linda. "*Le Programme De Coupons.* What kind of name is that, anyway? I don't trust them."

"What the officer said was true. I saw very few American officials the entire time I was at the hospital. Other countries were present, but the French oversaw most operations."

Dawn pointed out the window. "That pickup has circled three times today. If that's more of the *Le Programme De Coupons*, they just met their match with me!"

Linda joined her. The man behind the steering wheel puffed on his cigarette before flicking it out of the vehicle. He leaned out to look back as he drove by. She stepped sideways and bolted the door.

"Do you know him?" Dawn asked.

"No. We just need to keep the door secure, as you said." She occupied herself straightening the play table. Did he know she was here or was he just searching the neighborhood? She fought back the sting in her eyes. She'd never be able to forgive herself if harm came to the children.

"Poor Carter is in Maude's office now, answering why he decided to open the door without permission." Dawn sighed. "He's such a good kid. They all are. Somehow, I have to get more coupon books for them. I wonder where their fancy-named headquarters is?"

"Don't go poking around their facilities. Maude doesn't want to draw attention. It's dangerous."

"So, I'm supposed to do nothing?"

Linda put up her hand. "Stop pacing and listen. The authorities mean business. Bruce doesn't want their help for a reason. We don't know – they may not even let him come back here."

Dawn's nostrils flared. "He'll come whether he has permission or not. Not everyone is a deserter."

"I know you think –"

"Oh, no – you have no idea what I'm thinking, lady! You know what I think? You need to get over yourself and pull some strings at the hospital to get Bruce out of there. The least you can do is find help for these kids. And when Bruce gets here? Do everyone a favor and go home this time. I'm not leaving Maude."

Maude walked in. "You'll leave too."

Dawn twirled around. "I'm staying."

"No, you're not. I can't afford another mouth to feed."

~

The three women sat around the table staring at the two coupon books stacked in the middle. They reminded Linda of the WWII ration books her grandfather used to have displayed on his desk.

Dawn's head rested on the table. She hadn't spoken since Maude told them that they couldn't stay. Both women's positions were valid. Maude didn't need an extra mouth to feed, but she couldn't handle the children alone.

Linda propped her head up with one hand and massaged her temples. Maude knew her secret. Someone in her position regularly dealt with rocky relationships resulting in displaced children. Her little remaining dignity felt suddenly stripped away.

"What are you thinking?" Maude asked.

She rubbed her neck. "About what a mess this is. I think I

195

need to go see Fred – I mean Thomas."

Dawn looked up.

"His real name is Thomas. I stayed the night with him the day I left the hospital. He's in hiding so he won't be issued any coupon books."

"I'll send some provisions," Maude said. "Dawn can take them."

Dawn lay her head back down.

"Dawn! Will you do as Maude asked?"

"Like I have a choice." She stomped out.

"Don't be rough on her," Maude said. "She's been so concerned about Bruce. As much as the dear girl tries to put on a front, I know this whole situation frightens her."

"I know. She's confused. And it hurt when you told her she had to leave."

"Maybe so. But even if I had enough supplies, I can't have someone trying to help me who doesn't yet see what priority and loyalty look like. The child's eyes will be opened one day. Until then, I can't afford for Assurance Home to be scrutinized any more than it already is because she isn't careful."

"You need to leave before they make you."

Maude ran her fingers through her hair. "It's more dangerous to go than to stay, I'm afraid. You two are welcome to remain here until Bruce returns. I'll allow Josiah to scout around when I feel it's safe. He can get an idea of which route might be safest out of the city. Take Thomas with you. I can send some food, but you'll have to come up with a plan to leave without exposing us any further. Resolve your differences. It will take time to get home, and division will put you in more danger." Her lip quivered. "I'm afraid it will be like a lion's den out there."

Or a coyote's.

CHAPTER TWENTY

Dawn laced up the boots Kelsey gave her. "I hope I get to see him today." She giggled. "That guard should let me in just to get rid of me."

"Don't make him mad, child," Maude warned.

"I won't. I'm using all the charm I can muster – sweet smile, batting my lashes. See?" She exaggerated her blinks and curtseyed.

Carter laughed. "Do that again, Miss Dawn. You look funny."

"Funny?" She mussed up his hair. "Not exactly what I'm going for."

Maude pointed her finger. "Be careful. You've been to the hospital every day for a week. I don't want the patrol police to see a pattern and start trailing you. The less they see of us, the better."

"I'm careful. I promise. It's just that it has been over two weeks, and Bruce was so sick that I want to make sure he can find us when he's released." She picked up the bag sitting on the table. "I'll take this to Thomas on the way."

Linda walked in. "I'll take Thomas his meal."

"Whatever." Dawn dropped it back down and turned from Maude's silent reprimand. "Bye." She batted her lashes at Carter and laughed when he batted his back.

She headed toward the alley. Her boots fit well and wouldn't have to be broken in for the trip home. Maude had given Linda a pair of shoes. Hopefully, she would break hers in, too. *Seriously!* The woman was a stranger these days. A decent mother would ask about the trips to the hospital – be hanging on every detail. *Not once!* And anytime she mentioned Lostyn, Linda excused herself to another room.

Maude sided with Linda. It didn't surprise her. Everyone thought she was still young and immature.

Why not support her? God sided with them, too. Her life's mission was to help people. She had so much to offer, *but oh no!* Instead, she was being sent away with an ungrateful woman who acted like going home was torture.

News flash! When they got home, Lostyn could deal with his wife. She would get Thomas admitted to the assisted living facility. Then she would be free to help people who appreciated her. Mr. Bruce John Hugh Bonin would see that Dawn Finley wasn't still the naïve blue-eyed blond he still pictured. Frankly, it was time for him to either step up to the plate or – or what? She stomped her foot. Or, he could just go back to Nevada! He wasn't stupid, and she was not going to wait in the wings. *Seriously!*

The gate soldier started into the guard shack when he saw her round the corner.

"Hey!"

His chin fell to his chest.

Jerk. "I guess you know why I'm here."

He grunted and pulled out his clipboard. "Name again."

"Bruce Bonin. Please have good news for me today. May I see him now?"

"No one by that name."

"Yes, he is. His name has been on your list every day."

"Dismissed yesterday afternoon." The guard flopped his board onto the desk. "Escorted out by the authorities."

He held up his hands when she protested. "I do not know."

~

Thomas took the bag of food from Linda. "Tell Maude thank you for me, will you? She's a real nice lady."

"I will. I need to talk to you."

"Ain't nobody gonna stop you." He emptied the bag's contents on the table.

"The authorities are signing people up for something they call the *Le Programme De Coupons*. It enables a person to get food and other necessities."

"You can be counting me out. Not sure I want them to know I be here. I figure they would make me leave and I ain't interested in that. I got nowhere to go."

"I understand, but Maude won't be able to send many more supplies. She's going to be quite limited on what she receives from them, and there's a lot of mouths to feed at the home."

"Oh." He started putting the food back in the bag.

"No, I didn't mean it like that. She's okay for now and wants to help you. I'm just saying it's going to get worse before there's a turnaround."

"I figure that's the truth. No use expecting that life is gonna be easy any time soon." He opened the cabinet and set the pack of crackers and two cans of Vienna sausage next to a ration's box on the otherwise empty shelf. "I sure wish I was able to pay her back for the kindness. I can't think of no way, though." He pulled over two crates for them to sit on.

She rubbed the palm of her hand with the opposite thumb. "I've been thinking about what you talked about the other day. About mercy and grace – the coin thing." A nervous laugh slipped out. "I know all about needing mercy. I make a mess of everything. I – um, I'm just curious to know what else the preacher said, maybe

199

about grace."

"It's not about what the preacher said. It's more about what you know about yourself. You been thinking about your monsters?"

"I didn't say I had any."

"Everyone does. I know that for sure."

"Some people I know back at home have monsters."

He reached for his coat and shook it out to make his bed on the floor. "Well, when you decide you got your own, I'll talk with you some more about it."

She straightened. "I just came to tell you that Dawn and I will be leaving with Bruce as soon as he is well."

"That's good. It's time for you to be finishing your break."

His words tightened the invisible noose thrown over her head since being discovered. "Anyway, we want you to go with us."

"Thank you for the offer, but I think I be staying here. Like I told you, I ain't got nowhere to go."

"What about your son? We could help you find him."

He walked to the gate and pushed it aside. "Those police are pretty prompt. You should be going now."

"Why don't I stay here with you, then? I can find supplies, and you won't have to be alone. We can take care of each other. There's safety in numbers, you know."

"No, ma'am." He stepped out of the opening. "I'll take no part in that."

The gate grated as it closed behind her. The peephole latched shut. Linda set her jaw. No matter what Thomas said, some of his monsters still hung around.

A movement caught her attention. The skinny man was walking toward the apartment, looking in each window as he passed. Two apartments down, he stopped and lit up a cigarette. The long drag choked him, and he coughed profusely.

"Thomas, let me in," she whispered.

The gate slid quietly open, and she slipped back inside.

~

Maude set down the drink jug when Linda walked in. "It took you longer than I thought."

"I wanted to make sure I missed the patrol, so I came home by a different route." Linda picked up the jug. Her hand shook, causing water to slop out and onto the table. She retrieved a cloth from the sink and wiped up the spill.

"Is something wrong with Thomas?"

"I couldn't convince him to leave."

"Hmm. I guess I'll have to pay him a visit myself."

It was the first time she had heard the children's caregiver say she would leave the premises. Linda set the drink container back on the shelf. Eight full containers of water remained, even though they had served drinks every day and filled a pail to wash clothes.

"Did you hear?"

Maude's voice broke into her thoughts.

She swung around. "What? Is someone outside?"

"Are you okay?"

"Sorry." She smoothed her shirt. "I don't think Thomas will listen. I've decided I'll stay with him. Bruce and Dawn can go home."

Before Maude could respond, she said, "Hear me out. Thomas is old and set in his ways. The trauma of leaving may be greater than staying. I think I can convince him to move to the next block. There's an old house there in much better shape than his. That part of the neighborhood has been picked over for anything of value, and everyone has moved on. No one will bother us there. I'll get us enrolled in the *Le Programme De Coupons*. The police and hospital security don't communicate well so no one will question me being in the area. I'll tell them that we've been hiding out because we were afraid."

Maude stared at her.

"I think it's best. I mean, he isn't going to adjust well

201

anywhere else."

"You're telling me that you would stay here and send Bruce and Dawn ahead."

"Yes."

"And your son can explain to your husband why you've elected to stay in the city and live with an old man." Maude crossed her arms. "Look. I know what your problem is. I've witnessed many –"

"Wait a minute –"

"Dawn told me you sent your son away to live with your parents. You didn't go home after the quake. You've created a dozen excuses. Dawn isn't buying them, and neither will Bruce. I know I don't."

"You have no idea."

"Well, you're wrong. I do. And, do you think your son doesn't know? Let me tell you something. Of all the children that have come through here, I assure you every single child sensed the trouble in the environment they were leaving. Even those too young to talk expressed that something was wrong. You can't go back to your husband? So be it. But Bruce and your parents deserve better than for you to drop off the planet. They think they've lost their loved one and are hurting. Are you okay with that?"

"No! But it's called survival. Are you all right with that?" She marched out of the room.

In the bedroom, she shoved her meager belongs into the backpack. Before Bruce and Dawn got back, she would be gone. Contrary to what everyone thought, she never had intentions of putting Bruce, Dawn, or Thomas's life in danger and still didn't.

Why couldn't anyone understand she needed protection, too? The backpack tipped over the edge of the bed. Its precarious state summed up her life – reduced to nothing and ready to crash. No money. No job. No transportation. No contacts. The pack tilted in slow motion before plummeting to the ground. If only there were a cliff where she could do the same.

The front door slammed. Dawn yelled out. Linda ran to

the kitchen.

Dawn glared at her. "Good news, Linda. Bruce is gone. How do you feel about that? Here's even better news. He's been arrested. Gee. You won't have to worry about bumping into him for a while."

~

Linda grabbed Dawn. "Cut it out! I'm not going to listen to your drama. Who told you they arrested Bruce?"

Dawn yanked away. "The gate guard. Why do you care?"

She shoved her into the chair. "Stop it!" When Dawn tried to stand, she pushed her back down. "What did he say?"

"It's all your fault. Bruce is trying hard to help, and now he's in trouble. Again! And you don't even care." Dawn burst into tears.

She drew a long breath. Everyone accused her of not caring. It wasn't true. She'd simply chosen the wrong ways to care – repeatedly.

Bruce crossed five states to find her. She didn't know where to begin to search for him. Her father would know what to do. Her mother would pray.

All she wanted to do was run.

She sat across from Dawn. "You're right. It's my fault, but I never wanted to hurt anyone. Please talk to me. Do you have any idea what he did to get into trouble while you two were together?"

Dawn slung her braid back. "They told us to turn around and leave the area, but we made up an excuse, and they let us in. That's all I know."

The women fell quiet.

The rhythm of the bulldozers and cranes as they dumped rubbish into the endless line of trucks hauling it out of the city fit the melancholy in the room.

Last week, environmental engineers positioned giant recycling machinery at the edge of the business district to better distribute the millions of tons of scrap. Orange cones guided the construction teams past the street Assurance Home was located on.

Before long, though, construction workers would remove the cones and plow right to the front door. While the neighborhood shrunk, the odds of finding Bruce without drawing attention seemed insurmountable.

Maude broke the silence. "There's only one thing to do. No one is going to assist you. If you continue to look for him, you'll wind up in trouble yourself. What good is that? He's a strong young man and can take care of himself. He will be all right. I will pray for that with boldness. But I cannot bear the thought of either of you being apprehended for wandering the streets, and the possibility of that is growing every time you step out of this house."

She pulled out a handkerchief and dabbed her eyes. "I don't know how to say this, so I beg your forgiveness in advance. You have to leave without him."

"That's it?" Dawn asked. "Just like that? Too bad, Bruce, but that's life. Sorry." She shook her head. "No! I can't believe you're kicking us out without him."

"Sometimes we must make difficult decisions, child."

"Maude's right. We're putting the kids in danger."

"I don't get you, Linda. All the sudden, you're worried about these kids while your own son is in jeopardy. You hardly interact with them. I think you'd just sit here and fold clothes all day. It's as if you live in your own world where no one else is allowed. You won't talk about why you chose to stay. You don't worry about what Lostyn or anyone else thinks. It's like you're numb. Meanwhile, I'm going crazy! I can't lose Bruce. I won't!"

Suddenly Linda felt it – Coyote breaking through the barriers protecting her soul. Trying to stop him, she hugged herself tightly, but she was no match, and her head fell in shame.

Tüdampa consoled her, "Surrender to failure. It's okay – I'll help you cope."

Maybe she was numb. "You don't know me," was all she

knew to say.

"I know what I see – a selfish, heartless woman."

"You only see what I allow you to. You don't really know me."

"That makes no sense!"

Dawn's expression showed that she couldn't envision a world she'd never been part of. She couldn't see that the boy they saw in the restaurant the day of the earthquake lived the lifestyle Bruce had been spared. The boy's mother had never uttered a word to Linda, but the two understood each other. They had both worked hard but failed to create a loving home where everyone could be safe.

Maude stared until Linda turned away from the knowing gaze.

"What she means, child," Maude said, "is that we only see what we choose. Our subconscious warns us that looking beyond what we're comfortable with puts us at risk of seeing someone else's demons. We don't want to understand their problems because, frankly, we've fed the evil in us enough to know the danger. So, we close our eyes. Perhaps, that makes us the selfish ones."

"What? Is that what you think?" Dawn demanded. "While she hid out taking care of herself, I *chose* to look for her and Bruce. And Miss Kay!" Her voice turned sarcastic. "Talk about bearing a burden. It doesn't exactly sound selfish to me."

"Despite what you think, I love my son, Dawn. I'm going to do whatever it takes to free him so both of you can get back to a normal life."

"Whatever."

Maude smacked the table with both palms. "Give me your hands."

Wide-eyed, Dawn sat back.

"Both of you. Now!"

Linda gently but firmly took Dawn's hands and placed them on the table with her own.

Maude wove their hands together. "What benefit are you to Bruce fighting the way you are? He will find his way, and when you're reunited, he'll want you two on the same side. It's time to lay this aside. Pull together, ladies." She gave their hands a stern squeeze. "I'm going to tend to the children. When I get back, I expect you not only to be speaking civil to one another but also to have your escape route planned." She left the room.

Dawn jerked her hands away and rocked, pinching the bridge of her nose. "I feel like a traitor."

Linda kept her hands folded on the table, giving the distraught young woman time to compose herself.

Dawn went to the storage drawers and pulled out a paper and pencil. "I've walked these streets enough to know which route to take to get out of here." She drew on the paper and shoved it in front of Linda. "There's our escape route. You can figure out our supplies. Good luck."

Linda took the pencil. "That's not a problem."

Her problem was much bigger than that. The coyote wanted to be fed.

~

"I feel guilty sending you away," Maude said.

Linda drew tornados on the paper. Judges don't feel guilty. They hand down verdicts.

"Have you noticed that it's growing dark earlier?" she asked.

"We need to talk."

"Dawn needs to speak with Thomas again. I'm not getting anywhere with him."

Maude's volume raised a notch. "I'm not changing the subject, Linda. In the neighborhood where I grew up, I remember a woman named Thelma Lou Barkley who kept a barrier in front her – like you do. I didn't know what it meant at the time, but it made me sad."

206

Linda drew boxes around each tornado.

"One day, while helping my mother at the shelter, I walked into the shower room and saw Mrs. Barkley undressing. Bruises covered her body. I took her by surprise, and, for a split second, that false front came down. That's all it took for me to be afraid for her."

She turned the paper over and drew boxes inside of boxes.

"Have you thought about the consequences when you just suddenly show up – still alive? Oh, dear. I'm not good at this." Maude cleared her throat. "I want to know how Lostyn is going to react."

She pushed so hard, the pencil's lead broke. "He'll be shocked like everyone else."

"Do you have friends you can trust to help you, maybe at church?"

"Really, it's all right. Don't you know that home is where the love is? It's where I belong. Just ask Dawn."

"Please, Linda. Be careful."

"Honestly. Don't concern yourself. I'm sure I'll be welcomed home. After I face my consequences, everything will be just grand."

"Don't go home."

"Since you're the one making me leave, I don't think you have the right to tell me where to go."

"I don't want you to be anyone's punching bag."

"Shut up!" She bolted for the living room door, but Maude beat her there.

"I'm leaving. That's what you want."

"Listen to me."

"No!"

"I'm trying to figure out how I can help you. I've prayed and prayed about this."

Linda couldn't hold back the emotions erupting like a ferocious volcano. "You want to know how my prayers were answered? I prayed for a marriage just like my parents. Where love was equally shared by a husband and wife and any children they were blessed with. That's all I ever wanted. Was that too much to ask?"

Her newest friend moved to the kitchen table and sat, willing to accept whatever spewed out.

"I'm sorry, Maude."

Remorse singed the bowels of her spirit. *Tüdampa* stalked, calling for hellfire to declare her an unfit wife. *"You don't deserve the happily-ever-after,"* he spoke with authority. He mocked her, obscenities gushing from him, pronouncing her a loathsome mother and deplorable daughter. The onslaught burned with fury until her blistered core sizzled into molten resignation. She was guilty as charged. Convicted and waiting to be sentenced.

"My parents were happy," she said. "Always. When Dad came home from the fields, Mom would always prepare a foot bath for him. She'd rub his feet until his aching moans turned into praise. 'You did it again, my dear Wadonii,' he'd say. Whenever Mom worried about the affairs of the world, he'd kiss her forehead and insist she sit while he made tea."

When I was little, I'd crawl up onto the chair beside her. He'd serve us like we were his queen and princess. In the late evenings, I'd hear laughter floating down the hall, sometimes into the wee hours of the morning."

The only time it was any different was when Mom discerned it was time to pray. They'd go separate ways. But, I knew they'd come together again. While growing up, I never questioned their commitment and love for each other or for me."

Maude's eyes were moist.

The kids felt the same way toward Maude. In bed with their doors shut, they were tucked in with the assurance of a woman's unfaltering love for each one of them. Another pang of guilt hit, and Linda hoped she hadn't woke any of them with the outburst.

"Ever heard an inner voice so clear you thought it came from someone standing right next to you?" she asked Maude.

"God spoke to me like that once."

"My inner voice told me I deserved everything I didn't get. Is that God? If so, such a sense of humor, don't you think? Just answer one thing, Maude. Why did Bruce have to suffer, too?"

She went to the bedroom and locked the door. Stripping off her clothes, she stood in front of the mirror. Her skin was now clear. No bruises or cuts remained. Just tears dropping to her chest. They slid over her breasts and dripped to the floor.

It didn't feel like God wanted her to go home, but he apparently didn't care enough to intervene. She had wanted the fairy tale but realized now that it didn't exist for her – why had she believed the lie?

Chapter twenty-one

"We may be fighting a losing battle. Thomas swears no one is going to make him leave." Linda checked her watch. "It's almost time for patrol. Let's stop here and wait for them to pass."

She and Dawn climbed up the busted porch planks of the craftsman-style townhouse and went inside.

"I hope he'll change his mind and come with us," Dawn said. "He's lonely. I just know he is."

An oval rug lay in front of the fireplace. A bouncer seat covered with fabric of pinwheels in bright yellows, greens, and reds sat on it. A pink rattle, blue teething ring, and brown teddy bear with a Valentine's heart were scattered on the rug.

"Who do you suppose lived here?" Linda asked. "I think it was a young couple. I'm going by the box of diapers and the baby bouncer." She snickered. "And the gigantic TV and speakers. Guess about the baby – boy or girl?"

Dawn studied the items. "Tough call. I'm going to say, girl."

"Me, too. Lostyn would have never let Bruce play with a

211

pink rattle." She sat cross-legged at the edge of the rug, making sure not to touch it as if doing so would scar the family's last memories.

Dawn stared at her.

"Something wrong?"

"I haven't seen you wear a braid in a long time. With your black hair, it really speaks of your Shospokee roots."

"As in gray?" Linda teased.

"You don't have a bit of gray. Not one streak that I can see." She joined her on the floor. "I hope that whomever this family was, they're safe and can come back someday to a beautiful home. By the time that happens, I bet the little girl will be riding a tricycle."

"I hope you're right. New couples deserve a chance to build a life together. It may sound strange to you, but I think they will be happy anywhere. The young make changes easier than the elderly – like Thomas. Even people my age find it hard to make life changes." She pivoted to face Dawn. "Do you know who Thomas reminds me of? Remember Ernest, the man that used to sit on the bench by the Highland Park pond?

"Yes! He always brought a bag of halved grapes to feed the ducks. He would give the bag to Bruce and me and let us feed them."

Linda smiled. "Those were good times. Your mom and I took turns bringing dessert. When you two emptied Ernest's bag of grapes, we made you sit at the table for lunch. It was all we could do to keep you seated long enough to finish your meal. Then the men always walked you to the end of the pier to fish. I loved every minute."

"Lostyn always insisted Bruce bait my hook. He told him the same thing every time, '*You must always take care of girls. It's your duty.*' Bruce would cross his eyes at me behind his dad's back. Later, when it was just the two of us, he refused to help me. He said that if I learned to do it myself, I'd never go hungry."

Linda sighed. "Life took a crazy turn for all of us. But look

at you, now. I'm proud of you for helping Thomas and Maude."
She hugged her. "Thank you for finding me. I don't deserve a
friend like you."

Dawn squirmed.

"What's wrong?"

"You seem sad."

Linda caressed her cheek. "Maybe I'm sad that your
parents didn't get to see their little girl all grown-up and wanting to
follow in their footsteps. They would be very proud of you, too."

Dawn's lower lip trembled.

"I wanted to bring Bruce home after your parents'
accident, but I just couldn't do it." She stood. "Patrol will be by
any minute."

They watched through the cracked door as the police
lumbered down the street and climbed into the jeep parked at the
end of the road. When they were gone, Dawn led the way to the
apartment. "I'm going to tell Thomas about the pond. I bet it's
been a long time since he's seen ducks."

Linda knocked on the gate door. When there was no
answer, she knocked louder.

Dawn pushed the gate aside. "Oh no!"

Inside the apartment, stacks of old newspapers Thomas
used to cover for warmth at night were strewn across the floor. His
partially eaten lunch spilled off the toppled table onto the playing
cards.

Linda opened the cabinets. "It's not looters. The food is
still here."

"Who would bother an old man? What could he possibly
have that they were looking for?" Her face puckered. "I promise
you one thing, I don't know who's responsible for this, but they
will pay! You agree, don't you?"

Linda swallowed. It wasn't *what* they were looking for. It
was *who*. She left and ran down the alley.

~

Linda kept packing. "We can't waste any more time."

"I don't like it," Maude said. "There are too many ways for you two to get hurt. There are still troublemakers around. While you were at Thomas's, a man knocked on the door, asking if I'd seen a doctor and nurse missing from the hospital. When I told him no, he asked if I had any cigarettes. The nerve! I think he was trying to figure out what kind of supplies I had. He left in a pickup with other people. Two, I think, but I couldn't tell for sure."

"Was the pickup an old blue one?" Dawn asked. "There's been one of them circling the last few days."

"Yes!" Maude wrung her hands. "See? I just don't know. When are you leaving?"

Linda crammed the rolled socks into the backpacks. *Three were looking for her?* "As soon as possible."

"I wish Thomas would agree to leave. He's old, but a man traveling with you would make me feel better. Are you positive he won't change his mind?"

Linda and Dawn made eye contact.

"He won't," Linda said.

Dawn had insisted that the police found him, but the man Lostyn had sent was the perpetrator – the same one who questioned Maude.

Everyone was in danger because of her, and what was she doing? Running again. Deserting her son, again. If it was God sending her back to face Lostyn, who could argue? She zipped up the packs. "We're more worried about you, Maude. Two coupon books aren't enough."

Dawn rested her chin on the palm of one hand. "Maybe I should steal some supplies for you, too."

Maude's hazel eyes widened. "No! I didn't know you were sneaking around doing that. You should have known I intended to help you."

"We can't take your supplies. It would be stealing from the

children."

"That's right," Linda agreed.

Maude pursed her lips. "You don't need to worry about us." She pushed aside the utility cart from in front of the door that led to the back of the house. "Follow me."

"We shouldn't go in there," Dawn said. "You said the walls aren't stable."

"Come on."

They followed Maude down the hall to the last door. She narrowed her eyes. "Our secret, okay?"

They nodded.

Opening the door, she retrieved a flashlight hanging on a hook inside the door and clicked it on. The light shone on shelves that lined every wall from top to bottom. Each shelf bowed from the weight of supplies.

"I thought the fewer people that knew, the better. I've been stockpiling for a long time."

"Wow," said Linda. "Talk about being prepared."

~

Linda spotted the pickup parked at the side of the home an hour ago. There were definitely three occupants. She could tell from the occasional red glow of a cigarette being passed around.

She whispered, "Wake up. We have to leave now."

Dawn stirred.

She checked her jacket pockets one more time. "I gathered your things and spoke with Maude a few minutes ago."

Dawn hopped on each leg as she put on her jeans. "Why not leave when we planned? I want to watch the gate a few more days."

"It's a good night. It's cloudy. It'll make it easier to leave through the Third Street Gate."

"Are you nuts? That's the biggest transfer gate on this side!"

"Which means the road is better. Move quietly. Serene just fell back to sleep on the floor mat."

When they walked into Maude's office, the woman rushed to embrace Dawn. Tears streaked her face. Dawn reached for a napkin at the edge of the desk and dabbed the older woman's cheeks. "I don't want to leave you and the children. You need me."

Maude blew her nose. "Nonsense. It's time. Do you have all your supplies?"

"Yes. Thank you for everything." Linda hugged her. "You have my word, we'll check on you as soon as we can. We can't delay. We must leave now."

Maude turned off the office and entryway lights. Linda took Dawn's hand as they tiptoed past the sleeping toddler and out the door. When she hesitated on the porch, Linda pulled her down the stairs.

"This way." She cut through the yard, the opposite side of where the pickup was parked.

They moved quickly to the outskirts of the construction site.

"It's going to rain on us," Dawn muttered.

"Good. There will be fewer workers out."

A group of light posts lit up the staging area. Three trucks waited in line to leave. Another dozen was lined up waiting to load. Men stood around drinking from steaming cups.

Dawn huffed. "Creeps. Nice, warm coffee for them, but no milk or juice for the children."

"Stay low to the ground. See the truck at the end? It's not going anywhere for a while, so we'll have time to cut through the fence behind it. Then we'll head to the tree line and make our way to the road. We'll be long gone by daylight."

"Okay," Dawn said. "Here goes."

They ran behind a crushed rock pile to the closest truck. Two men stood by the cab, one giving the other directions.

"Stay to the right as far as you can. There's a new hole big enough to swallow the entire truck. You're clear after that." He joined the men waiting for loads, and the driver climbed in. When he reached behind the seat, they ran past the truck.

"Keep going," Linda murmured.

At the fence, Dawn pulled out Maude's bolt cutters and cut the barbed wire while Linda rocked back and forth watching to see if anyone noticed them.

Beyond the line of big trucks, a smaller vehicle turned onto the street. Even in the darkness, she knew who occupied the vehicle that drove slowly, almost coming to a stop.

"Hurry."

"I can't get it. It's too thick."

Linda grabbed one side of the cutters, and together they pushed until the fence wire snapped. They made four cuts.

Dawn pushed against it, making a gap for Linda to crawl through. "Go!"

She scooted halfway through. Her coat caught on the fence. "I'm stuck!"

Dawn unhooked the jacket and crawled through behind her.

A truck door slammed. When the motor turned over, they ran into the tall weeds.

Linda caught a quick breath. "We're not far from the road. When we get to the pavement, run down the street between loads."

Following the noise of the truck's motor, they went deeper into the trees. The brush thickened, and Linda was suddenly turned around.

As if reading her mind, Dawn said, "I remember a crossing not far from here when Bruce and I came in. We'll turn left there. Then, I bet it's at least three days to the bridge if we don't get a ride."

Moments later, they broke through the other side of the trees. The road was just steps away. A light flashed. Linda shoved Dawn back into the brush.

~

The flashlight's beam bounced in rhythm with the guard's footsteps. Linda didn't move for fear the twig under her foot might snap. The man's labored breathing caused the beam to shake as it swung like a pendulum, searching the roadside. The light lifted and penetrated the brush. She turned her head away as it passed back and forth in front of her black clothes and hair. The moon threatened to break through the clouds. *Please, no.* When the flashlight beam grew dim, she lifted her foot. The twig didn't snap.

"You're too close to the road," Dawn whispered behind her. "Keep moving but stay inside the tree line. Remember – the moon to your right." Slipping off the backpack, she handled it to Linda and gave her a small shove. "Go! I'm going back to the fence and cover our tracks. They're suspicious. If they see the breach, they'll be hot on our trail."

"We should stay together."

"It's better if there's some distance between us. Less noise. Remember – the moon to your right. I'll meet you at the crossroad." Dawn disappeared back into the brush.

A thorn bush grazed Linda's face, and blood trickled down. Wiping it off, she pushed into the thickening growth, stopping every few steps to listen for Dawn. Unable to go any farther into the thicket, she backtracked.

The branches rustled in front of her. "Dawn. Is that you?"

The only noise was raindrops beginning to hit the higher tree branches. The moon was behind her. Turning to reposition, she collided with a tree and fell backward.

The jolt sent a tingling sensation all the way to her jaw. She sat motionless, waiting for the pain radiating up her spine to subside.

After this, they were not going to separate anymore. Not until they were close enough for Dawn to get to Ozark Ridge safely on her own. Then, she'd confess that she was leaving Lostyn. It would end their friendship. Dawn wouldn't bother to try to find her again.

Once Bruce was released and discovered his mother had deserted him, he wouldn't look for her anymore, either.

She pulled herself up, glad to see that the moon was to her right again. On the first step, her left leg became entangled in the thorns, sending her tumbling forward. All she could do was what she'd always done. She threw up her hands to shield her face.

Chapter twenty-two

Dawn still wasn't at the crossroads. If they didn't hurry, it would be daylight before they reached Highway 61. Linda worked her way back, staying out of sight as loaded trucks drove by until she came to the fence and followed it, trying to find where they had crossed through.

The solo hum of the generator at the gatehouse was muted as the massive gate whined opened. A truck's motor revved and popped before groaning under the heavy load as it moved forward. She knelt behind an evergreen and waited until it passed. When the noise diminished, she heard Dawn yelling.

"I said let go! You can't stop me from leaving."

Linda snuck closer to the entrance.

Two guards dragged Dawn toward the gatehouse, her screams growing louder and the kicking fiercer.

"You kick me one more –"

Dawn twisted so hard, the guard slipped, and her foot landed hard on his shoulder.

"*Aie!*"

The other guard laughed. *"Vous êtes si faible!"*

"Aidez moi!"

They pulled her into the building and slammed the door. The gate guard in the window leaned back in the chair and folded his arms behind his head.

She moved closer but stopped when the guards walked back out. One rubbed his arm while the other spoke on his radio.

"I have a female 10-15 in custody. Need a 10-16 at Third Street Gate." He clipped the radio back in place. "I'm not going back in there. *Non!* Let McKellar handle her."

An SUV drove up and stopped in front of the building.

"Ah, he is lucky not to have to deal with her long. *Au revoir* to the troublemaker." He motioned. "Come. I do not think our bird tried to fly the coop alone. *'Elle n'est pas si courageuse.'"*

~

Pulling the backpack straps tighter, Linda ran to the crossroad. Turning away from the driving rain, she almost stepped off into a vast crater that had swallowed most of the road. Her arms flapped backward to keep her from plunging into the black void.

Covering her nose from the rotten-egg smell that rose from deep within the earth, she peered into it. Asphalt edged its first layer before it turned into an abyss. The hole stretched to the treeline. At the brink of the woods, glowing green eyes flashed at her.

Tüdampa!

Rain-streaked moonlight bounced off the predator's back as he stepped into full view and stalked the perimeter of the hole. Drool dripped from his tongue. His panting echoed across the divide, sending her body into convulsions. The beast stopped. His eyes paled to blue.

She stilled, spellbound by the mesmerizing stare.

He settled too, shoulders first, to the ground. His head

lowered to sniff the sulfurous smell rising from the gateway to Hades. The fragrance seemed to calm him, and he appeared at peace – something she'd long forgotten. One of his paws dangled over the edge, pointing downward as an invitation for her to be at peace, too.

Her own toes lined perfectly with the brink of the gulf that promised to swallow up her worries. Just one move and evidence of her failed existence would vanish.

Tüdampa tilted his head. *"I'm only trying to help you. That's what a man is supposed to do – protect his wife."*

Lostyn had lost his way a long time ago.

He rose and paced. *"No promises on the pie, Mom . . . just letting you know 4 emerg."*

Why should Bruce feel obligated to her? She could end his burden tonight. She examined the hole again. Did loved ones suffer more if a person's remains were never found?

Noise from an oncoming truck rumbled down the road ahead of it.

Tüdampa paced faster. *"I know what I see. A selfish, heartless woman."*

She covered her head. "Leave me alone!" But, Dawn was right. No one saw *Amigota* in her. They only saw a woman who didn't know how to love.

The rank fumes enticed her to act quickly – one step to make everything right. Her search for an acceptable path would be over. Mercy for her – for others.

The truck trudged toward the intersection.

He stopped. *"Take the step. It's your victory run,"* he taunted. *"Your moment."*

Wanting to step forward, she hesitated. Her mistakes could be judged, and justice served for all the people that had been hurt because of Linda Bonin. People like Thomas who had only tried to help. He had said, *"People don't need to go wasting life figuring out their monsters . . . just know they got some."*

The elderly man's words broke the hypnotic spell. The

truck cab bounced as it geared up, its headlights flooding the road. *Tüdampa's* countenance was reduced to that of a shabby coyote, slinking back to the woods with its tail lowered.

"Trickster!"

Linda ran until she was out of breath. She limped off the road and fell prostrate to the ground behind a rusted gas tank sunken halfway into the earth.

"Koiyah! Duwaniitehai!"

The engine noise from the truck drowned out her voice as it passed, its taillights disappearing into the black of night.

The rain turned to hailstones that inflicted punishment on her backside. The relentless chastisement came as a relief – almost comforting because it felt deserved. She didn't move while the stoning changed to a cleansing of cold rain.

She wanted a sip of soothing tea with horsemint or chamomile. To be young again. To walk the path and play in the clearing while Mother danced around the rock, swaying, as her soft chant reached a crescendo of joyful song. The aging, squinty eyes searching the heavens, her prayer shawl stretched out to catch the answers to all petitions.

Linda's voice sounded hollow as she uttered the familiar chant. *Wa hee na hai ho.* Her shoulders began to sway. *Wa hee na hai ho.* Her voice grew stronger. *Wa hee na hai ho. Na ho!* Rising, she stumbled into the dark void, gaining strength with each verse.

When a parked car came into view, she dropped and belly-crawled to it through the soaked, overgrown ragweed. The back-door handle to the vacant sanctuary gave way. Pulling it open against the tall grass, she crawled in just before a ball of lightning struck the middle of the road and bounced over the car.

Peeling out of the wet clothes, she draped them over the seat and pulled the extra set of sportswear out of the backpack.

The furious wind rocking the car was no competition to the fear shaking her body. She spread out the *Saturday Bulletin* newspaper that was dated the day of the earthquake and curled under it into a fetal position.

It was too dark to see, but Linda knew she was far, far from anywhere she wanted to be.

~

Dawn bolted out of the chair.

"Stop her!" the officer behind the desk ordered.

The young man walking in blocked the door when she tried to push him out of the way. She kicked his shins.

He swung her around and yanked her arms behind her back. They wrestled her to the ground and bound her hands and feet, but not before she landed a kick to the officer's ribs. The blow doubled him over.

"You okay, McKellar?"

The officer limped back to the desk. "Take her to camp."

"Why?"

"You have a problem with that, Adler?"

"I just figured I was going to Hold One, that's all."

"I have the authority to ship problems anywhere I want," he snapped. "I'm not in the mood to fill out a load of paperwork and camp has none." He scowled at the younger guard. "Problems come in all shapes and sizes. Even boys with poorly shaved heads can be problems, isn't that right?"

"Yes, sir."

McKellar left, slamming the door behind him.

The one named Adler ran both hands through the stubble on his head.

"I get a phone call!" She demanded.

He studied her. She matched his inspection until he dropped his gaze and dusted off his shorts.

"There's mud on your socks."

He grumbled but bent to adjust them, folding the muddy part down. "You got my uniform dirty. It's four days until rotation. McKellar will be on my back the rest of the week."

"Sounds like a problem. Maybe you're like me. Maybe your

225

boss left to find someone to take *you* to camp."

He stuffed his shirt back in. "I'm not scared."

"Should I be?"

"It's nothing to joke about."

"I guess not. Let's try another route then. Adler, your boss isn't a fair person. I mean, you did most of the work with me. But now, you're going to have to put up with his attitude about your appearance. What's it like not being appreciated? Never mind. You don't have to answer. I say we leave through the gate and be on our merry way. You won't have to worry about your dirty uniform. I won't tell anyone. I promise. I'll cross my heart on it if you untie me. You could just get lost. I don't see anyone stopping us, do you?"

"I can handle McKellar." He pulled a pistol out of the cabinet and strapped the holster belt in place. He loosened her leg rope and led her outside. "Turn around. I'm going to untie you, but it would be a big mistake to run."

"I don't understand why we can't leave the city."

"Because it's crazy out there, that's why."

She rubbed her wrists. "Please. Let me sneak out of here. It's still dark enough that no one will notice if I slip away. I can at least go back to the orphanage."

He blinked. "What orphanage?"

"Forget I said anything." She just put Maude and the children in danger again.

"Assurance Home?"

"I'm not saying another word."

"Good. Walk fast." He pushed her onto the freshly grated road running along the riverbank. They walked until they came to a hill of crushed metal. He led her around to an opening. "Watch out." He bent her head under the razor wire wrapped around two steel bars and nudged her forward.

The night turned more gray than black as morning approached, shedding light on the clearing. It was surrounded by the crushed metal on one side and chain-link fences running to the pitch-colored river on the other.

"If this is camp, I have a feeling we're not going to sit around, singing *Kum Ba Yah*. Not that I see anyone to share a campfire with. You know what? I don't think that McKellar guy likes you too much. I'm telling you, it's me today, you tomorrow. You don't have to put up with that. What are you doing with them, anyway? You took the job for hot meals, I bet. I doubt that it was the uniform. What do you know about Assurance Home?"

"Sit."

"That's a good idea. We can slow down and think this through. I'm sure there's a way for this to work for both of us."

Adler's bulky figure became more defined as the sky lightened in the east. His head was down as he circled her.

"Your socks are filthy. Don't think you're going to be able to hide that. For a week, did you say?"

"Stop talking."

"I'm just trying to figure this out, that's all. I mean, what's wrong with people leaving the city? It makes no sense. You can't tell me that the refugee camps are too full for one more person. Take me to that Hold One place."

"I said be quiet. No, I tell you what. You have a problem with that. Come on." He pulled her up. "Start walking. If you've been around Maude, you're sure to know *Amazing Grace* by now. Sing it!"

"You do know Maude!"

"Any kid around town that's ever had a problem knows her." The slight rise in his voice revealed more about himself than he meant to.

"This whole camp thing would really upset her."

"Ma'am, shut up and sing."

"You'll regret it. Just because I've been around her, doesn't mean I can carry a tune." She belted out the song's first line. "Amazing grace, how sweet the sound . . ."

She pushed stray hair off her face. She couldn't sing as well as Maude but could be just as stubborn.

Adler pushed her toward the water.

"You can take me to the real camp, now. You and McKellar can have a good laugh when you get back."

"Walk straight ahead and keep singing!" He prodded her with the gun. When she hesitated, he poked again. "Don't stop. Don't turn around."

"That saved a wretch like me . . ."

Grandmother once told her a story about the martyrs of Sebaste. Not that she could compare herself to anyone close to a saint. Far from it. She just wanted to leave the city. Grandmother told her that the soldiers were marched to a frozen pond just like Adler was pushing her toward the river. Had they experienced the same palpations that threatened to explode her heart into millions of pieces? *No way!* They were the real deal – persecuted because of their faith. Did they sing?

"I once was lost, but now am found . . ."

Her throat tightened. Dread for the six-foot kid with the gun pointed at her back rose above her fear. The young guard thought he was finished with her, but his actions were going to haunt him forever. Different grief than she had ever experienced before overwhelmed her. What a heavy burden for a young man to carry.

The next steps were more difficult, her feet sinking further in the black mud leading to the Mississippi. The fast-moving current moved trash downstream where most of the debris crashed into the pile stuck in the bend, sending a maddening echo through the air.

She gulped. Why was God finished with her so soon? Why not allow her to carry on the mission work her parents loved?

She threw back her shoulders. Adler could shoot her down. Dawn Finley would follow the call wherever it led, even in a camp where no one spent the night. She sang out. Grandmother would be proud. The black muck sucked her down to the knees.

". . . was blind, but now I see."

CHAPTER TWENTY-THREE

The foursome approached what had been Linda's fortress for the night. The long-haired man, who looked about Bruce's age, kept his rifle aimed at the vehicle's windows as he circled it. Keeping the gun raised, he turned to survey the barren farmland. A large crack zigzagged across the field to her hiding place, a clump of uprooted Magnolia trees that leaned on top of one another like a giant game of Pick UP Stix.

Everyone heard the semi-truck at the same time. The young man hesitated, as if considering running back to the car for refuge, but then changed his mind and hurried the group onto the field. Motioning them to stop, he approached to inspect the trees.

When he spotted her, she held up her hands. "I'm alone. Get your family on this side. The truck is coming."

Trucks hauling trash from the city were the only traffic on the road, and by the traveler's action, he shared her discomfort of being exposed to the environment.

Scooping up the smallest child, he rushed his charges behind the trees. Not taking his gaze off Linda, he bent on one knee and nodded for the others to sit. The gaunt woman tightened her grip on her plastic sack. The children leaned against a fallen tree trunk and closed their sunken eyes, too tired to show interest in the stranger.

Linda first thought the adults were married, but now that they sat within a few feet of one another, she decided they must be blood relatives. Their features were similar enough for them to be siblings, both sporting big eyes narrowly spaced above slim noses.

They wore layers of loose-fitting, dirty clothes. The woman wore a long denim skirt with pants under it. The scuffed hiking boots hinted at a rough road traveled. The children wore shorts over pants. As warm as it was, none of them sweated under the layers of clothing.

She reached for her packs.

The man raised his gun again.

"I have water." She pulled out four of ten remaining bottles. "You're dehydrated."

"We have nothing to barter in return."

"Seeing your determination is payment enough."

He nodded and opened one bottle to pass around.

"Don't try to ration. You need it now."

"Get ready," he told his group. "We move on as soon as the truck passes."

He looked at Linda.

She sensed he would allow her to travel with them, but she said, "I'm doing this on my own." She pulled out a Ziploc bag with snacks and handed it to the woman. "I insist. My traveling partner couldn't come. She would be horrified if you didn't take the food."

"Thank you, ma'am."

After the truck passed, the man slung the rifle's leather strap over his shoulder. "A rowdy group followed us for a while. Steer clear of them. Anyone who knows you are alone will track you down till they find you."

He led his group to follow the dissipating dust cloud behind the truck.

She gulped down two chalky tasting *chèques*-issued meal bars, having elected to bring them, and leave the food that the children preferred with Maude.

The bearing down heat made her groggy. Dead leaves crunched under her feet as she spread out the thin thermal blanket retrieved from the emergency basket in the trunk of the car. The blanket's instant warmth penetrated her skin.

Lula, Mississippi was over an hour's drive on a good day. The night before, she'd barely traveled any distance in the pouring down rain. It was still at least fifty miles to the bridge which meant be two hard days walking at a brisk pace. A power nap would help.

When her eyes closed, the scene of Dawn struggling to be free haunted her. Sleep threatened not to come as punishment for leaving her friend behind. Her body finally relented, but only after she gave up trying to pray. *Duwaniitehai* for Dawn's safety. *Duwaniitehai* for Bruce's forgiveness.

Mostly, she desperately wanted to find the right words to ask for mercy.

They never came.

～

Past the river, the skyline grayed as the sun rose behind her. Dawn obeyed and didn't turn around. If able to look Adler in the eye, she would explain that life was meant to be spent laughing and encouraging others. For taking hikes, discovering a spring, or watching turtles cross a pond.

People weren't problems to be dealt with – to be washed downstream. He needed to hear about Grandmother, who said serious issues were merely opportunities for God to smack the enemy down.

Her legs were mired deep in the mud. Adler was stuck, too. That's why the young man was taking a long time to finish his assignment.

"Pour le bien commun."

He didn't respond.

The French slogan might have been inspiring before the earthquake. After all, humanity was supposed to help its own. That was the Peace Corps' appeal.

Then the earth moved, changing her life as quickly as the river changed course. It wasn't easy to stand firm on a foundation that moved.

She would do everything again if given a chance. Being silly with the girls or talking them through their hurts at night had been worth every minute. They loved her. No matter what, Lindsey, Lucy, and the others knew that she loved them, too.

Bruce's face came alive in her mind. He smiled and wanted to touch her. She tugged at her braid to squelch her sudden giddiness. He spoke to her heart what she already knew. He had stayed in Nevada to work through his feelings.

Memories scrolled through her mind like an Instagram feed. She heart-tagged each one.

Time passes but memories live on. Maybe that truth would encourage Adler to make decisions that wouldn't haunt him. Sharing that thought was her final mission. Holding hands out to signal movement, she slowly turned her upper body.

Adler wasn't there. Dawn's gaze followed the tracks all the way back to where they formed a circle. Only one set of footprints marked the life journey she just took.

She stepped back to firmer ground, one leg at a time, retrieving her boot from each hole before the mud buried it.

She blushed at what just happened. If she spent less time talking, she would have noticed her demise was of her own making.

She stood still and quiet as a thought warmed her. God wasn't done with her yet. He just wanted her full attention.

~

Linda winced. Blisters were as predictable as old people – like the owners of the abandoned car. The pristine condition of the full-size, ninety-eight Oldsmobile convinced her an older couple owned it. When the tires went flat, they must have caught a ride to the nearest town. As predictable as seniors were, it surprised her they had left it unlocked. Too bad they didn't leave the keys – she would drive it on all flats. She stopped.

Sloshing back to the car, she searched under each wheelwell until finding the small black magnetic key case every other senior in the country used to hide their spare. She slid it open and held her breath as she inserted the key. The motor turned over. *Thank you!* The front tires spun to gain traction before pulling the vehicle out of the weeds.

As the car bumped down the highway, she turned on the radio, searching in vain for a local station. She'd heard no outside communication in two months. Barely past the first turn-off, the bumping changed to a grinding that forced her to pull off the road.

She moaned and lay her head on the steering wheel but jerked back up at the sound of a vehicle. It was too early for another truck. A pickup appeared in the rearview mirror. Dust whipped behind it as it slowed to a crawl. She stuck her arm out the window to signal it to go around, but it pulled behind the car and stopped. When the doors didn't open, Linda rolled up the window and locked the doors.

The man had warned her about a rowdy group. But, the old blue pickup wasn't carrying a random group. Trying to stay calm, she retrieved her things out of the passenger floorboard. When she sat back up, the skinny man stood at the driver window.

He gazed at the empty seats. "Too bad for your friend," he said. "We watched the scuffle at the gate. Maybe they'll be real nice to her. It took some convincing to get through the gate ourselves, but," he rubbed his thumb and fingers together, "it turns out your hubby was generous enough with the cash."

Swaggering to the back, he waved to the passengers. A woman, followed by the fat private investigator climbed out. He lit up a cigarette and took a long drag before passing it to the others. The woman spoke with exaggerated hand gestures, causing all of them to talk at the same time. A roar of laughter followed a round of whispering.

She cracked open the door.

"No need to run, Linda. We're just here to help you get home."

CHAPTER TWENTY-FOUR

Dawn pulled off the muddy boots and set them by the door. She slid the gate-door shut and opened the small crack to allow light in. The coffee pot still lay where it landed when the table had been overturned. Strewn playing cards covered the floor.

"Thomas, are you here? Are you okay?" The man in the pictures tacked to the wall didn't answer.

Thomas wouldn't mind her company. His heart was pure gold. The two Army commemorative coins that he gave her as payment for finding him the liquor when they first met proved it.

Sweeping the small area with a broken-handled broom, she up-righted the table and set the coffee pot in the middle. After folding the blankets and gathering the trash, she wiped her hands. *There!* If given a second chance, Thomas's home was ready to welcome him back.

He needed more food. That wasn't going to be a problem. The station where she'd stolen supplies from earlier was unattended most of the time. The guards would just have to order additional food to replenish Thomas' *chèques* allotment.

She closed the apartment door and pulled her boots back on. The next thing to be done was to warn Maude to stay away from the boy name Adler.

Hiding behind buildings each time a guard came near, Dawn otherwise ran through the condemned area with ease. She tiptoed onto the porch of the home. Through the window, she watched Kelsey play with the toddlers. Carter and Josiah sat at the work table, their heads bent together as they whispered in each other's ear.

It was past time for studies, but Maude wasn't in the room. *See?* The children needed help with homework. Maude was apparently too busy in the kitchen, sidetracked with meals. The home had to have help, even if she wasn't allowed.

A man spoke on the other side of the door. She jumped off the porch and hid behind the azalea bush at the corner of the house.

Maude stepped outside with the visitor. "I'll be watching. I'll tell her what you said. But, Dawn is stubborn, so I can't promise anything."

"It's the best way. I'll be back soon. If she shows up, try to keep her here. Send Josiah to tell me."

"Oh, I will. You can trust me on that."

The guard looked both ways before heading toward Third Street Gate.

She sighed. Maude sided with the authorities, her only interest to protect the children. As many times as the home had been put in danger because of her, who could blame the woman?

She didn't dare ask to stay there, but Thomas's wasn't an option anymore, either. Surely, Maude told the guard about that place, too.

"You're not going anywhere."

She looked up. Maude still stood on the porch watching the guard walk down the street.

"I know you're there, and I know what you're thinking. As soon as he's gone, get in this house. We need to talk." Maude walked inside and left the door open.

The soldiers would carry Maude off for harboring a criminal and force the children onto a bus to be separated forever. It would be all her fault. Why was it so hard for her to learn that there was a time to tell stories and a time to keep your mouth shut?

Dark dots appeared and danced in the bright sun, interrupting the self-reprimand. Her body ignored all resolve and slumped against the house. The dots grew until everything went black.

Someone spoke. Did they say, "*Curse her?*"

The soldiers couldn't be trusted. *Save the children, Maude — don't let them go to camp.* Something wet covered her face. They were going to suffocate her.

"Shh, don't talk, child."

The world wobbled back into focus. Kelsey squatted beside Maude. Carter peeked over them.

Maude dabbed Dawn's face with a wet cloth. "Bless your heart. What a horrible ordeal you've been through. Let's get you inside."

Josiah appeared from behind. Lifting her up, he bore most of her weight as they climbed the stairs and went inside.

"Want me to do something, Miss Maude?" Carter asked.

"No, thank you. She doesn't need to be disturbed."

Or seen. They helped her into the bedroom.

"Thank you, children," Maude said quietly. "Now, tend to the others until I'm finished here. Serene's meal is already on the table."

Maude undressed Dawn, then washed her legs before pulling the bed's blanket up. "I'll be in the next room. After you rest, we'll talk."

She whimpered. Maude was a beautiful woman to take care of a person who caused so much trouble.

"Don't try to talk. There'll be plenty of time for that. And don't cry. When you wake up, I'll tell you all about my precious Adler sent by God to rescue you. Oh, praise be."

~

Dawn choked up. "I've prayed to God since I was in sixth grade to send me to a mission field. I begged Him every night. I read, studied, and then read some more. Well, guess what, Maude? He sent me here. I can't go home while there's work to do. Don't you see? He let Linda get away, but not me. I'll help you. I promise I will. I'll be very cautious. I'll make sure I never open my mouth again. I've learned. I promise I have. Your business is my business. The children will be my priority. I'll keep them safe."

Light filtered through the stained-glass window protected from vandals by an outside board.

"I can help rebuild churches here. There will be a tremendous need, don't you think? I'll help lay the blocks. I'm stronger than I look."

"Or?" Maude asked.

"Or what?"

"Whatever else that mind of yours can come up with. Child, the best thing you can do is quiet down, so you'll be able to hear what God has to say."

"I want to help, but I don't know what to do. I know I talk too much. I don't know why, but I do."

Maude grinned. "You do talk a lot, child. But I didn't mean it that way. You need to quiet your soul. You're so excited to help, you aren't waiting for direction. Just slow down. You've slept most of the day, but more rest will help put things in perspective."

"You have to admit that it's a little too handy of a coincidence for me to wind up back with you because of a soldier who used to live with you."

"I'll admit you may be right about that."

Adler, who sat quietly across the room, walked over and stood next to Maude. "I owe this woman my life."

She kissed him on the cheek. "You are precious to me, child. I'm glad you came back to check on us."

Adler pulled the woman's hand to his heart and looked at Dawn. "She took me in when everyone else said I was worthless. I'll do whatever I can to help her and keep the children safe. You, too."

"Thank you, Adler," Dawn said. "No one will ever know you let me go. I promise I'll never tell. I'll stay hidden if the authorities come."

"You don't need to worry about that. No one is going to look for you. I took care of the problem, remember?" He checked to see if the children were listening. "But we got bigger problems than that."

"Not *we got*." Maude shook her finger. "I taught you better than that."

"Yes, ma'am. There are bigger problems to deal with."

"Such as?"

"They'll be clearing this section much sooner than later."

"Nonsense."

Dawn nodded. "You need to listen to him."

Maude sat. "I don't want to hear what you have to say, but let's get it over with."

"They're going to turn this part of the city into a staging area for the rebuilding phase. I've not only heard it talked about, but I've also seen the blueprints."

"They'll level this place over my dead body!"

He put his hands on her shoulders. "Please don't let them hear you say that."

~

"Say something." The skinny man shoved the phone against her bruised cheek.

Linda moistened her swollen lip with her tongue. It left a copper taste. "It's me, Lostyn."

"Where are you?"

The room looked like a tavern. A bar ran across the width

239

of one end. Empty shelves with broken mirrored backs lined the wall.

"I don't know."

The scraggly haired man jerked the phone away and covered the speaker. "That was real good," he whispered. "Now, if you know what's best for you, you'll be quiet while I finish these here negotiations."

He pulled a stool from the bar and plopped down on it, facing her. A dirty sock stuck out of the toe of his tennis shoe that bounced on the seat's rail. "I told you she was with me, partner. I hate that I couldn't bring your wife straight to you, but I got this small problem. It's one those minor inconveniences that pop up in business. I'm sure you'll be able to fix it in no time flat. You see, there's someone here who wants – let's call it a transportation fee, and I ain't got no control over that."

He listened for a minute and then shoved the phone at her again. "You tell him we ain't alone." He pointed across the room. "Tell him they mean business."

The P.I. crossed the room and stood over her.

"It's true," she said. The –"

"No, no, no. No details, lady."

"They want a transportation fee." She turned away from the pasty face.

"I told you I ain't lying. I wouldn't do that to you. The way I see it, this here is just a bump in the road. So, let me tell you how this has to go down. You send the money, just like I said. I'll give our friends here their fee. Then I'll take mine and get your fine little lady home."

Lostyn's voice grew louder over the phone.

"Sorry man, but it can't work that way. I gotta tell you. Our other partner here doesn't have my patience. Your woman's been playing dodge with him, you know what I mean? Seems like she's had a whole lot of practice."

What was Lostyn's punishment going to be for making him pay a recovery fee for her? Dodge or dance – they both hurt.

"Great! That's good, real good. We'll be in touch." He hung up and tossed the phone to the other man. "Remember. If it weren't for me, you'd be getting nothing. I found her first. But I'm happy to share and all. The way I see it, we'll work this, split the money, and you can finish any other business you got with Lostyn."

"Shut up, Sammy."

"You said my name in front of her, dude. That ain't right. You don't want me spilling your name, do you? Play by the rules, man." He coughed. "I think you messed up by the way. You should give him a week or something. You know the banks ain't letting the cash flow, yet."

"Three days is enough. We don't want time for people to notice what's going on, do we? That would be a problem for you."

"I ain't wanting no problems." Sammy's hand twitched as he lit up a cigarette. "I gotta see if there's any booze around here," he muttered. He motioned, and the woman who had been standing in the corner slunk out of the room behind him.

The P.I. ran his grubby finger down her chin and neck. "I've been keeping tabs on you for a long time, but you know that, don't you?"

When she didn't answer, he continued, "Before you discovered me, I watched you through every window in the house. I liked what I saw. I like you best in red, but what you've got on suits me too." He leaned closer.

Linda glared at him. At least, with Lostyn, she knew what to expect. She spat in his face and braced.

He responded just like Lostyn would have. The first blow mercifully knocked her out.

Melissa Kirk

CHAPTER TWENTY-FIVE

"Are you sure this will work?" Dawn asked as they approached the rations tent. She glanced back at the pickup Adler had located. The beat up black truck with a rusty fender barely hanging on didn't look like any of the military trucks. "Do you think they'll say something about the vehicle?"

"It's too late to change our mind," Adler said. "We need those boxes." He frowned. "Do you want to get Bruce out of Holding or not?"

"Yes, but we're not even sure he's there."

"He is. Follow my lead and please, please, don't talk." He pulled one clean sock higher to match the other before stepping around the stack of pallets that blocked the path to the tent entrance.

A soldier inventoried supplies as they were unloaded from a delivery truck.

Dawn swooped around Adler and called out, "Excuse me, sir."

"Careful," Adler hissed. "He's strapped, and I'm not."

"Sir!" she repeated.

The soldier threw down his pen. "What?"

"I'm sorry to bother you, but I need a supply box."

"Where's your requisition form?"

"Officer —" She cocked her head to read his name tag. "*Soldat* Lin. I, uh, we work at —"

Adler cut in, "North Gate's last load was short three boxes."

"No supplies without an order." He turned back to his checklist.

"Don't dis me, man. We're just counting hours to clock off, like you."

The soldier puffed out his chest and spread his words out evenly. "North Gate acquisitions will have to make a new order."

Adler strung out his words in response. "Field Commander Dubois doesn't bother with orders."

Soldat Lin rolled his eyes. He barked an order to the female soldier who was emptying the truck. She tossed three boxes to Adler.

"Sign." The soldier held out a clipboard to Dawn.

"Um —"

"I sign all paperwork." Adler scribbled *Will Smith* on the paperwork and motioned for Dawn toward the truck. "You drive."

When they were south of the business district, Adler told her to pull over.

She opened the door to climb out, but he yanked her back in.

"No way, Chatty."

"Quit calling me that!"

"Quit talking so much! You stay here. If I'm not back in ten minutes, drive back to the Home."

"But you don't even know Bruce."

"I'll find him."

"Let me describe him to you, then."

"You already have a dozen times. Sit here and chill." He

hoisted the boxes onto his shoulder and cut across rubble to the soldier guarding the front of the brick building.

Dawn alternated rubbing her hands together and checking the time. Five minutes passed. Then ten. Maybe she could bribe the guard. She checked her hair in the mirror.

Adler ran back across the clearing and jumped in. "Drive!"

"Where's –"

"Go!"

She sped around the first corner.

"Turn left."

"That's not the way."

"Pay attention! Go back toward supplies and take the north road. We can't take a direct route back." He ran his hands over his smooth head. "Whew! That was too close. Bruce took off into the woods. I don't think anyone except for the front guard got a good look at us. I hope his eyesight stinks." He grabbed the door handle. "Drop me off here. I've got to be on duty in less than an hour."

"What do we do now?"

"Get back to the house and stay out of sight." He jumped out and ran, disappearing behind a stack of crushed metal.

Dawn drove to the storage bins where Adler had found the truck and wedged the vehicle back in behind them.

When she arrived back at the home, Maude was in the kitchen.

"Where did you and Adler go?" she asked.

"We took care of some business."

"What kind of business?"

"We picked up supplies."

"And?"

"Maude!" She moaned. "Please don't be upset. Adler knew where Bruce was being detained and had a plan to get him out. It was an excellent idea, too."

Maude crossed her arms. "Where are they?"

"Adler went to work."

"And Bruce?"

Dawn chewed her fingertip. "I'm not sure."

"If you have brought more trouble to this home, young lady, I will —"

"No, ma'am. I didn't. Adler took care of everything. I don't even know what happened. He made me drop him off and told me to come home the long way so no one could follow me, which they didn't because I was careful. I promise."

She stared at the front door. *Where are you, Bruce?*

~

A woman's face faded in and out before Linda's eyes drifted shut, again. Her ears throbbed, muffling the conversation in the room. The pain in her legs pulsated in rhythm with her heartbeat, each vying for the most attention.

"She's waking up."

"I'm sorry," she wept. "Don't hurt me anymore."

"I can't understand you." A male voice floated over her. "What did you say?"

"Please."

The voices floated away as her body begged for more rest.

When she woke up again, the room was darker. An empty chair was positioned at the foot of the bed. Partially closed blinds covered the window. A single streetlight shone through the slats.

Something bit her hand. Her fingers worked over the bump. *An IV?* She gazed up. A solution bag hung on a pole.

The door opened. Light from the hallway flooded the room when the woman in scrubs cleared the doorway. "Good," she said. "You're awake."

Linda licked her dry lips. "Where am I?"

"You're in the hospital."

Back at the field hospital? She was under arrest, then.

"Can you tell me your name?"

"I'm sure you already know. Janice Mitchell."

"I can barely understand you, but I think you said Janice.

Is that correct?"

She gave only a tiny nod, intensely aware that any more than that would shoot pain through her head.

"Janice, you are at the Long Lake Health Center. We've been functioning as a hospital since the earthquake. My name is Betty, and I'll be taking care of you through the night. You suffered a nasty assault, but –" She patted Linda's hand. "You're going to be okay. If you need anything for pain, please let me know. The doctor will be in later to see you." The nurse adjusted the pillow.

"I'm thirsty."

"I can take care of that." Betty raised the bed and held the straw steady as she sipped water from the pink plastic glass.

"Thank you."

"You're welcome, dear. Do you remember what happened?"

The rocking motion of shaking her head created a wave of nausea.

"That's understandable. Our minds like to rest after trauma. It's perfectly acceptable. Your memory will return to you what it wants as it sees fit. I can tell you that a man brought you in. A thin man – nervous. He claimed he found you on the side of the street. We all agreed that he wasn't the person who attacked you. Do you know anyone who fits that description?"

"No."

A doctor came in and stood by Betty.

"Hello, Janice. I'm glad you're awake."

"Randall."

～

Dawn flew off the porch into his arms. Bruce swung her around. When he set her down, she poked him in the chest.

"It's about time you got here. I've been scared to death."

"Can we get out of sight?"

"Absolutely." She grabbed his hand. "I bet you don't

remember anything about the home. I'll introduce you to everyone again."

Inside, Bruce shook Maude's hand. "Your prayers worked, ma'am."

"If I remember right, you weren't too interested in those prayers."

He ran a hand through his matted hair. "I've been humbled a little since then. Please forgive me."

"There isn't anything to apologize for, child. I'm glad you're here and safe. But, I must ask. Were you followed?"

"No, ma'am. I ditched the guy chasing me long before I got to the district."

"Good! Come in. I'll have Carter get you something to drink."

The stocky boy jumped up. "That's my job!"

Maude signaled the children to go out the back door. Ignoring the round of protests, she passed the drink from Carter to Bruce. "We'll leave you two to catch up. There's enough work in the backyard to keep the children busy for quite a while." She held open the door, giving instructions to each child as they went out.

When the door closed, Bruce pulled Dawn to him. "I told God that if I ever got to see you again, I would do this." He kissed her.

Her arms went limp.

He snickered. "Is that okay?"

"Yes. Maybe. I mean, can we do that again?"

He stole a look to make sure the kids were busy in the yard, and kissed her again, lingering until she finally pulled away and giggled.

"What's so funny?"

"I don't know. Well, I do know." Her cheeks warmed. "I couldn't help it. It just popped into my head. I thought of when we used to catch lizards and try to feed them to the fish."

"Well, that's really romantic."

"I know, right? But, I mean, you and me? I never expected us to be standing here like this, even though I've dreamed about it forever, it seems."

"I decided I better start paying attention to what's important."

"I'm glad I'm important to you."

He moved a stray bang behind her ear. His thoughts had also drifted in recent days to the young friend he remembered playing with at the pond. She was too vulnerable to be in this environment.

"I had to get out of that place," he said. "You wouldn't believe the nonstop gut-wrenching groans from the men who lost their family. They talked about digging through their homes only to find their baby's lifeless bodies still in their crib. And wives —" His voice broke.

Etched with concern, Dawn's moistened gaze didn't waver.

He looked away. Barred windows in the room overshadowed the innocent children's paintings that were tacked to the wall. "Life takes on a new meaning when you lose the people you love." He cleared his throat. "While I was in there, an enormous cloud that I wasn't even aware of lifted. My idea of *what* matters changed to *who* matters."

"You've not lost anyone, you know. Just temporarily displaced from some, like me – and your mother." She touched his arm. "She's alive, Bruce."

He dropped his head back and let the relief soak in. "Thank you, God."

"She was working at the hospital. It's a long story, but she found me here.

While Dawn filled him in on what had happened at the home, he soaked in her sparkling, sapphire blue eyes. When she paused, he waggled his eyebrows until her cheeks turned bright pink. "Maude was wrong, you know. I am more than okay."

"Oh? Well, we'll see," she teased back but then turned

serious. "We didn't want to leave, but Maude insisted we go and said you would be okay. I had no choice but to trust her. Your mother made it out of the city. They caught me at the fence line."

She assumed a front stance position. "I remembered the karate lessons you gave me. I kicked the living daylights out of one officer. I bet he's still limping!'

He held his breath. "Did they send you to Holding?"

"No. To a place that they call the camp."

"Crud! I've heard stories. People with no regard for others – packed in like sardines."

She stared at him. "There's nobody there."

"Huh?"

"No. The young kid that helped you today? That's Adler. He let me go free."

"Why in the world are you hanging with him? That's dangerous. You have no idea what is going on."

Her hands flew up. "Like you do? Seriously! I may not know much, but I know that Adler is on our side. You're standing here with me, aren't you?"

Bruce rubbed the back of his neck. They were safe. But, Adler would have to do more to earn his trust. "When did Mom leave? Is Dad picking her up somewhere?" he asked.

"Five days ago. And she never tried to call him that I know of."

He didn't blame her. "I need to let my grandparents know what's going on."

Dawn held up a finger and disappeared. She returned with a phone. "Adler keeps my portable charger juiced up for me."

He fidgeted while waiting for an answer on the other end. "Hello?"

"Granddad, it's me! Mom is okay." He put his arm around her. "Dawn too!"

Granddad sobbed.

"It's all right, Granddad."

"You've been missed, son. May we please talk to your

mother?"

"I'm sorry, but Mom isn't here. I have to catch up with her. I know that doesn't make sense but please don't ask. I'll get her home safe."

"God will direct your steps, Son."

"I've started to notice that. I have to go. Kiss Grandmother for me." Bruce handed her the phone.

"Don't you want to call your dad?" Dawn asked.

"Maybe later." He squeezed her hand. "Let's leave as soon as we can. I have to get to Mom."

Dawn lowered her eyes.

He tilted her chin up. "Hey. What's wrong?"

"I can't go."

"What do you mean?"

"Maude is refusing to leave until God tells her to." She spread her arms out. "Until then, this is my mission field. My *India*."

"How can I leave, then?"

"I can't go, Bruce."

He wrapped his arms tightly around her, praying this was just a trick. But he knew the truth.

"I can't stay."

CHAPTER TWENTY-SIX

The patients sat in a semi-circle laughing at the ruddy-faced man attempting to tell a joke. Linda balanced with the cane as she crossed the large, open room to sit in the corner seating area. A bent-over man in a red and gray checked robe walked over.

She waved him off. "That seat is taken."

He joined the group, instead. He mumbled something, and they all turned to stare.

With deliberate defiance, she ignored their murmuring and went back to her room. If meds weren't so sparse, she would ask for a pain pill. Instead, she gingerly pulled one leg at a time onto the bed.

Randall passed by the door and backtracked. "I thought you went to the group room."

She lay back.

He pulled the chair over and sat. "Do you want to talk about it?"

"There's nothing to say."

"Have you recalled something?"

"I haven't, but it doesn't matter."

"It *does* matter. I'm going to find the heathens that did this to you."

"I doubt it. It has been a week."

She could tell her words irritated him but he moved on.

"For now, we'll concentrate on getting you well. You're doing much better. Your legs are stronger, especially the left one."

He stewed over the chart. "The last x-rays show your ribs are healing nicely, too. It looks like you've suffered some earlier events."

"I fell when the earthquake hit. I told you that."

Randall tapped his pen while reviewing the information. "That's what you said." He stuck the pen in his pocket. "Physical therapy again in the morning. Staples out in three days."

She pulled the cotton blanket to her neck. "Is this where you've been since you left me?" That didn't sound as she intended.

"I caught a ride to Tupelo. The police at the station weren't interested in hearing what I had to say. The roads to Birmingham were blocked, so I turned back."

Linda concentrated on her feet, wiggling her toes, and rotating her ankles. Pain radiated into her hips. *Take the beating and move on.*

"It's rough out there, as you, unfortunately, discovered. It's not even safe for a man to hitchhike. I traveled mostly on foot. It's a sad day when you can't trust anyone with a vehicle."

A picture of a blue pickup flashed in her mind. She twitched.

"Is something wrong?"

"No."

"I stopped here to give myself time to catch my breath and replenish supplies. I was coming back for you."

"When can I leave?"

"I'm gathering supplies. When you're able, we will travel."

"You didn't answer my question, Doctor."

A scowl crossed his face. "As your *doctor*, I would say in a few days. However, I'm not just your doctor. I'm telling you that we aren't going anywhere until I decide it's safe, Janice. You are under my care again."

She was sick and tired of being a mishandled care package. "I'll be ready in two days, Doctor."

~

Adler and Bruce had been in deep conversation for three hours.

Dawn couldn't take anymore. "Can I talk now? I know what I'm talking about."

Mischief danced in Bruce's eyes. "Like when Adler took you to camp?"

"Not fair, Bruce John Hugh Bonin!" She narrowed her eyes at Adler. "My whole life flashed before me."

Adler's gaze dropped. "I'm sorry, Dawn. I was just trying to keep you safe and not get caught doing it. I didn't know you thought I was going to – well, you know."

"I admit I was delusional. But, it's crazy around here. It feels like a whole different world. Stuff like that play tricks with your mind. I imagined you a lot less kind and smart than you really are. I owe you an apology."

They exchanged peace signs.

"So, can I talk now?"

The men leaned back in their chairs.

"I can at least tell you which way Linda and I were planning to go."

"You already did," they answered in unison.

"Well, did I tell you which way I told her to turn at the crossroad?"

"Yeah, you did." Bruce smiled.

She moseyed to the table and glanced at their notes. "You've been planning your route north and considering places along the way where she might have stopped. Right?"

"That's right," Bruce said.

Adler latched his hands behind his head. "She probably found help around Millington and made it to Dyersburg. She should be along Interstate 155 waiting to be transported across the river. I've filled Bruce in on all the truck routes I know of that are open that way."

"Our pal here even slipped a transport map out for me." Bruce pulled it out of his pocket and spread it on the table.

Dawn put her hands on her hips. "That's all fine and good, but I'm afraid you've wasted your time."

Bruce's eyes glazed over. "Here we go."

"If you had let me join in, I could have saved you a lot of worthless work."

"Good grief. If you have something important to add, please do so," he said. "Otherwise, we need to get to work again."

"You're going the wrong direction."

He smirked. "Why would you think that?"

"I *know* that because I know that your mother didn't want to go home. You would have known too if you had let me talk. But, oh well. I realized that long before we left. She went south. So, there. I guess you two can work another three hours planning your new route."

Bruce scratched his temple. "Are you sure?"

"Don't ask me why, but your mother wasn't going home."

He turned to Adler. "What do you know about the southern routes?"

Adler plopped the chair back on all four legs. "That's tougher. Few trucks are going that way. Highway 61 is a mess."

"Mom would have taken the shortest route."

"The bad news then is she probably hasn't had much help. The good news is you should be able to catch up with her pretty quick. The best news is that your route out of here is pretty straightforward." Adler drew lines on the map and slid it to him. "I've got to go. Everything on my end is the same. I'll be ready for you at 2100 hours."

Dawn's stomach knotted. "You're leaving tonight?"

"I have to if I expect to catch up with her." Bruce shook Adler's hand. "Thanks for everything, man."

"It's all cool. Stay safe." Adler slipped out the back door.

Bruce rolled the map and tapped the corner of the table with it. "Why do you think Mom doesn't want to go home?"

"I just know it deep down. I'm sure Maude would tell you the same thing."

"I'm going with your instincts. Let's hope you're right." He scooted his chair back. "I better get some supplies together."

"I'm not ready for you to leave." She slipped onto his lap. "The minute you got here, my mind rested. I was just one step from crazy thinking that I might never see you again."

His gaze outlined her face and stopped at her quivering lips. He leaned until his lips brushed hers. "This thing with us – it's real, right?"

"Yes."

"I don't want to leave you here. Not even long enough for me to get Mom to safety. I don't like us being apart."

"Let's pretend we aren't. Why don't we say we're going to work – to fine-tune our responsibilities?"

"I like fine-tuning." His lips touched hers again.

Her head swam as the touch pressed to a deep kiss. It spoke everything she needed to know. His heart belonged to her. He would never have to guess her feelings for him. That was a promise.

She sniffled. "I don't know what to say."

He leaned back and winked. "That's a first."

She raised her hand, but he stopped it in midair and held it to his mouth. His gaze cut across the room.

Carter was propped up against the wall. "Sure looks like he's your boyfriend to me."

~

Linda shut the beveled-glass door and slid her weary body into the mahogany bench closest to the back wall. She stretched her left leg under the pew and lifted the corner of the gauze wrap. The superficial wound covering the knee was healing. But, the jagged gash on the calf was still inflamed around the staples. She timidly scratched around it. Experience told her that her leg wasn't ready for a lot of walking, but Randall's paranoia of a government takeover was escalating, as was his obsession with her.

During the morning rounds, he demanded that she stay until he dismissed her to leave with him. She wanted to say emphatically no but didn't. Her body couldn't handle any more trauma of any kind.

He wasn't due back until the next evening, but she had informed Betty she wanted the staples removed first thing in the morning. The nurse examined the leg and protested, but Linda threatened to do it herself, so Betty relented and agreed to reconsider on her next rounds.

The softly lit square room contrasted the rest of the bright hospital. A crucifix hung on the front wall between the only two windows. Arms stretched outward on the cross. The head was fallen to one side, the body totally spent. The person's crime? Claim as King. His passion? Hurting, broken people. She grunted. That didn't appear to be the case.

White candles in glass holders sat on the lace covered wooden table centered below the crucifix. The Virgin Mary statue on one back corner of the table balanced the vase of silk Chrysanthemums on the other.

The noise of a rolling cart and gossiping nurses in the hall diminished, making the music in the room too loud, but she didn't see the source to turn down the volume.

Most patients rested this time of day, and the staff took the opportunity to savor a cup of coffee. She'd purposefully picked the slow time. God was going to hear her complaint without interruption.

Her leg couldn't handle the stress required to kneel on the

bench in front of the table, so she limped to its edge and stood with both hands glued to her sides. It was good enough. God knew her thoughts weren't that reverent.

Nailed to the wall beneath the body of Jesus, an inscribed golden plaque read: *"He who knows how to forgive prepares for himself many graces from God. As often as I look upon the cross, so often will I forgive with all my heart"* - *St. Faustina.*

Forgiveness was Lostyn gifting flowers after bringing the smallest infractions to his wife's attention – *with all his heart.*

Nothing came out when she tried to speak. She glared at the crucifix. Her point would get across even if the words resonated only in her heart.

When was the last straw – the moment God turned his back on her? There were a lot of evil, vicious people in the world. Humans who acted like monsters. She was not a monster.

It didn't surprise her that God didn't respond.

The chill in the room caused goose bumps to pop out on her arms. Her leg tired, so she returned to the pew and rubbed her thigh. At least, the stabbing pain meant life still coursed through her veins even though *Tüdampa* had almost convinced her that there was an easier way. The coyote thought she was a failure. But, he had failed to recognize that she never chose the easy route.

The door squeaked open. The chaplain walked in, wearing Diesel jeans with a black short sleeve shirt and white clerical collar. He paused by the entrance to turn down the music volume at the intercom.

"You're Janice if I remember correctly." The priest stood waiting to see if she offered to shake his hand. She didn't, so he continued. "I'm Greg Patters, pastor of St. Bartholomew Catholic Church and the chaplain here at Long Lake Health."

"I know."

"I've watched you improve every day. Prayers are being answered."

Not hers.

After taking the handful of cards out of the prayer box, he

sat near her. "These are difficult times." His mouth turned down. "Yesterday, I lost a dear friend due to injuries he sustained during a rescue effort. I was the only one able to grieve for him. His family is still buried under their home. The bulldozers haven't made it to their street yet."

She chewed her lip.

"There's not a day that goes by that I don't want to question God." He arched his eyebrows. "Doesn't seem to fit the occupation, does it?"

"It's been bad."

"What is man, that God is mindful of him?"

"Quotes about God taking care of humankind seems out of place right now."

"You know scripture."

"Some."

"It does seem odd that my mind would be consumed with that verse, but I haven't been able to shake it." He leaned his head against the wall. "King David said, *When I look at the night sky and see the work of your fingers – the moon and the stars you set in place – what are mere mortals that you should think about them, human beings that you should care for them?*"

He turned his attention to the cards, silently reading each one before stuffing them into his shirt pocket. "There is heartache everywhere. Yet, God hasn't lost sight of us."

"There's a whole lot of decaying bodies that would beg to argue if they could. He wasn't exactly mindful of them."

"I'll be honest with you. It's been hard for me to absorb that. All I know is that he is still mindful of me. It's humbling."

"I'm sure he's aware of you. You're a priest."

"A title that reminds me daily how much I fall short." He grunted. "If I were to write what's bad about me on a piece of paper, it would fill up fast. But God is merciful. If I made a list of the good I've done," he shook his head, "it would be pathetically short. But he shows me grace."

Thomas had battled with the preacher. *Mercy! Grace! Mercy!*

Grace!

"Like two sides of a coin?"

His eyes and mouth turned up in unison, friendly creases appearing to outline his cheeks. "I heard it explained that way one time by a fellow who pastored a church in my neighborhood. We had many conversations on Saturday mornings over pancakes and coffee. He often commented that mercy and grace were different, but both equally part of Father God's debt-payment plan."

She twisted a non-existent ring on her finger. She hadn't worn her wedding ring for so long, the skin tone under where it had been was now tanned evenly with the rest of her hand. "My good page would be non-existent."

"You have the opportunity, then, to be thankful because there's an endless supply of grace." He changed seats to face her. "May I share something?" He smiled again. "Something that was a game-changer for me."

He waited until she nodded.

"A while back, I helped a man bury his family. We dressed all five of them in their favorite clothes that we dug from the rubble they once called their home. Then we laid them to rest in the backyard under the shade tree. You know what? We didn't care about the safety environment announcements. The United States with all its resources, with all the foreign aid coming to help – none of it mattered. We couldn't fix it."

She didn't dare look up because of the mournful tone of his voice.

"I got angry. What use was this collar if I couldn't provide relief? I didn't sleep for weeks. I found myself counting how many days it had been since my world collapsed. Forty days. Forty days that the church hadn't been able to hold the flood of people attending the Holy Mass."

He put his elbows on his knees and clasped his hands together. "It took that many times drawing near to the mystery of Christ before it finally struck me. Since the earthquake, the sun had never failed to rise, and the stars still hung in place. That evening, as the sun set, surrounded by brilliant red and purple hues streaking toward the heavens, I fell to my knees."

She stole a glance at him.

He stared in earnest to a space occupied only by his mind. "King David spoke the truth. This isn't *my* world. I didn't create the earthquake, didn't allow it, and I have no power to fix the aftermath. It's been twenty-eight more days, and I'm still powerless. My only choice is to accept God's sovereignty – his full authority. He created the big plan and knows the details from beginning to end."

He raised his hands palms up. "What do I know? I remember things from *my* past – I didn't know anything about *yours* before you arrived here. I have no idea what decisions I will be asked to make this evening, tomorrow or the next. I don't know if I will live to be one hundred or die before the week ends. I don't know what will come next for anyone.

"But I know the one who does. When I see the works of his hand, I know he is close by. When I think that something or someone needs to be fixed, often just to make my life more comfortable, I know God's grace can sustain me while he works – if I let it, that is. The day I stepped across the line where mercy and grace met me, my burdens were taken by the God who created this world. He set me free. Why should I hold myself in bondage?"

The priest paused for a long while. "He never promised we wouldn't suffer, but he did promise we could run to him. He even promised to work everything together for the good of those who love him. The way I see it, we have two choices. Turn to him or turn bitter."

He stood. "I'm going to visit a gentleman down the hall. If you want to talk later, I'll be around." The door snapped shut behind him, locking out the rest of the world.

Linda limped back to the front and examined the statue of the Virgin Mother, dressed in white and blue garments. Did the young mother pray for mercy from the doubters and gossipers? They were probably no different than her neighbors. What went on behind closed doors wasn't anyone's business, but rumors always landed on willing ears. How had the mother of Jesus handled the unfairness of life?

A bare gold cross lay on the table. She picked it up and held it next to the crucifix nailed to the wall. A battered body hung on one. Mercy. The other was empty. Grace. Father Patters had said the pastor called it the debt-payment plan. Thomas would have said the same thing if she had acknowledged her monsters with him.

She owed a tremendous amount of debt for all her wrongs. There weren't enough hours in a lifetime to right them all. With her track record, she would fail miserably anyway. Was there enough mercy for a mother who selfishly sent her son away? Would God extend grace to a prideful woman? Did the one who guided the sun and moon really care about people who lost their way?

She wanted mercy. Desired grace. She needed them because she didn't want to be bitter.

Bracing with the table, Linda carefully knelt on her better knee. Already, she had been in conversation with God, and he was gracious enough to look beyond the irreverent outside to see her hurt inside.

As she lit a candle, the Spirit of *Amigota* flowed into the crevices of brokenness, flooding her whole being with the promise of hope and healing.

She visualized her mother kneeling by the rock at the end of the pathway, and wished she had a prayer shawl.

"*Koiyah*," she whispered. "Can you hear me, Mom? You're much better at this than I am. Pray with me. *Duwaniitehai*. I want to be free."

Melissa Kirk

Chapter twenty-seven

Betty pushed aside the bedside service table. "Are you sure you don't want to wait? Doctor Gipson is going to be upset. He seems quite attached to you."

Linda stepped into her pants. "I'm ready. Thanks for the excellent care. Your patients are spoiled."

Betty grinned. "Yours were too, I bet."

"I guess the doctor told you I was a nurse."

"Would have known it anyway. You know the drills, front, and back. Here, don't forget the cane."

"Keep it. I'm out of here. Take care." She stuck her head out the door. A CNA, arms loaded with fresh linen, walked into a room down the hall, leaving a clear path to the front doors.

"I'm going to hear about it later you know," Betty called out.

Linda waved over her shoulder but didn't stop until the door closed behind her. She paused in the crisp morning air long enough to slip on the thin sweater claimed from the pile of clothes donated to the facility.

The fog resting over the river was clearer than it had been just over a week ago. The sudden memory scared her. She picked up her pace, setting a goal to reach the bridge ahead before stopping to rest.

A cattle guard lay across the damaged bridge to support crossing traffic. Below, creek water riffled over the cobblestones and green vegetation that lined the bottom. Overgrown ragweed spotted the bank. It was a much different view than the black abyss she had almost succumbed to after escaping the city limits.

She surveyed the open field. There was no evidence of *Tüdampa*. She wasn't going to feed him anymore so there was no reason to fear him. But, the uneasiness she experienced from being unable to remember anything after encountering the coyote still settled over her like the fog blanketing the river.

A vehicle appeared, heading for the narrow crossover. The sudden recollection of a blue pickup stripped away any remaining calm, and she quickly hobbled to clear the bridge.

A horn blared out. Linda pushed forward until leg pains forced her to hop off the road. Brakes squealed the vehicle to a stop. Its horn honked a prolonged blast followed by several short ones.

Bruce jumped out. "Mom!"

She turned around. The healthy, tanned frame ran to the bridge and picked her up. His bear hug rivaled her father's. She buried the spasms it caused under the sheer glee of his presence.

Without effort, he carried her to the car. "I've been driving up and down this road for days trying to find you. What happened?"

"I'm fine. Really."

His worry lines only slightly softened.

"I'm glad you're okay, Son."

He shut the door and climbed behind the steering wheel. "Dawn told me you would be traveling south."

"She's okay, too?" Linda couldn't hold back the flood of tears.

Bruce dug through the pile on the floorboard until he found a paper napkin, which he refolded to pat her cheeks dry.

"Can you ever forgive me, Son? I wanted you back home the same day you left for the ranch. I missed you so much. I just couldn't, I mean, I didn't know how –"

"Listen, Mom. We need to talk. Dawn said that you didn't want to go home. Maybe you shouldn't. I know Dad can be – no, you know what? We don't even have to talk about it." He squeezed her shoulder. "I'll take you anywhere you want to go. He doesn't have to know I found you."

"I've had time to think, too. I have to go home, Son."

"No, I won't let you do that. Whatever's going on, we'll work through it together."

"Take me home."

"Look, you don't have to play brave around me. I'm not a kid anymore."

"No, you're not. And I'm not the same person either. I am not running anymore."

He started the car. "I'm taking you to the ranch. You can stop being afraid there."

"Stop! You do not know what I need, and you will not dictate my future."

~

Linda's hands shook.

Lostyn walked along the sidewalk, inspecting the flower beds that were overrun with weeds.

The wrought iron porch light automatically flickered on with the arrival of dusk.

Bruce took a deep breath and exhaled slowly. "You don't have to do this, Mom."

"Yes, I do."

"Stay in the car." He stepped out and shut the door too hard.

267

Lostyn raised his jaw. Bruce squared his shoulders. Neither spoke while staring each other down.

She wanted healing – for all of them. Perhaps it was too late.

Bruce finally opened the passenger door. Taking her arm, they walked to the sidewalk, he keeping his body slightly ahead to shelter her.

Lostyn's right hand flexed in and out of a fist. "It took you a while to find your mother. I assume the delay was necessary."

"Yes, sir."

Her husband stepped toward her.

"Now, Dad."

"It's all right, Son. Your father just wants to know where I've been."

Lostyn's gaze bore into her. "Why did it take you so long to come home?"

"Good grief," Bruce said. "It's not exactly a joy ride to get around Memphis these days."

She shook her head in reproach.

"I needed time to heal, Lostyn."

"What happened to you?"

"I'm not sure. Someone found me unconscious and took me to the hospital."

Bruce did a double take. "You didn't tell me that!"

"You don't know what happened to you?" Lostyn demanded.

"No."

She braced and promised herself she would not cower down this time.

His demeanor suddenly changed. "I'm sorry, dear. I'm glad you're home." He put his arm around her and directed all of them into the house. He sat across from her in the living room.

His facial expression betrayed his stiff back to reveal the emotional roller coaster he was on. He was coasting now, but experience had taught her that the steep climb just ahead always led to a furious downward spiral.

"I'm recovering," she said. "The doctor told me that I might never remember what happened. Which is okay. Too much has gone on this summer for me to absorb anyway." She sat straighter. "Son, would you excuse us?"

"I'm staying right here."

"Please. I need to speak to your father alone."

He locked an icy stare on Lostyn. "I'll be in the next room if you need me, Mom."

She waited until she heard the guestroom door shut. "I have to start by telling you that I could have come home right after the earthquake. I'm sorry I didn't send word with Dawn that I was okay."

Lostyn stroked his mustache.

"I thought I was running away, but I learned it was only a break. I had to have time to sort through my thoughts – my life. I've been ignoring the truth, pretending that the problems we have are all because of me." Her hands trembled. "I'm sorry for the times I didn't do my best and ask for your forgiveness."

He pressed his lips together.

The room was filthy. The television was on the floor, propped against the bookshelf. Empty drink bottles and food wrappers covered the table by the chair. The floor hadn't been mopped, probably the entire time she had been gone. She understood what Father Patters meant. Being able to stay in control of everything was a myth.

"I'm glad you took the time to think things over, Linda. I can help you –"

"You can't fix me."

He stretched his neck muscles. "You've suffered a severe trauma of some kind. But, we'll work through it, as I see fit. You need me. You know that."

In the chapel, the plaque under the crucifix had read, *"He who knows how to forgive prepares for himself many graces from God . . ."* A strength she'd never experienced was born. She sat taller. "I've been living a lie. I can't be perfect. Not even for you."

Fear threatened to shut her down, but the growing courage inside her demolished it. "I came to say that I forgive you."

He snapped back as if she'd slapped him. "I didn't know you were brave enough to talk to me like this."

When she didn't offer an excuse, he stood and walked to the wide picture window. His muscular frame swallowed the light, casting a larger than life shadow onto the floor. Beside him was a chair from the kitchen that had been placed to face outside.

"I thought running away would free me. It was the wrong decision. Running away never freed anyone. I gained nothing by ignoring the obvious. The truth is that you abused me, and I allowed you. I believed my actions dictated yours. It was all a lie. Those beliefs kept me in bondage."

"You ran out on me."

While he stared out the window, she recalled when they were young and adventurous. Lostyn's personality had been overly abrasive. It excited her back then, her naivety mistaking it for boldness – not abusive behavior.

He nodded toward the backyard. "Unlike my wife, my friend has been here every night."

She didn't have to look. It was *Tüdampa*. She could tell by his demeanor that he was still feeding him.

"He understands me. And I can always depend on him to point out my enemies." Lostyn scooted the chair back.

"I'm not the enemy. Thirty years ago, we stood side by side in Soquili Temple Church. We committed to love each other forever. I'm not going to break that commitment. But, our problems are too big for us to handle alone."

"I can only imagine what my father would have said if he knew I had been sleeping with the enemy. He taught me to be on guard, and I almost blew it."

Linda saw the shotgun as Lostyn reached for it.

"Don't." Bruce came around the corner. His raised arm pointed a handgun at his father.

Lostyn froze.

"You haven't blown anything, yet, Dad. So, just don't."

Bruce cocked the gun.

"Take it easy, Son."

Bruce motioned Linda back.

"You surprise me, boy. Didn't know you'd grown a backbone. That's good, though." Lostyn moved slowly away from the shotgun. "Be careful, now. We don't want any accidents."

He dove for Bruce's legs.

The force threw Bruce's body over Lostyn, tumbling them to the ground. Bruce kicked the shotgun across the wood floor. Lostyn flipped to his back. They rolled until their bodies collided with the fireplace. Matched in strength, the men wrestled for control of the pistol. The muzzle aimed downward.

"Stop!" Linda screamed.

The gun went off.

~

"911. What is your emergency?"

Linda gave the address and hung up Lostyn's phone.

Her husband lay face down, arms and legs spread out amongst the shattered picture window glass. His face was turned away from them.

Bruce stood with the pistol aimed at his father. He rubbed the sweat dripping from his chin with his shoulder.

"Listen," Lostyn said. "Let's just calm down and –"

"Stop talking!" Bruce barked. His arm shook, tired from the wrestling match. He adjusted his stance.

She stood at the back door. The coyote was gone. Hints of a coming sunset were all that remained of the day as the sun settled behind the tall fence.

The Chaplin had been right. A person didn't have the power to fix anything or anyone – not even themselves. She had chosen to love her husband, but the bondage he kept her in

271

distorted the true meaning of love.

"Not enough men have gone to jail for treating women like you did me. Your actions aren't excusable." She stepped closer, but Bruce waved her back.

"Everything is confusing right now, Lostyn. I'm going to have to let grace take over. To be honest, I don't even know what that looks like. I just know that I'm not running anymore, but I am going somewhere safe. I know that's what I'm supposed to do."

"You are not leaving me."

"Don't move, Dad."

"I'm going with God's help," she said. "My perspective has to clear up."

Lostyn's left heel bounced as he fought to stay still.

The gravity of the evening pressed the final truth into her. "I need help. You do, too."

She didn't feel the Spirit of *Amigota* for the man she'd just recommitted to love moments ago. She just felt tired.

"God cherishes love and commitment. I know that," she said. "I don't know the future. I just know that today, this ends."

He swore. "You are making a mistake."

Blue lights flashed into the darkening room.

"Knowing the truth is never a mistake."

CHAPTER TWENTY-EIGHT

"Hey, it's a new day so don't sleep it away," Bruce whispered.

Dawn giggled. "Where are you?"

"Almost to the Rocky Mountains. Mom has been making me stop every other hour. She says it's nice to use facilities that work well." He laughed. "Hey, do you remember when you visited the ranch, and we drove to the school? There's a ten-acre plot of land for sale near there. The owners are crazy to sell it! The Mustangs graze in the pasture every morning. If it's still there, I'm going to buy it. What do you think? I – we could, um . . ."

"Yes."

"That's it? One word? Are you sick or something?"

"Bruce John Hugh Bonin! I set a goal to listen more and not talk too much. I want to last an entire day. Don't mess me up, because if –"

"Shh."

"Okay."

He turned serious. "What did Adler find out?"

"We have to hurry! The contractors are almost to our street. Adler was blunt when he explained to Maude that she wouldn't be able to stop them from taking over the home. She threw a fit! But, we told her your plan, and she finally broke and agreed to leave. We've started packing."

"Whew!" Bruce ran his hands through his hair. "Good. I'm ready for you to get out of there. Tell Adler to call me when he finds a service truck big enough to transport everyone. Don't over pack. We need the children to be able to move quickly to the pickup point. Which, by the way, has changed. Commander Obright gave orders to move the North team seven miles farther up the road."

"That's impossible! We would have to travel through the worker's camp to get there. There's no way to do that without being caught."

"It'll work. Trucks go through there all the time."

"Yeah, through a checkpoint!"

"Adler won't go through the gates. Just make sure he finds a truck that won't be conspicuous. A utility vehicle, or better yet, one that he can paint *HAZMAT* on the side. No one messes with them. I need you to trust me. I'll keep you safe."

"Where are the children going to stay?"

He scratched his chin.

"You still there? You found a place, right?"

"Yes. Well, that's not exactly true. But I will."

"You can't expect –"

"Watch out. Don't mess up your word count for the day."

It was quiet on the other end.

"Ah, come on, Blue. I won't let you down."

She sniffed. "So, how many Mustangs are there in the herd?"

He smiled. "Twenty-four. They're beautiful. But, I've got my eye on a blond, blue-eyed filly."

"Wow, I can't wait to see her."

"Seriously?" He snickered. "You don't have to wait. Just

look in the mirror! Gotta go." He hung up.

Once outside the city limits, getting the children to a shelter wasn't going to be hard. Evacuees on the west side had moved far enough away from the city to ease safety concerns. But, sneaking a truckload of kids through the worker's camp was a challenge he'd just as soon pass on.

~

Bruce exited off the expressway. "Less than an hour until we're there." He winked. "That didn't take long, did it?"

"Not at all. And what a pleasure to ride for a week in the car with your stinky feet." Linda plugged her nose.

He laughed. "Hey, now."

She stretched her leg that they jokingly dubbed *There Yet* because every few hours it complained like a child anxious to reach their destination. The drive had taken twice as long as usual. Traffic routed around the disaster area merged onto backed-up interstates. Construction barrels lined the highways, easing motorists into single lanes to travel one direction, then reversing where Interstates crossed. They had counted fourteen different flags from other nations that bordered selected portions of the highway with a banner that read: *"Helping - For the Common Good."*

"What did Dawn have to say when she called back?"

"Adler found a black passenger van that would hold of all them. They tore out the seats and covered the windows to make it look like a hearse. It's safe enough."

The worried look creasing his forehead spoke anything other than safe.

He continued, "Chris is delaying the helicopter at Springfield, Missouri until Thursday. I have to find two hops to get there – first stop Denver."

Her son had been like a healing balm. Since leaving Ozark Ridge, he hadn't once brought up the horror that unfolded at home. Instead, he had shouldered all the responsibilities, filing a report with the police, and obtaining a restraining order. Then, he'd contacted the utility companies, winterized the house, and forwarded the mail.

They had talked about the ranch and the balloons. About the Mavericks and his work. And about Dawn. She hid a smile. The tone of his voice when he spoke of her was the same as when he was a child experiencing a new adventure with unadulterated passion.

Now, his hands clutched the steering wheel tight, his thoughts wrapped up in his next mission.

"Look at the Sierra," she said to distract him. "I've missed the view."

"Dad doesn't know where I live. Why don't I take you there instead of the ranch? I'll work out the details with the apartment management."

"I'm not a detail." Linda bit her tongue. "I'm sorry. I know you're trying to keep me safe. It's just that, the entire time I was on the run, I knew I would see your father again."

He grunted. "Trust me, it wasn't necessary."

"Yes, it was. To be free, I had to stand up to him." She wondered if the pain that once again shot through her side at the thought of facing Lostyn would ever stop. "I was crazy to think I could have faced him without help. That was foolish. You saved my life, Son. I promise never to put you at risk like that, again."

"I would have never forgiven myself if Dad had hurt you. The courts wouldn't have excused my actions." He shook his head. "I about choked with that whole love and commitment spiel you gave."

"I meant what I said. Your father and I have been living together with a warped definition of love. We will never be able to learn the real meaning without being apart."

"Can I suggest something?"

"As long as it doesn't require me to go into hiding."

He smacked the steering wheel. "You know he'll come looking for you."

"I'm not running anymore." Her spirit lifted her resolve. "But, I'm not going to try to go it alone, either."

Bruce adjusted his cap.

"Son, the truth is that God sees a person's needs. Even the ones they don't realize they have. I have faith he will direct my next steps. I'm going to trust him with your father's, too."

He turned toward Soquili.

She didn't know what to do or where to go, yet. But, how many times had Mom shown her how to trust God? It was time she did.

She glanced at Bruce, whose focus seemed already buried again under the burden of getting Dawn and the residents of Assurance Home out of Memphis. Hopefully, her child would learn much faster than her to place his confidence in the Creator.

"My *nahuto*, what makes you worry? The Creator of *Amigota* sees beyond what is not learned to what can be achieved by the Spirit."

He cut his eyes toward her. "Sorry, Mom. I didn't understand you."

It was true, but there was no failure in that. He had the right spirit in him and would learn much faster than her. She spread her sweater over her arms. "I will always pray for you, Son."

CHAPTER TWENTY-NINE

Bruce parked the small bus and jogged a quarter-mile to the roadblock. On the other side, in the open field, a new, bare-bones treatment plant pumped water from the river.

The area would succumb to darkness in an hour. He punched in Dawn's phone number. The call went straight to voicemail, again. *Come on!*

He propped one foot against a Box Elder that stood out from the tree line. Behind him, leaves rustled as some small critter scooted farther into the woods.

Grandmother's prediction of *Gehetmo* came true. But it wasn't as he had pictured. The battle line had been drawn between self-reliance and trust. The mark was somewhat skewed. Looking for his mother had uncovered the dangers of his misguided independence while catapulting him straight into Dawn's arms.

Thoughts of Dawn had overtaken his mind to the point he understood his mom's insistence that you can't be with someone for a long time and not have deep-rooted feelings.

They had known each other for nearly twenty years. They

experienced childhood together. They both suffered loss. For every time they fought like cats and dogs, they had made up with a pinkie finger promise to stick together.

He broke off the small dead branch above him and flicked off the ants. It was already October. The hike in the Sierra Mountains never happened. There, the leaves would be changing color, and now, rain would interrupt most walks.

The top of a black van crested the sand hill. *TRUST TRANSPORT* was painted in white on the side. The lettering with a swirl under the first letter was Dawn's trademark.

The bubble lights of a police car topped the same hill and followed the vehicle as it crossed the open field.

Bruce stepped back into the shadows. As the van drove by, the driver's window lowered, and Adler shook his head. The window went back up, and the vehicle kept going.

He jumped the A-frame barrier and ran toward the police car, aware that Adler made a right turn and disappeared behind the water treatment plant. He whistled. The cruiser drove to him and stopped.

"Do you know if there are any auto shops open in the area? I've got engine problems." He thumbed behind him. "I'm parked down the road."

"The closest one open to the public is twenty miles north on Highway 61."

"I was afraid of that. Going to be a long walk."

"I suggest you stay with your vehicle and leave in the morning. It can be dangerous around here at night. You may be able to catch a ride at the Brook Road exit. Just be careful whom you climb into a vehicle with. There are still a few nuts around."

"Thanks for your help, officer." Bruce hopped back over the roadblock. The police car turned a half circle and slowed, before leaving the direction it came.

When the cruiser was out of sight, the van sped across the field and jerked to a stop. Adler jumped out and shook Bruce's hand. "Fast thinking! So, let's do this. I don't know what time the guards make their rounds at the plant." No sooner were the words out of his mouth than a patrol jeep appeared. He cursed.

The vehicle pulled up, and a guard climbed out. "What's going on here?" The driver directed the question at Adler while scrutinizing Bruce.

Bruce nodded a greeting. "Got car trouble. I'm looking for the nearest repair shop."

"Why are you driving a hearse, Adler?"

Adler pulled at his collar. "I'm just making a few bucks on the side. North East Arkansas called for more bodies. It's not interfering with my job or anything."

"Be sure it doesn't. The dead aren't our concern."

"Yes, sir."

The guard's stare demanded Bruce's attention. "Where are you parked?"

"At the cutoff. I guess I need to get back."

"You do that. And take a word of warning with you. Do not cross the roadblock anymore. Not every guard is as nice as I am." He climbed back into the Jeep and crossed the field, swerving to miss a sand pit.

Adler peeled off the too-tight suit jacket. "I don't know what McKellar is doing out here, but the boss just found a new reason to hound me."

The passenger side door slid open, and Dawn climbed out. "I could have gone the rest of my life without seeing that man again. I can't imagine what would have happened if he had seen the *dead* bodies."

Bruce barely heard, his thoughts on wanting to grab and kiss her. Instead, he offered Maude a hand to step down. The children followed one at a time and put their packs on their backs. Josiah and Bruce traded fist bumps.

"Me too!" Carter held up his hand.

Bruce bumped it and ruffled his hair.

"Come, children," Maude ordered. She handed Serene to Dawn and directed Kelsey to take Abay's hand. The rest of the kids lined up.

"There's a bus at the end of the road," he said. "We've got a two-hour drive ahead of us before I will feel comfortable. The mobile unit that Commander Obright issued is set up and ready for the kids."

"I thought you didn't know Obright," Dawn said.

"Chris does. Now, let's get out of here."

Maude motioned to Adler. "Hurry and get your things."

"I'm not coming."

She gasped. "What!"

"I'm staying. I'd be extra weight, and besides, I'm in a good position to keep up with what's happening on this side of the fence. I can keep you updated on anything that goes on in the neighborhood."

"No, sir. When I agreed to leave, I committed to leaving my worries behind. I'll not have you staying here and disturbing my rest."

"There's no time." Bruce gently took Maude's arm and saluted the young guard. "Appreciate you, man."

"No problem. I'm headed back before McKellar goes into a frenzy." Adler closed the door to Maude's protest. The van sped across the field.

Dressed in a pink plaid shirt, jeans, and knee-high boots, Dawn took the lead. The last rays of the day's sun cast highlights on her blond hair. He couldn't wait to unbraid and run his hands through it. To hold her and promise always to be there. He exhaled. *Commitment wasn't too hard, was it?*

The children followed Dawn single file.

"Time to go, ma'am. Adler will be all right."

Maude sighed. "I will have to pray before I have peace about that. Meanwhile, I must continue my work." She pointed down the road. "See my Abay? He is a handsome little boy, isn't he?"

"Yes."

"When his grandfather traced the child's bloodline, he

determined the boy and his mother unfit and sent them away. Abay's mom committed suicide. That's how the precious child came to be under my care."

Bruce scowled. "That's terrible."

"And Carter? His mother had three men in her life. None of them would claim the poor child as theirs. When the man she lived with ran off, she gave her boy to the authorities."

He adjusted his cap. "We should —"

"Before the earthquake, Josiah's mother called me every week. Sometimes twice. She desperately wants to reunite with him. She just hasn't figured out how. He's been with me four years. I hope and pray that Julie – that's her name – is okay."

Bruce pulled at his collar.

"You've faced a similar battle as one of my boys, haven't you?"

"We need to go, ma'am."

"I've learned many things since I opened the home to the first child. The most challenging lesson has been that the enemy isn't easily dissuaded."

She held up her hand when he tried to interrupt.

"It's time to go, I know. But, I'm supposed to help one more young man before I leave Assurance Home behind." She accepted the crook of his arm. "You're older, so I'll just share this piece of wisdom. There is one war, one enemy, and one winner. But the battles are countless and as varied as the number of people who have walked this earth. The enemy's strategy is to confuse you – to satisfy his appetite with your struggles. Do not feed him. Don't live what you feel. Learn what is right and live it, instead."

They walked to the bus in silence. The woman's words could have come straight from Grandmother's mouth.

The children were already loaded. Maude climbed in, voicing a list of instructions to them as she did.

Dawn stood by the door. Her eyelids were weighted down.

"The kids will be safe with Obright's team," he said. "They're going to Cape Girardeau. An orphanage is making room for them until other arrangements can be made."

"I'm ready to get out of here. This whole place is getting creepier by the day. Did I tell you about the coyote that started hanging around the home? It got into the fenced backyard." She shuddered. "It even followed the hearse until the patrol car got behind us. It's like the nasty, stinky animal is stalking us."

"Get in." He shoved her into the bus and pulled the door shut. Feeling his waistband for the pistol, he stepped into the center of the road and circled. *Tüdampa* should have gone down the first time they met. Not that it would have stopped the trickster. Its spirit played by rules outside the realm of human knowledge. He grunted. It didn't matter what dimension the adversary came from. If it messed with Blue, he'd shoot just to make his point.

He jumped the high step into the driver's seat and adjusted the rearview mirror. Josiah and Kelsey sat in the middle of the bus, entertaining the children while the two women conversed.

Successfully engaging in *Gehetmo* required the soldier to know the enemy. Maude and his grandparents were right, and he had no choice but to live the truth. He started the engine and made a U-turn. Grandmother didn't know it yet, but as soon as he got back to the ranch, she was taking him to the rock.

There was more truth for him to learn.

Epilogue

Linda sat in the turquoise and orange striped chair. The Aztec carpet with coordinating colors it set on was worn thin from shoes rubbing back and forth. She crossed her feet at the ankles and leaned back.

"Thank you for sending the wild turkey plumes," she said to the woman sitting across from her. "Mom loved them. She wants you to come for fry bread tacos on Friday."

"There should be enough feathers for Wadonii's winter solstice prayer sticks. If not, I have plenty more. Please tell your mother that I would love to come." Martha Deer Cloud matched her client's position and leaned back in the executive chair. "I'm glad you decided to confide in me as soon as you arrived." She smiled. "This is week six. Where would you like to begin this morning's session?"

"Choices."

"All right."

"I made a decision that not everyone is pleased with."

"Let's discuss it."

"Mom called me into their bedroom yesterday. I expected another story about the tricks that *Tüdampa* plays. Instead, she pulled out my baby papoose board and set it beside me. Then, she wrapped her prayer shawl around the board and us and prayed."

"How did you react?"

"I cried like a baby. I hadn't seen the cradleboard in years. I couldn't resist tying and untying its leather straps while she prayed. Mom recalled every painful experience in my childhood – didn't forget a one. She voiced over me every annual prayer she'd ever recited. When we finished, I felt like I had been bathed in prayer."

"Was that a comfort to you?"

"Not at first. I wondered why God allowed me to be hurt by Lostyn when one of his fiercest prayer warriors had prayed with all her might for my protection. But, then I wondered what would have happened had Mom not worn out the path to the rock on my account."

The counselor draped the cream sweater from the back of the chair over her shoulders. "Would you like a cup of hot tea?"

"No, thank you."

Martha dropped a sugar cube into her cup and stirred. "How does all this tie in with choice?" she asked.

"Mom and Dad choose to accept me as I am. They could rebuke me for staying with Lostyn as long as I did. Or, for having to raise their grandson. They certainly have the right to be angry because I let them believe I died in the earthquake. So, for them to accept me and my decision? I haven't felt this much love since I was a child."

Martha didn't speak, so Linda continued. "They told the elders what was going on, and now the entire Shospokee tribe is on alert. If Lostyn shows up, we'll know immediately." She chuckled. "Dad has never been big on words. But, every night, he makes me sit to watch the evening news with him. And when he goes to bed, he locks the doors and says, 'See, my dear? I have bolted the doors. I will pray that God Almighty rests his hand of protection on us while we sleep.'"

"I'm aware that Mr. Shamo follows you every day. The new responsibility redirected his life to a positive perspective." Martha leaned forward. "How do you feel about being watched all the time?"

Some things never change. "Watching Mr. Shamo try to be incognito is endearing. It reminds me that I'm no longer on my own. Friends and family have chosen to rally around me. Except for Bruce."

"How does he feel?"

After all she had put him through, he loved her. Remorse streamed toward her eyes, but sheer exhaustion dammed up the tears. It was just as well. Martha had already helped her understand that healing sometimes came after tears were held prisoner long enough to process the pain that produced them.

"Bruce wants me to go into hiding."

The counselor was quiet.

"I refuse to be a casualty. I will not allow Lostyn to have that hold on me. Besides, I could blame everything on him, and no one would criticize me. Matter of fact, most people applauded my decision to leave. But, how did that help me face the fact that I stayed so long? I sent my son away. I prided myself on being able to handle a situation much bigger than I could handle, and then self-imposed a guilty verdict for failing.

"You can fail in life and not be a failure."

She shrugged. "I suppose if I wanted to remain a victim, people's applause would be enough. But, their praise does not erase the memories of being thrown against the wall or of my son having to hold a gun on his dad to protect me. No, I want to do the right thing."

"What do you believe is the right thing?"

"I'm going to be a survivor. And, forgive myself. As far as Lostyn is concerned? I'm going to let God deal with him.

Tüdampa's spell over her was broken. She nodded to affirm the thought. "I'm free to choose."

Martha typed notes on the computer. "Can we continue this discussion?"

"Next week."

~

Linda pulled up her collar. That morning, the meteorologist predicted snow flurries, but it was almost noon, and the sky was still clear.

On the way home, she stopped at the small grocery store on the reservation to buy a sandwich. After convincing Mr. Shamo that they were close enough to the ranch for her to be safe, she drove alone through the fields and parked by the lake. She faced the car east to warm the interior with the last of the morning's sun. Mustangs grazed near the water's edge, ignoring her intrusion.

There was no escaping the past. Her short time on the run had proved that. She couldn't bury thirty years like they never happened without denouncing her very existence. Her scars would never agree to stay buried, anyway.

The sun's face slipped above the windshield, and she raised the visor. As if signaled, the horses galloped to the other side of the lake to continue grazing near the tall rock formation jutting out of the water's edge. They were free to run.

The sessions with Martha had been helpful, but meetings with the Almighty at the rock were teaching her that instead of trying to entomb the painful memories, she could embrace them as markers pointing to the finish line. Life was a race, and each day was training for the next.

She started the car. Linda Bonin was going to run again, too. Only, from now on, she was going to carefully choose the paths that had God's footprints all over them.

Arriving at the ranch, she laughed while sprinting toward the gate. Being able to stretch her legs again was another affirmation that a new season of life had come.

"Wait!" Wadonii shuffled off the porch and hurried across

the yard. "Here." She handed her a bundle of cloth.

Linda unfolded the white cotton material. An eagle surrounded by ruby and yellow flowers was embroidered on it. Yellow fringe lined the lower edges. "It's beautiful, *Koiyah!* Did you make this for me?"

Wadonii waved off the question. "Put it on."

The prayer shawl draped perfectly, its fringe swaying in the light breeze. The petite woman raised to her tiptoes to pull Linda's hair from beneath the cloth and smoothed it.

"Now." Her mother pointed to her own ear. "Listen."

Linda closed her eyes to shut out the distractions. The wind whistled, trying to decide which direction to blow.

"Harder," Wadonii said.

A faint chorus of yelps sounded from far off and grew in intensity. Her eyes flew back open.

Her mother nodded. "This is good, my *pai'tiompu!* It means you can hear."

"But I hear *Tüdampa.*"

"Yes. The trickster is always there, barking his folly to draw attention to him. When *Tüdampa* succeeds, truth is hidden. But you are ready to receive truth. Listen again." She patted her chest. "From here."

She had come for the truth.

Father Patter's words broke through the growing howls. *"When I think that something or someone needs to be fixed . . . grace . . ."*

Pulling the prayer shawl tighter, she closed her eyes again and listened. Amid *Tüdampa's* loud discord, she heard a faint whimper. Another whimper came, preceded by a sharp bark. The yelping stopped.

"I hear the wolf."

"Yes! It is *Kuha-cho* – the Wise One. He delivers words from Almighty."

The words from Almighty God came quietly, yet they blocked all the other noises clamoring for her attention. He made a request. As simple as it sounded, she hesitated.

"He is saying, 'Give me your hurt.'"

Wadonii's warm hands cradled her face.

"I don't know that I can, *Koiyah,*" she whispered. "I feel so much pain. I'm afraid if I give it all up, there won't be anything left of me."

Her mother shook her head. "Your fear does not come from truth. Daughter, you now wear an eagle on your back. How does he display his wings? Is it true that they are spread wide?"

"Yes."

"This means you are to be brave. Release your heavy burden to the creator of the wind. My precious *pai'tiompu* – you were not created to run. Like the eagle, you are meant to fly."

A gust of wind sent her mother's pronouncement heavenward in confirmation. Suddenly she ached to feel lighter and freer.

It was time to let God fight the battle.

Before her lay the flat stones that paved the path to the clearing. "I'm going to the rock, Mom. Do you want to go?"

"This is your time to pray. I will go to my room." Wadonii spread her shawl out, the sun shining through the worn-thin material. "Victory has come, and it is time for me to dance."

The end.

"We now have this light shining in our hearts, but we ourselves are like fragile clay jars containing this great treasure. This makes it clear that our great power is from God, not from ourselves. We are pressed on every side by troubles, but we are not crushed. We are perplexed, but not driven to despair. We are hunted down, but never abandoned by God. We get knocked down, but we are not destroyed."

2 Corinthians 4:7-9 NLT

DISCUSSION QUESTIONS

1. Because of Wadonii's Native American roots, her ways are unique and sometimes obscure. Yet, her family understands her love for the Almighty and listens to her warnings about evil. How easy is it for you to accept people who are different? Is it easier to accept a person's personal expression when they share your beliefs or harder?

2. Linda fears failure the most and feels that everything bad that happens is a direct result of her incompetence. Other than Lostyn's abuse, what are some negatives that she experiences because of her feelings?

3. Lostyn's focus is on success and respect. His ideas of protection are distorted and severe. What causes him to feel and act the way he does?

4. Dawn is young and naïve. Do you see any qualities in her that are mature?

5. Bruce doesn't want commitment. Why do you believe he feels so strongly about it?

6. At first, Linda is attracted to Dr. Randall Gipson who appears to have similar character flaws as Lostyn. Why do you think she is? Is it common for people to follow a pattern when developing relationships? Is it easy or hard to break a bad cycle? Why?

7. Other than Linda's family, some people have a positive impact on her life. Who are they and how are they influential?

8. Have there been times that you thought evil would destroy you? If so, did you receive help and from who?

9. Did you see divine protection on Linda at any time? When?

10. Do you believe there is spiritual warfare between good and evil?

11. Do you have a favorite scene from the novel? Or a favorite character?

12. What is your takeaway message from the story?

A NOTE FROM THE AUTHOR

I thought I had life figured out. Then stuff happened. You know, those annoying interruptions that throw everything off track. You've been there.

During a particularly big interruption, I threw myself a long pity party. Finding no relief, I finally had a talk with God. It was more like a complaint session. But he was merciful. He listened, and he answered, assuring me that he could take care of everything.

So, I handed it all to him.

Admittedly, surrendering my preconceived idea of what life was supposed to look like was difficult. Burying the notion that I had control of anything went against every grain in my take-charge personality.

I still occasionally want to tell God what's best. That's when Paul's conversations with the Almighty come to the forefront of my mind. Here is what he writes about the response he received and his reaction:

"Each time he said, 'My grace is all you need. My power works best in weakness.' So now I am glad to boast about my weaknesses so that the

power of Christ can work through me. That's why I take pleasure in my weaknesses, and in the insults, hardships, persecutions, and troubles that I suffer for Christ. For when I am weak, then I am strong."

II Corinthians 12:9-10 NLT

God's grace gets me through the day. God's grace opens opportunities for me to help people. It helps me understand and love others despite our differences.

God's grace is all-sufficient.

Sharing the message of grace is my ministry. My aim is to always be the GRACE WARRIOR. With all that I am. With all that I have.

As an author, speaker, and life coach, but mostly as a GRACE WARRIOR, my encouraging words to you are these – God's grace is all you need.

Melissa Kirk

ACKNOWLEDGEMENTS

Thank you to my husband, Larry, who has always supported me through each writing journey. You are a gem and I will always treasure you.

Thank you to my family and friends, who encourage me daily. You are precious to me and your prayers are greatly appreciated.

Thank you to my editor, Susan Mary Malone, who is one tough cookie. You really stretched me to write to the best of my ability. Your knowledge is as invaluable as your supply of red ink is endless.

Thank you to my fellow writers in 10 Minute Novelists who provide a vast supply of input and support.

Thank you to Writer's Ink for critiquing my blurb. I look forward to our future meetings.

Thank you to my beta readers, who gave me valuable insight.

Most of all, thank you to my readers. I wish you the very best in all seasons of your life. May you always call on God's grace.

WHERE TO VISIT ME

My Website:
www.TheGraceWarrior.com or www.MelissaKirk.ORG

Facebook:
MelissaKirkAuthor

Twitter:
@melissackirk

Instagram:
Melissackirk

Google+:
Melissa C Kirk Grace Warrior

Pinterest:
MelissaCKirk

To visit author page or leave a review:
www.amazon.com

GRACE WARRIOR DEVOTIONAL SERIES

GRACE WARRIOR – *Bathed in Mercy, Clothed in Grace*

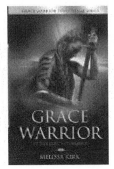

GRACE WARRIOR – *At the Kind's Command*

ADVENT– *Celebrate the Coming*

74605453R00183

Made in the USA
San Bernardino, CA
18 April 2018